WEREWOLF

WEREWOLF

Peter Rubie

LONGMEADOW PRESS

Cover design by Joe Curcio
Interior design by David Rosenthal

Library of Congress Cataloging-in-Publication Data

Rubie, Peter.
    Werewolf / Peter Rubie.
        p.   cm.
    ISBN: 0-681-41394-8
    I. Title.
    PS3568.U185W4   1991
    813'.54—dc20   91-5034
                                                          CIP

Printed in United States
First Edition

0 9 8 7 6 5 4 3 2 1

I would like to thank Mr. John Kennedy Melling, British police historian of London, England; Dr. Harry Lodge; Syd, Jim C., Jim D., and Carol, who were kind enough to advise me on this; and my agent and good friend, Lori Perkins.

For Stephen, Anne, Paul, and Sophie

Author's Note:

Smiths Common does not exist in the East End of London, and never did to my knowledge.

The same is true of the Mary Kitteridge Home.

"The presence in the human spirit of werewolves can direct the culture, the society, the individual human being to sources of healing. If it does so, it is a myth, not of despair, but of hope."

—*Charlotte F. Otten*
A Lycanthropy
Reader: Werewolves
in Western Culture
(Syracuse University
Press; 1986)

"Nothing is easier than self-deceit. For what each man wishes, that he also believes to be true."

—*Demosthenes*
(Ancient Greek
Statesman)

AUGUST 30, 1931

11:30 P.M.

T hey had a euphemism for it in the Job—"Illegal Ops." But any way you looked at it, abortion was a godless, sinful act, thought Detective Constable George Llewellyn. He trudged through the chilly evening air toward the Gypsy encampment on Smiths Common, his thoughts in turmoil; an act of murder, sure as if a baby had been stabbed to death with a coat hanger in its crib.

Now in his late twenties, George did not consider himself a religious man; indeed he had largely abandoned his Welsh, fire-and-brimstone Chapel upbringing. Yet at times like these—late at night, close to danger—the mysticism of his strict religious childhood reared up in the most unexpected ways. For a moment, he felt like a damned Papist.

He had even been involved in the arrest and conviction of several abortionists before moving to London. He remembered the faces of all of them.

Still, as much as George could not sanction nor forgive the grubby back-street goings-on, almost against his will he was able to conjure up situations in which it was probably better for a mother, especially an unmarried one, to be rid of the burden she carried within her. God knows, he had seen enough suffering of unwanted children. He quickly put aside such mutinous thoughts as he and the plain-clothes woman police officer beside him neared the muted lights of the Gypsy encampment. Now was not the time for such reflections.

The woman and he were sunk deep in their own thoughts as they followed the dark form of a young man leading the way ahead of them. A flashlight beam lit their way, but otherwise the three figures were hidden in the shrouds of a moonless night.

Such brooding uncomfortably led George back to thoughts of his wife and five-year-old daughter, the joy of an otherwise joyless union, snug at home and ignorant of his nocturnal misadventures.

Earlier, the woman—constable Sybil Goringe—and George had each nursed a drink while they waited in a nearby red-brick, spit-and-sawdust pub, The Wolf and Lamb. They had sat at a far corner table, ignored by the noisy gathering, until the young man now leading the way through the starless, cloudy night had approached them. Outside, George had reluctantly handed over £50. The young man had looked WPC Goringe up and down, given George a contemptuous glance, then brusquely muttered, "This way," and set off toward the common.

By now the trio had reached the first of the gaily painted caravans, and George snapped, "Which one is it, then?"

The young man ignored him, continuing through the camp past shaggy, tethered ponies sleeping on their feet until he reached several caravans close to each other, parked near bushes at the rear of the large circle of

3

wagons. "Wait here," he said to George, and, taking Sybil by the elbow, led her up the stairs of the nearest caravan, where they disappeared inside in a brief flare of interior light.

George slapped his hands together, glancing nervously toward the road where he imagined but could not see a group of waiting, uniformed policemen. *Waiting for me,* George thought uneasily. *Waiting to pounce.* He was hoping to make detective sergeant soon, and a lot was riding on how things went tonight.

A voice called from the darkness, making George jump. "Lost, are you?" It carried a tone of suspicion.

"I was told to wait here," George said defensively.

The disembodied woman's voice went on, "Why don't you just piss off. We don't want your kind 'round here. Just cause us trouble, that's all."

"Piss off yourself," George muttered. There was no reply and George was again left alone in the darkness, waiting for a signal from Sybil that everything was all right. She'd been inside an awfully long time. He began to imagine things going very wrong. . . .

His vigil was interrupted by a rumble of voices at the head of the camp, growing louder and accompanied by the beams of flashlights. *What the hell?* George thought.

"We're gonna get shot of the bastards, once an' for all!" a man's cockney voice yelled. "You with me, lads?" A roar of approval went up.

The night air was split by the shrill sound of a police whistle summoning help, angry voices growing more raucous. "Stay where you are!" someone else bellowed. *Sounds like Sidney Tanner,* George thought. "Damn you, you ignorant bastards!" he muttered angrily, glancing around, wondering what to do.

"You 'ear me? The lot of you. Stay where you are. . . ."

4

The darkness of the night was dispersed by the beams of flashlights, and the silence dispelled by angry shouts. More police whistles, and then the revving sound of car engines, alarm bells clanging, driving onto the common toward the caravans, their headlamps lighting the scene. George stepped into the shadows of the nearby caravans, looking around anxiously, wondering if he should shout to the other officers or stay out of sight.

"This is the police," a voice announced through a loud-hailer. "Stay away from the camp."

"Bollocks!" a voice shouted back.

George saw a group of locals at the head of the encampment shouting and shoving angrily at policemen who were trying to restrain them. Several constables went down, and the locals put their shoulders to vigorously rocking a caravan. Lights came on in other caravans, and Gypsy men began jumping to the ground, sticks and ax handles in hand, to see what the noise was about. A woman began screaming, and George knew things had become well and truly ballsed up. "This is all I bloody need," he muttered.

He could see the affray spilling toward him as locals from Smiths Common, policemen with truncheons swinging, and Romany men boiled together, crashing against caravans that rocked heavily on their springs. George realized he no longer had a choice. He had to get Sybil out of the caravan.

As he made his way up the steps the door opened, and at the same time a woman's voice yelled, "George!"

The young man stood silhouetted in the doorway, while from inside the caravan came wails and blood-curdling screams. The young Gypsy blocked the stairs, shouting, "Keep away." George ignored him, pushing onward. The Romany lashed out with a boot, catching George on the shoulder. He felt himself sailing backward, hitting the

5

ground hard. The young man jumped beside him, aiming another kick. "You set us up, you bastard. I'm gonna bloody do for you!"

Gasping for breath, George nevertheless rolled to one side, feeling the wind of the steel-capped boot as it stomped the earth by his face. Despite the pain in his chest, George heaved in air and wrapped himself around a leg, bringing the young man crashing down.

Around them the encampment was now in an uproar. George heard the crackle of flames, the odor of smoke wafting on the night. Inside the caravan, the screams grew louder and more frightening, sounds of someone being murdered, George was certain. He scrambled to overpower the Gypsy and clawed for his truncheon, deep in a special pocket in his trousers. Above him, he heard a woman scream, "Leave him alone!"

"George, help me!" he heard Sybil call. Lashing out with a fist, George managed to free himself enough to roll backward, still gasping for breath. He glanced up and saw Sybil struggling in the arms of a Gypsy woman who was shrieking at the two men on the ground. "He ain't done nothing, leave him be, you black-hearted bastard!"

The moment's distraction was all the young Gypsy needed, and he crashed on top on George, knocking him against a wagon wheel. George managed to bring up a knee, holding off his attacker, while the Gypsy, sobbing with frustration and rage, swung wild punches that mostly fell harmlessly on George's shoulders. A blow caught George on the side of the head. As the blips of silver before his eyes disappeared, George realized he was no longer pinned to the wagon wheel. Gathering himself, he saw the young Gypsy, still struggling, being dragged away by two uniformed coppers. Inside the caravan the screams were becoming more rapid and acute.

"George, get in here!" Sybil yelled, her voice near panic. He scrambled up the stairs, his truncheon now drawn.

George paused in the doorway, adjusting his eyes to the gloomy yellow light of the oil lamps swinging wildly from the ceiling. His companion was holding down a struggling Gypsy woman, while in the corner two other women leaned over someone prostrate on the floor.

"Get away from her!" George yelled, as another scream filled the small interior.

"She having a baby," Sybil shouted. George dropped to his knees, pulling out his handcuffs and snapping one bracelet around the exposed wrist of the Gypsy woman. "You, missus, are well and truly nicked," he said, by way of arresting her. "You all right, Sybil?"

As he spoke, George pulled his companion to one side, and, deftly snapped the other bracelet on the Gypsy woman's free wrist behind her back.

With a wrenching scream that jerked up George's head, the woman on the floor at the rear of the caravan gave birth. Moments later came an infant's wail. Pausing to catch his breath, George turned back to the handcuffed Gypsy woman. "What the bloody hell's your game?"

The Gypsy woman spat at him, then said, "God damn you, you evil-hearted devil. You ain't got no right treating that lad like that. He was only protecting me and them." She indicated the other Gypsy woman, now swaddling the newborn in a blanket, the exhausted mother, and her companion.

George leaned out the door of the caravan and shouted, "Oi, Sidney Tanner. This is George Llewellyn. Get a medic up here on the double. We got a woman in labor."

"Bit late for that, isn't it," Sybil said quietly. "She's had it, in case you hadn't noticed."

"Who's that?" George said, indicating the Gypsy woman still holding the baby protectively.

"Mother Isabelle. One of the abortionists we come to arrest. This one here's Mother Celina. The other two were here when I got here." She indicated the mother with a tip of her head. "All the ruckus was too much for her. Dropped it like a stone, didn't she, with all that hollering and carrying on outside. What's going on?"

Propped up against the caravan wall, the handcuffed Gypsy woman said, "You black-hearted son of a bitch." She stared malevolently at George. "You'll be sorry for this, an' that's a promise. It's all your fault." She squinted her eyes into slits. "I put the Evil Eye on you and curse you for the vicious animal you are."

"Shut up," George said, raising the back of his hand as if to strike her.

"George!" Sybil reprimanded.

"Just get her out of here," George said, and lurched out of the caravan to catch his breath, letting the rage burning within him cool down.

"I *curse* you down the generations," he heard the Gypsy woman yell after him. "You'll be sorry you was here tonight. I know *what* you are, you evil-hearted bastard. I know you for what you *really* are.

10 YEARS LATER

THURSDAY

January 2, 1941

I *t looks like snow again,* Nevil Stimpson thought. It was easier considering the weather than what the woman across the table had just told him. He shivered in anticipation of the worst. Despite the glow and crackle of a coal fire in one corner of the room, the chill in the air was a smothering damp that seeped into his bones, twisting him into painful, gnarled shapes the older he grew.

He unconsciously rubbed his aching left knee as he peered out of his front-room window at 23 Sebastopol Street, holding aside the heavy blackout curtain with the other hand. He was greeted by a bleakly gray English January, made worse by the wreckage that surrounded the street's otherwise anonymous half mile.

During the recent Battle of Britain, Nevil and others had stood with hands shading their eyes, squinting into the blue sky, at first unable to grasp the importance of the dogfights going on overhead, that their survival hung in the balance. After a few weeks, when an oily gray death plume erupted from a German plane, or a parachute opened, guiding to earth a hapless pilot, airgunner, or bomb aimer, the crowds cheered, though Nevil did not. He remembered the fighting at Vimy Ridge during the "last lot" and saw nothing to cheer about. Lonely men were dying above them.

Nevertheless, he watched the plaiting curly white exhaust trails of the overhead battles between British Spitfires and Hurricanes and the German Heinkel bombers and their Messerschmidt fighter guardians, faintly heard the stuttering of cannon shell as the airplanes seemed to weave in and out of ground-tethered silver barrage balloons shaped like miniature zeppelins.

Although it had been quiet for the last two weeks, the effects of months of intensive nighttime firebombing on London by the Luftwaffe was taking its toll, strewing corpses into strange and obscene shapes, impaling civilians with twisted shards of shrapnel, burying them beneath bricks, shattered glass, burning rubble, and personal effects, creating a landscape of desolation.

Where once in Sebastopol Street there had stood two rows of lower-middle-class prim identical houses, like Siamese guardians of the street and its secrets, there was now mostly ruin. Forlorn, disheveled figures wandered amid ten-foot-high piles of rubble, searching, disbelieving their eyes and their fortune. Chaos had descended. The remaining Victorian frontages looked like dirty teeth in a diseased mouth, defiantly upright against a white, lowering sky. Mushroomlike numbus clouds sailed past, driven by a cutting, icy wind.

Nevil forced himself to turn and face his client, a lady in her fifties with a brittle, groomed appearance. She wore a high-collared, navy blue ankle-length dress, almost defiantly Edwardian in style.

Blast, he thought angrily. *It isn't fair!* He couldn't meet her eyes, and instead, glanced past her at the grandfather clock ticking the minutes loudly in the corner by the dusty floor-to-ceiling bookcases. It was 4:30 P.M. Along the pelmet line grotesque carved masks leered down. Nevil felt they were malevolently mocking him this afternoon, rather than the evil spirits they were supposed to scare away.

The woman sat primly in the wooden chair across the table from him, partly hidden by stacks of books, exuding iron-willed patience. Her crocodile-skin handbag was placed neatly in her lap, long, slender fingers clasping it tightly. Beneath her veiled pillbox hat, adorned with several chiffon flowers, her pale expression was split by thinly compressed lips, determination etching deep lines into her face.

Nevil fidgeted, but still could not bring himself to speak to her—what she had suggested so appalled him.

He was a squat man, with black hairs that curled from his nostrils, bushy eyebrows, and thick curly hair that had receded until its boundary was now halfway up his skull. His lack of money was evident in his patched, ember-singed tan baggy cardigan; his gray flannel trousers, shiny with age and overironing; and the frayed shirt collar and cuffs he carefully trimmed with nail scissors, an old-school tie carefully tucked into his cardigan and held in place by a large tiepin just below the Windsor knot.

His hands shook, small palsied quivers almost in time with his pulse; his left eye began to twitch, both permanent reminders of his fragile nerves, shattered in the shelling in France twenty-odd years earlier. There had been times recently, because of the aerial bombardment London was suffering, when Nevil was convinced he had been transported back in time, enduring once more the terror of crouching in the mud as shells shrieked like enraged demons around him.

Nevil slapped a hand to his face, feeling the beginnings of a beard stubble. He massaged his left cheek until the tic subsided.

At fifty-two, Nevil looked more like a teacher now than when he had been in a classroom ten years before, pounding Cicero and Plato into the thick, unwilling skulls of sixteen-year-old shopkeepers' sons bound for the lesser universities. Nevil's pupils had been gleefully happy at his failure as a teacher and as an individual, proud that their virgin imaginations had been unsullied by lessons of history or a desire to embrace new ideas. He was certain their adult lives would mirror the structured boredom of their school days.

It had finally become too much for him. He had collapsed weeping in a classroom filled with jeering boys and had subsequently left the employ of the school enveloped in a cloud of embarrassed whispers about doctors, sickness, and the welfare of young minds that still followed him around. Nevil abandoned England for an extended holiday in the Greek isles.

While he was away, he had learned to read Hebrew and Arabic, studied Spengler and Steiner, Crowley and the *Necronomicon*, discovering new worlds of darkness and light, metaphysical ideas that seemed to speak directly to his experiences. Then his widowed mother died and Nevil returned, still a bachelor, to take up his inheritance—the house he was now living in.

He looked again at the woman across the table, his palsied hands feeling more noticeable than ever. Getting further involved with her would be a big mistake, he just knew it.

Between them lay several leather-bound tomes, the

pages spiderwebbed with annotations and comments, some of them written in his own neat, minuscule handwriting. Nevil looked at the astrological charts he had painstakingly prepared, spending the morning absorbed in the exacting craft of calligraphy, symbols, and lines carefully marked in red and green ink, their tags in black. The charts made him shudder even after days of checking and rechecking.

"This premonition I have of disaster is so *strong*, Mr. Stimpson," she said at last. "I beg of you. You must help us."

Nevil turned to the window again. *Damn it!* he thought. The urge just to let the situation drop and have nothing more to do with this woman was overpowering; but, as ever, he needed money badly; and, as a result, he was prepared to ignore his better judgment. If it wasn't for the woman, now glaring at him as though her silent determination were enough to force her own way, he would have been down-and-out, he was sure.

He let fall the curtain and returned his attention to the two charts. They were superfluous now, but he had to say something. *Why me?* he thought. He could see her agitation mirrored in the writhing, gloved hands, partly hidden in her lap.

He took down the top book of several stacked to one side. The paper made a cracking sound like snapping slender bones as he carefully turned the discolored yellow pages, hoping he would look up and she would be gone. He ran a finger down a column, peering through thin, silver-rimmed spectacles to recheck his calculations.

He stared at the first chart: a child born August 31, 1931. There was such a sense of malevolence emanating from it Nevil frankly doubted he was reading it correctly. Doubting his own abilities was easier than facing the terror the chart engendered in him. The afflictions of this nine-year-old were simply crushing.

"As you can plainly see," he said at last, his voice cracking slightly, "the Sun, Mercury, and Venus are all in Virgo; Mars, Saturn, Uranus, and Pluto form a Grand Cross, with Pluto in Cancer and in opposition to Saturn, all four planets square to each other."

He could have been speaking Chinese, for all the sense it made to the woman, he thought. Or for all she appeared to care at the moment.

Nevil stared at the chart. What he saw there was a person excessively influenced by dark forces, a person with no conscience, no saving human graces—a demon!

Unable to tell her what he saw, instead he rose and crossed to his bookcase, pulling down his locked, leather-bound copy of the *Necronomicon,* the book of demons and primeval forces worshiped and summoned six thousand years ago, long before the creation of the Cabala. It was the book of the Ancient Ones of the Sumerians, who lived on in the magick of the great Sorcerer Aleister Crowley and the stories of H. P. Lovecraft.

Nevil's hands began to sweat; his facial tic returned. He flipped through the pages, searching for *what,* he wasn't quite sure, divine guidance perhaps. The pages flipped and fell open, as if delivering a message from beyond—a warning to Nevil from the Mad Arab Abdul Alhazred himself. In large red letters at the top of the page lying open before him, like a branded warning from Hell, Nevil read: *There are no effective banishings for the forces invoked herein!*

Below it he read:

The wolves carry my name in their midnight speeches, and that quiet, subtle Voice is summoning me from afar. . . . I must put down here all that I can concerning the horrors that stalk Without, and which lie in wait at the door of every man.

The volume slipped from Nevil's trembling fingers. For a moment he found himself staring into a black maw, a dark, cramped tunnel. He heard the steady drip of water somewhere, and the scampering splashes of rodents, and saw, for a brief instant, a flash of someone's head, caught by a beam of light, saw blood spurting from a gash in the throat. . . .

"Are you all right, Mr. Stimpson?" his client asked. The cultured voice, with its edge of impatience, startled him; he had forgotten she was still here.

"Yes, yes," he mumbled.

Then he recalled the Nazi bombing raids; *that* must be what the vision meant. The bombing would start up again soon. . . . A Voice within him chuckled.

Returning to the table, he stared out at the weak light, his eyes tearing, then, taking a deep breath, he pushed aside the child's chart and turned to the next.

He became more brisk in his manner. "This person was born on June 19, 1906." He looked up at the woman, sure now that the chart before him was hers. She had been unwilling to give him much detail, even after all this time.

"This really isn't necessary—" she began, but he interrupted her.

"As I explained earlier," he said, "without a precise time of birth it makes things much more difficult. I see tremendous intelligence, intensity, dexterity, a musician perhaps?" He raised an eyebrow in question and looked pointedly at her fingers. Long, slender, coming to a point—a pianist's hands.

She ducked her head in agreement, as though pledged not to speak further. Nevil found her silence extremely disconcerting, overbearing almost. She reminded him of his mother—the *self-control,* her severity. He looked back at the charts. "I wish to God you hadn't said anything," he muttered. "There's nothing I can do for you."

He straightened in his chair, but his resolve weakened, and he added, "I'll call you in a few days, how's that, Miss Stepan?"

She rose, finding her most haughty demeanor, hiding any disappointment she was feeling, her dark eyes peering at him, probing. "Very well, Mr. Stimpson. If you feel that is best." She thrust her handbag at him, pressing it on him until he took it. "Please, at least look after this for me, until next week."

"I don't want any trouble, you understand? My position is very delicate. . . ."

"Of course. You are quite correct. I just didn't know who else to ask."

Nevil could think of no more to say to her. He stood awkwardly, glancing around, rocking slightly on the balls of his feet.

He escorted her to the door and watched as she entered her chauffeur-driven Bristol and drove down the street. No need to worry about petrol rationing for the likes of her, he thought enviously. *There was one law for the rich and another for the rest of us.*

Returning to the sitting room, Nevil stared out of the window again, watching the exhaust clouds dissipate slowly as the car paused at the end of the street, stark against a background of huge, camouflaged circular storage tanks, then turned into the main road. His fingers tapped the handbag, lying closed on the table. He had

17

read her Tarot cards once a week for nearly two years now. Yet he knew very little about her, even so.

He thought back on the strange afternoon. Her voice had been edged with panic, though she had controlled it with varying degrees of success, submitting to him readily as usual as he took command of the relationship in the crisp, schoolmasterish way he had retained.

He unclasped the handbag and pulled out a tan, leather-bound journal. After what she had intimated, he did not want to read what was in it. He stared at the unopened diary, his fingers dancing indecisively along the edges, but never alighting long enough to flip a page.

A cold draft whistled through the ill-fitting window frame. He hugged his heavy cardigan around him for warmth, but still he shivered.

□   □   □

Two miles away, Detective Sergeant George Llewellyn of the Smiths Common CID was also waiting impatiently and shivering from the cold. He and a plainclothes detective named Angus Campbell stared across mounds of rubble at a warehouse. *We should just go in,* George thought. *Bugger those bureaucrats in customs, and bugger this by-the-book stuff the inspector's insisting on.*

In the darkness, all George and Campbell could really see were shadows, darker shapes layered over lighter. As the night dragged on toward Friday, a full moon began to rise through the cloud cover. Bomber's Moon they called it nowadays.

The two policemen were slumped in silence in the front seats of an unmarked Austin, the interior lit sporadically by little red glows as each man drew on a cigarette. The Austin was a large square vehicle that rattled. It was also drafty as hell. Inside, the windows were misted from condensation except for small patches the men had rubbed clear. Tobacco smoke hung in layers from the ceiling like cumulus clouds.

George pulled out a hip flask, uncapped it, and took a deep draught. Then he tucked in his scarf and unconsciously brushed his thick mustache to the sides as he peered out the window. He blew into his hands and rubbed them together vigorously. *It's bloody freezing!* he thought.

No one could guess by looking at him that he was a miner's son, had spent five years as a teenager in the pits before joining the force. He had labored away his puberty, but now his muscle was going to flab, and the drinking had begun to burst the small veins in his face, reddening his cheeks and giving him a paunch. George had been a pasty-faced, eighteen-year-old wag of six foot two when he had first been a beat bobby in Cardiff, but now that he was just shy of forty the years had worn away some of his native charm, and thinned his fair hair until the widow's peak had receded above his furrowed forehead.

So what were those two geezers doing in that warehouse? he thought. *I'll be damned if they've managed to slip out the back; they'd need a bloody boat. Then the launch would get them.*

He let his worries subside. His suspects weren't going anywhere. More important, where had young Williams got to? How long did it take to interrupt a JP's supper and get him to sign a search warrant? Despite himself, George glanced at his wristwatch. It was five minutes later than the last time he had looked.

It had begun simply enough: George had been sent round to inform a Mrs. Anderson that her husband, Thomas, had been killed by a taxi in the blackout. It was a common enough story these days. Dozens of people a week were being killed or injured in the darkness as busses and lorries drove on pencil-thin beams, hard to spot from the air—or from the ground for that matter.

Because of Mrs. Anderson's inability to explain what her husband was doing late at night near the dockyards, it had finally become a toss-up whether Tommy Anderson was one of those IRA gits, a German agent, or a black marketeer. After several days of questioning in the interview rooms of the James Street police station, Mrs. Anderson had admitted her husband's involvement with a gang of East End mobsters.

The police had charged her with being an accessory and after a brief appearance in a magistrate's court let her go home on her own recognizance. Two days later—yesterday—Mrs. Anderson had been visited by two young men. An hour later she had left her home in a hurry, carrying a suitcase.

Meanwhile, Detectives Campbell and Williams followed the men to the dockyards and watched them enter a derelict building. Detective Constable Campbell had then sent young Williams sprinting for the nearest police box to telephone George at the station. Fifteen minutes later George had arrived in the Austin.

Now they waited for Williams and the search warrant, praying that the two men were still inside what George was certain was an Aladdin's cave of contraband goods.

The silence of the night was broken by the banshee wail of an air-raid siren, swiftly joined in a mournful chorus as others took up the warning. The bombers were coming.

Campbell looked up, startled from a doze. "Christ, Sarge, bloody Hitler's back. What do we do?"

"We go and have a look, boyo." As George spoke he opened his door and was chilled by the sudden inrush of icy air. The night sky was already crisscrossed with swaying searchlight beams, and in the distance they could hear the first faint thumps of anti-aircraft fire as the bombers made their way up from the coast.

"Do what?" Campbell said, forgetting his fear for a moment in astonishment. George was already making his way quickly but carefully toward the warehouse.

"Bloody mad Welsh git," Campbell muttered, and reluctantly stumbled behind, climbing over the rubble strewn in his path, his flashlight firmly in his hand, though no beam shone from it yet.

□   □   □

As Nevil cycled through the dark gloom of the London streets, he felt at once a part and yet also removed from the surreal ordinariness of the landscape. Everyone acted as though it was business as usual, as if the Nazis weren't but a few miles away across the Channel, poised to strike. They were softening up the English like wolves circling a tethered lamb, bolting in unexpectedly to bite viciously, then darting out of range again.

The cold air stung Nevil's face, fanned by the whirring speed of the bicycle ride, his clothes flapping like flightless wings.

Every few hundred yards, the main road was dotted with large black shelter signs—metal plates clamped to lampposts with a big white *S*, and below that, in small letters the word SHELTER. A large white arrow pointed to the building in front of the sign. Above each sign was a small V-shaped roof to keep the dim night-light from shining upward.

Nevil concentrated on cycling. The effort had warmed him a little now, and the calming whir of the wheels' spokes as he was propelled down the almost deserted streets helped to calm him, blocking out nearly all thought. He passed building after building with sandbagged doors and shuttered windows, defaced with hastily pasted large white posters declaring SHELTER HERE DURING BUSINESS HOURS or SHELTER FOR FIFTY PERSONS AFTER 5 P.M. There were buildings in central London that descended six floors underground. When the banshees wailed in the West End you wouldn't have to run farther than fifty yards in any direction to find shelter. At the Ritz, they brought you breakfast in bed, even in the shelters.

Not like that out here, Nevil thought, as the closeness of the buildings gave way to tracts of land like badly spaced dentures. Nevil cycled on. He was worried about calling on his client, but he had made up his mind. He would try to forget what she had hinted to him, her ridiculous premonition, and return her journal unopened, unread. It was important to get the relationship back to a simple client-reader, undemanding, lucrative. For as badly as he needed the money from the various Tarot card and tea-leaf readings he did for her every week, he didn't want to get involved with the police, couldn't afford to get involved with them again—and what she was asking of him would surely mean that eventually. Nevil shuddered at the thought.

Money had always been something Nevil aspired to despise, "an obscene distraction of the lower classes," an acquaintance at university had once described it. Nevil had winced inwardly, feeling embarrassed he could not be so blasé, feeling angry and ashamed of his poor background as his years at university drew to a close and he was faced with returning to Sebastopol Street; money for him had always been contentious.

As a youth, Nevil recalled his mother telling him she and his father had found a job for him. Five evenings a week, plus all day Saturdays, he had helped out at the local brewery doing menial labor. His parents had been deeply suspicious of Nevil's inclination for books and academia, even when he matriculated and won a scholarship to Oxford to read classics. "Damn nancy-boy," his father had complained. "You got no balls! Can't be no son of mine."

As if the dull humping of barrels and crates on and off the drays was not demeaning enough, Nevil had seen little of the five shillings a week he had been paid. His father, a clerk in the brewery who had lost an arm fighting the Boers in South Africa, took care of all that, doling out a shilling every Saturday and insisting Nevil "save" the rest of his earnings. Nevil well remembered how that money was "saved."

When, at sixteen, he had made a scene about using his savings to buy a bicycle, his mother bluntly told him there were none; they had nearly thrown him out of the house, and when he went to work his boss, a friend of his father's, had given him hell for a week. From then on, what Nevil earned was contributed as his "upkeep." He was an ungrateful wretch, a thankless child, always had been. The echoes of their scorn remained with him still, after all these years. *Stupid really,* he thought. Never a forceful person, Nevil had capitulated easily enough, the unfairness of it all still rankling him.

They were right though, he thought, as he cycled through the encroaching evening. *I am an ungrateful, wicked person.* He had amounted to nothing, just as his parents had predicted. From the hindsight of middle age Nevil could see that now.

Night seemed to descend while he wasn't looking. One moment the evening had been shadow-filled, but if he looked carefully he could still see his way unaided by the thin, flickering beam he was allowed on his bicycle. Then in a blink of an eye almost, the world was a mass of dark shapes, and only when he got close could Nevil make out a lamppost or a fence. He paused by a street sign and peered up. He realized he wasn't far away now—a street or two at most. The rubble had been cleared into piles, and, although it took only a moment to orient himself, Nevil did not feel sufficiently brave to continue riding. He removed his bicycle clips from his trouser cuffs and wheeled the bike down the street. The house he wanted was at the very end of the cul-de-sac, backing onto the river, separated on one side by the rest of the common that began behind Nevil's house, and bounded in a horseshoe shape on the other by the river, warehouses, and dockyards.

To his left, Nevil saw a large brick wall had been breached by an explosion. It revealed the interior of a warehouse, a black maw where Nevil's imagination fantasized all kinds of sinister dangers lurked. He hurried his pace, bumping the bike over unseen obstacles that occasionally wrenched the handlebars sideways.

The unlit house he headed toward was a massive mansion-like place. Iron railings shaped like spears around the edge of the garden and an iron gate—which had so far escaped armament-factory melting pots—separated it from the rest of the world. Although it was too far from the center of London, it looked grand enough to have once been a candidate for an embassy.

Nevil leaned his bike up against the railings and was about to push open the gate when the airraid sirens began. Their wails, like howling wolves, sent a shiver of dread through him. He glanced around desperately, looking for a hiding place, a haven from the bombs. He heard the thumps of antiaircraft fire as it burst in the air with the dull whump of exploding cement bags, and then the growing throbbing bass of hundreds of aircraft approaching their targets. Nevil felt the gentle vibrations of the ack-ack gun emplacements along the river. Then he saw an upper window curtain move, and he dashed inside the gate and ran up to the front door, yelling to be let in, battering at the wood and ringing the bell.

The noises of the air raid grew louder; the boom, crump, crump, crump of Luftwaffe bombs ripping apart buildings across the river, drawing closer.

The door to the house remained firmly closed, the curtains firmly in place.

In the distance, Nevil heard the soft muffled sounds of bombs whistling down, causing the earth to shudder as they exploded in gouts of fire. On the horizon an orange glow was imperceptibly growing stronger as the flames caught hold. With a fear verging on panic, Nevil realized there would be no help from the inhabitants of this house. He was caught out in the open, unprotected and doomed. He sank to the ground, leaning against the closed door, sobbing, his arms uselessly shielding his head.

The grinding sound of the approaching bombers grew deafening, and the sky was lit like sheet lightning by detonating bombs.

Nevil crouched in terror in the doorway, gibbering. Amid the cacophony of destruction raining around him he heard an inhuman, cracked wail, as if the very Earth was howling from rage. The sound was like that of a creature in pain. It was followed by a high-pitched scream of terror, so near it destroyed Nevil's inertia, galvanizing him into movement. As the explosions drew closer and the first bombers passed overhead like a swarm of enraged wasps, Nevil bolted from the doorway, running into the street, blind to the direction he was heading, wanting only to be somewhere else, somewhere safe. There was a hideous whistle, a shriek that was almost triumphant, and behind him the house erupted in a hailstorm of bricks, glass, and splintered wood.

Nevil felt the shock of the detonation more clearly than he heard it through the thunder of guns and aircraft engines and explosions. The concussion was like a sledge-hammer in the kidneys, tossing him into the air like an offering to angry gods. The last thing he remembered as he sank into oblivion was being pursued by an echoing version of that unholy howl. Then, mercifully, the echo faded.

□   □   □

George Llewellyn and Angus Campbell approached the warehouse warily. Every few moments, George nervously peered into the night sky as crisscrossing beams from the searchlights tried to illuminate the bombers. The nearby antiaircraft fire detonated with a deafening ringing. This was madness! They had to take cover. What had he been thinking about, for God's sake? Then a movement in the warehouse distracted him.

"There!" he shouted above the din, banging Angus on the arm to attract his attention. From the rubble of the building they saw a figure dart away into the darkness, making a run for the breached wall.

The two policemen gave chase, Angus quicker off the mark than his sergeant. He disappeared through the gap in the wall after the figure. George stumbled on loose rubble, painfully cracking his ankle. The sound of the bomb was shrill and sharp, and George knew instinctively it was almost on top of him. He dived for safety, the night illuminated bright as daylight. George saw a figure flung into the air; then the concussion of the explosion hit him like a careering car. The last thing he remembered was flying backward.

□   □   □

An icy mist was falling when Nevil awoke. The dew had begun to collect on his face and hands and freeze, and his muscles felt locked and knotted. He could hear the loud ringing of church bells, and in a moment's euphoria wondered if he had missed the armistice—the war was finally over!

Then, as he came more fully awake, and, oddly, felt warmth on one side of his body and ice on the other, he wondered whether he had died. All he could hear was the torment of booming bells inside his skull. He was finally in Purgatory, he was certain.

Above him, the night sky was veiled by scudding clouds that flirted with the moon. As he fully collected his thoughts, Nevil realized he had gone deaf. He could hear nothing but the ringing. Feeling trapped, he glanced around frantically searching for the bombers he could no longer hear. There was no sign. He discovered that the source of the strange warmth to one side of him was the blazing remains of the house he had crouched near when the raid had started. It was a good fifty yards away, but the fierceness of the blaze lit the night with tall quivering spearpoints of flame ferociously devouring what was left of the mansion.

The landscape was from Nevil's worst nightmares: the desolation of the muddy trenches of France—but at home. There was no escape now, nowhere to hide.

Bits of walls and wooden posts thrust into the air at strange angles, supporting nothing, charred, smoking mysterious stumps. Buildings on either side of the street for about a hundred yards' radius had been damaged by the blast. The gate and fence to the big house on the commons were buckled and twisted and mostly flattened, and in between the flames and the smoke he could see the vista of the river where before had stood houses—people's homes like his own. The thought made Nevil feel suddenly even more vulnerable.

A tug was anchored offshore, ineffectually spraying water on the blazing dockside like a little boy peeing. As Nevil painfully sat up and looked around, he realized belatedly he was lucky to be alive. Close by, a large shard of glass had come to rest intact after scything overhead. He brushed himself off, removing small pieces of wood, glass, and rocks, wincing at every movement.

As he moved, the ringing in his head became worse, though faintly, as if in the distance, he could hear the crackle of the inferno behind him. Perhaps he wouldn't end up stone deaf after all.

Staring with astonishment at the wall of flames that reached out toward him with lascivious tongues, he was startled to see a figure materialize in the mid-distance and stare at him. It was crouching, its shape distorted and partially hidden by curling gray smoke and ash, glowing embers and sparks drifting across the ruined scenery. Then it disappeared. Nevil was left wondering whether he had seen a human being or an animal. He couldn't be sure. He cried out for help, hoping to catch its attention, but there was no answer that he could hear, and nothing approached him. He would have to force himself to stand up and try to make safety on his own. God knew what might collapse on top of him if he stayed where he was for much longer.

He scanned the scene and saw the figure again, to the left of his original sighting. He tried to shout, "Over here!"

but it sounded faint amidst the ringing in his ears and he was certain his voice could be no louder than a whisper. Besides, the figure paid him no attention.

Nevil cautiously hauled himself to his feet, leaning against an unstable pile of bricks. It occurred to him that he had probably just seen a prowling dog, judging from its size. It might be wounded or crazed or something.

Nevil carefully picked his way among the splinters of ruined buildings and steaming gouges in the earth, the icy mist continuing to gather at the edges of the fire. He tried to keep his mind off his aches and pains as he stumbled toward the blazing house. The crouching figure, the dog Nevil thought he had seen, reappeared, then ducked away.

Nevil halted. He didn't like dogs under normal circumstances. Dog bites hurt. Dog bites, he recalled vividly, could kill you. He had been bitten by a neighbor's slavering Alsatian as a child and had never forgotten the pain, nor the panic his mother had instilled in him as she rushed him to the doctor's surgery.

Nevil looked around anxiously, catching sight of the animal again as it made its way closer. With a sudden flash of fear, he thought, *It's stalking me!*

He could not stop his hands from shaking. He looked around for a weapon and with difficulty retrieved a length of piping from under a large swath of wallpapered plaster. Nevil peered at the grotesque silhouetted shapes the light from the fire threw around him. Somewhere among them, he was sure, lurked something dangerous.

He hefted the lead piping, drawing little comfort from it, and edged toward the flames, hoping the animal would be too afraid to follow. As he moved, he continually looked to his sides and over his shoulder, reeling and tripping as he wretchedly tried to keep his balance in the darkness

29

and make up for his lack of hearing. Every few yards he was forced to leave his back unwatched as he stumbled.

The fire was burning fiercely still, and Nevil was forced to skirt its edge, moving to the east and onto the grounds of the house. The view opened toward the river and the warehouses. There was no sign of the animal. Nevil's hopes revived—perhaps it had slunk away somewhere. Keeping near the fire had been a good idea after all. His nerves steadied a little.

Nevil paused to catch his breath, hefting the dirty pipe. Perhaps there had been no dog. Perhaps it had just been tricks of the light and his shaky nerves. The ringing in his ears had subsided a little now, though everything else sounded muffled.

He saw a movement not too far to his left and cautiously made his way forward. From the cover of a wall stump he peered into an opening before him.

In one corner, a fire blazed from a hole in the earth, like a ruptured volcano. The light from the fire flickered across the scene, throwing huge, writhing shadows.

What Nevil saw immediately was the body. It protruded out of a pile of debris from the waist, trapped on its side facing away from Nevil. The top half of its clothes had been shredded and tatters swayed in the cold breeze. Beyond, Nevil spotted another, smaller figure, curled fetally against a large chunk of squared masonry, staring at him, though without any sign of recognition that help had arrived.

With great trepidation, Nevil eased himself into the clearing, ready to run at the slightest hint of danger. He had heard the rumors like everyone else—the Nazis had parachuted maniacs and diseased things into the ruins to terrorize the survivors of their bombing raids; there were animals living like starving rats among the desolation, ready to destroy anything that interfered with their scavaging, crazed from the massive destruction, the noise, the flames. . . .

Close to, Nevil saw by the flickering light that the body had suffered the most gruesome wounds. The face was shredded and blood splashed on the rags still covering the visible portion of the body. A dark, syrupy pool, had gathered by its head and neck, only the remnants of an overcoat, jacket, and shirt suggesting that this had once been a man in civilian clothes. Unable to look longer at the ghastly sight, too late for any kind of help, Nevil suppressed his nausea and quickly turned away, facing the second figure.

He approached at a crouch, unsure at first whether this victim was also dead. The figure lay curled and twitching spasmodically with its thumb in its mouth, its face bathed in shadows and partially obscured by strands of wild dark hair. Nevil realized with a start that he was staring at a child, maybe eight years old, it was hard to say—and that he or she was still breathing, though shallowly. The child made no sign that it had seen Nevil, nor that it knew where it was or what was happening. It simply lay curled, its whole body quivering, thumb in its mouth, drool dribbling from one corner, glazed eyes fixed on the butchered corpse a bare five feet in front of it.

Nevil spent several apprehensive moments deciding what to do. The realization that he was faced with a child had sent another spasm of dread into him. Getting involved with children had been the cause of all his troubles before and he *knew,* intuitively, that this one would bring him a lot of grief. But he couldn't just walk away. The child was in shock, probably traumatized by what it had been through. Nevil could not help but empathize with it. Shell shock was something he knew intimately, and having suffered from it he could not wish it on his worst enemy, let alone this pathetic innocent, obviously driven into its own world by the force of the violence it had been subjected to. Nevil spent several minutes examining it for injuries, discovering in the process that he was dealing with a prepubescent boy. The child was so covered in caked filth it had taken a while to notice that it was naked. The discovery caused Nevil to quickly remove his coat, and despite the biting cold, he gently eased the boy forward and slipped the coat under his shoulders and drew it closed. The child growled softly, as though in warning, but otherwise did not react. The boy's skin was hard to the touch, and despite the poor light, which revealed shapes clearly but not details, Nevil could see that it was mottled in places, covered with scabs and cracks. Once he had finished, Nevil wiped his hands against his jacket in case he had picked up something contagious. He stared at the child. Where had he come from? How did he get like this?

Nevil gazed around, as though the desolate ruins could somehow provide the answers he so badly needed. What was he going to do? All Nevil saw was the man lying close by, his injuries nauseating, even to someone who had become hardened to the sights of maimed and dead in France during the last war and here in London over the past few months. Perhaps the dead man and the boy were connected, Nevil thought. Father and son, maybe. Or uncle and nephew . . . too many questions without answers.

Nevil waved a hand before the boy's eyes, but to no avail. *I should just pick him up and take him to hospital,* Nevil decided. But a warning instinct told him to stop and consider what he was going to do before it was too late. He remembered days of police holding cells and intensive, grueling questioning before they'd finally been forced to let him go for lack of evidence. Nevil could still see vividly the CID officer who had arrested and interviewed him, almost snarling that he might have got away with it *this* time, but *next* time—and he was sure there would be a next time—they'd make sure he'd swing for it.

If Nevil took the boy to hospital, he would inevitably end up having to explain to the authorities—and ultimately the police—how he came across the boy, why he was in such bad condition. . . . *No, no, no,* Nevil thought. "I can't go through that again," he muttered aloud. He sat on his haunches shivering with the cold, and stared at the boy, who was oblivious to his surroundings or Nevil's awful dilemma.

Perhaps I should take him home? Nevil wondered. Whatever he did to try and help this child would land him in dire circumstances, Nevil was certain. He couldn't be *seen* to be helping this child, it was too dangerous. But to do nothing was just as dreadful an option. If Nevil brought him in, there would be questions—questions he could not answer; and even those answers he had, like the last time, wouldn't be believed.

It was all too horrible to contemplate. Christ! What was he to do? *Can't just leave him here like this,* Nevil decided. Whatever else, he could not turn his back on someone in such obvious need of help. Not again. He would have to move the boy, take a chance. Put him somewhere safe, or relatively so anyway, until Nevil could work out a way to get the boy the medical help he obviously needed.

There was a bombed-out series of houses backing onto the common that might do, Nevil decided at last. He would take the child there, get him some food and blankets, and then set about seeing to his other needs.

Nevil leaned forward and awkwardly gathered the boy into his arms. He did not weigh a great deal, all skin and bones really, Nevil saw, but heavy enough nonetheless. The child groaned and again made a growling sound low in its throat, but otherwise it did not react when Nevil manhandled it over his shoulder in a fireman's lift. Thus braced, Nevil clumsily staggered through the ruins toward the black mass of the common, certain he was making a terrible mistake but not knowing what else to do.

□　　□　　□

What George recalled most about being down the pits was the suffocating dusty blackness—a blackness so total that the weak beams from pit-helmet lamps scarcely lit anything but the swirling motes of coal dust, through which weaved the strangely inhuman shadows of the other miners as they hacked and carved the thick slabs of coal from the exposed face of the lode, then heaved them onto the trucks George helped to haul. For some reason, George knew he should not be fifteen years old again and underground. The dust made him cough too much and ground its way deep into his skin. It made picking up girls much more difficult. Scrubbing could not get rid of it, nor could he banish the slightly sweet, choking smell that clung to his nostrils. Besides, he resented the brutal monotony, he was afraid of the claustrophobic darkness, of the hacking coughs of the older miners as they chipped away chunks of rocks and coal with heavy iron chisels and pickaxes, terrified of hearing once again the rumble of collapsing walls and ceilings, the caging pitch blackness of a cave in. . . .

George opened his eyes and through swirling orange-tinged dust stared impassively at an approaching fireman making his way carefully through the rubble.

Propped up as he was, it took George a moment to

realize the brick wall in front of him was no longer standing. He could see other firemen in the background, shouting instructions, rolling out hoses, and in a couple of cases already playing jets of water onto a blazing house and the dockside.

Christ, I could do with a drink, he thought. *My mouth feels like a wrestler's jockstrap.* He tried to summon up some spit, but the dry metallic taste remained. Belatedly he tried to move his hands to get at his flask, but the movement caused him too much pain. *Oh, God, the bastards have done for me,* he thought. *What a stupid way to die!*

"Are you all right, old son?" the fireman said, his sooty face looming over George. He smiled reassuringly. "You're a lucky bloke, ain't yer? You should be dead after that big bleeder. Took out half the bloody street." As he spoke, he expertly ran his hands over George, looking for blood and broken bones.

George tried to sit up, crying out at stabbing pains in his chest and left side. He tried once more and found he could move, though the fireman gently pushed him back to the ground.

"Best just lie there for the moment. Make sure you ain't damaged nothing internal, like. You hang on, chum, I'll get someone who can help yer."

George nodded agreement. He lay quietly, collecting his thoughts. He licked his lips again, in anticipation of a large scotch he was going to have once he was out of this ridiculous situation. He was a policeman, for God's sake. It was his job to help other people, or so they'd have you think anyway, not lie down on the job.

It was only then that he remembered Angus Campbell. *Christ, he must have taken the full force of the blast!* Sitting up carefully and leaning against a beam that jutted from a hole in the ground, George examined his surroundings. It was the wall, or at least what was left of it, that must have saved him, taking the brunt of the explosion. Somewhere near that raging fire, poor old Scotch Angus was lying under a ton of masonry. And probably that toe-rag he had been chasing, as well. George shut his eyes again, a fatigue crashing him. What a way to close a case.

His reverie was distracted by sounds of tumbling masonry. Opening his eyes, he saw three men hurrying over the jagged stump of the wall toward him, backlit by flames whipping hundreds of feet into the air, and rolling gray-black clouds girding the blazing buildings.

A half hour later, his ribs bound by a field nurse and pronounced okay enough to make his own way to hospital, George sat on a pile of bricks with several other victims near a motorized canteen, watching water gushing in spraying arcs onto the barely contained fire still raging in the west wing of what had once been a large house. Behind him, George heard others tackling more fires, though smaller, along the street. He shifted the blanket around his shoulders and sipped sweet strong tea from a chipped, heavy mug. Civil defense volunteers and uniformed bobbies were busy digging out both bodies and survivors, while others ranged through the rubble in bewilderment. Feeling stronger now, George stood up and handed his blanket to the nurse, still in her red-lined black cape. She looked pale and drawn, and her auburn hair kept falling in front of her face from under her white starched scarf. She was really too busy organizing the care of the survivors to do more than pause for a moment to catch her breath and stare at George. It was apparent from her appearance that she had been on her way to work before the air raid had forced her to remain for a while and help out.

"I'm okay, really," he said. He flashed her one of his

winning smiles, though it didn't appear to affect her. "Just needed a cuppa, that's all. Thank's for this." He indicated his bound chest.

She nodded in absentminded acknowledgment before continuing with her ministering, talking soothingly in Hungarian or French to those bombing victims who did not understand English.

George limped toward the police officers, on the way managing to borrow a tin hat from one of the air-raid wardens wandering around. The streets were now semiilluminated from the glow of the fires, and immediately above them the sky was an angry red, the smoke changing into a pink cloud as it rose. The cloud was peppered with tiny white pinpoints of light as antiaircraft guns in the distance fired at the last of the retreating bombers. A moment after seeing the flashes, George heard the thumps of bursting shells. The barrage balloons hovering over London stood out clearly, and as he looked carefully, George realized that through the gaps in the ranks of the balloons he could see the incongruous twinkling of real stars above the roof of pink that held bursting shells, flares, and the fading grind of vicious engines.

Somewhat in awe of the terrible beauty he was witness to, George recalled it was said that the magnesium-clad thermite bombs burned at a temperature of two thousand degrees, and that if one was left on the floor it would eat its way through just about anything. That was why sweating gangs of men were throwing sand and dirt on the base of the flames, trying to smother the heart of the fires.

About the street there were a dozen small motorized water pumps, carried in two-wheeled trailers, their whirring sound so loud George could hear little else as he drew nearer. Firemen were working methodically, calling instructions to each other, or taking a break, their faces blackened, tin hats pushed back on their heads, sharing a cigarette and ignoring the civilians wandering around. It didn't seem like war somehow, George thought. It was more—he paused, groping to clear his thoughts—more "normal" looking, as though these were not firebombs but natural disasters. Little fountains of spraying water squirted up from leaky pipes, soaking the ground, and, George noticed belatedly, his shoes and socks. He continued to step carefully over the bulging pipes strewn across the ground. He passed one young constable chucking up his dinner over a wall, and then an older sergeant, steel-gray hair peeking from beneath his tin hat, recognized George and waved him forward.

"You'd better come and take a look at this, Taff," said the sergeant. Like many Londoners, to the sergeant all Welshmen were Taff, regardless of their given name. George could still hear the constable heaving as he made his way over to the sergeant.

By the time George reached the body he knew why the young copper was throwing up his guts in the corner. It took a moment's horrified fascination with the terrible wounds on the corpse for George to realize he was staring at the barely recognizable remains of Detective Constable Angus Campbell. Half his throat and neck were ripped away.

George went to kneel beside the corpse, buried to its waist in fallen masonry, to get a closer look, gasping at an unexpected stabbing pain in his side, but stopped when he spotted the pool of blood—and a footprint. "Well, well, well," he muttered. He was still trying to make sense of it all when the uniformed sergeant took George by the arm.

Directing him toward the smoldering remains of the east wing of the house, he said, "There's another one."

George's eyes widened. "Jesus Christ, Fred." One victim

with such terrible wounds could have been a freak of the explosion—maybe. Two, so far apart, was something different.

The sergeant looked back at the now shrouded body, unable to completely suppress a shudder. "It ain't enough we got bloody Hitler bombing hell out of us."

The sergeant stared into George's face. His brown eyes were sunk in black circles on either side a bulbous, pocked nose, and George saw his own fear mirrored there as the sergeant added, "That poor bugger looks like he's been *eaten*."

□　　□　　□

As George and Station Sergeant Fred Medford neared the smoldering remains of the east wing of the house on the common, the all clear sounded. A harmonized wailing was now proclaiming the end of the air raid, and the sound made the city seem to moan with an agonized relief, finally able to cry out at the fiery wounds inflicted on her. Both men glanced into the night sky, as if reassuring themselves that it was really safe again, then quickly looked elsewhere, chagrined. The bombers were only a faint drone, barely recognizable amid all the shouting, rattling engines, and clanging alarm bells.

"Thank Christ for that," Sergeant Medford muttered.

"Too bloody right," George murmured in reply, each man talking more to himself than the other. *It's like being in the trenches,* George thought as he trudged through the mud and slime. *Bugger being out in Burma, they should try living here for a while. We're like ants, waiting to be squelched.*

They waded over soggy, blistered earth, curls of steam rising into the hazy night, and weaved their way over hosepipes lying like tangled arteries. The blue light from

their flashlights bounced crazily, making it hard to illuminate where they were going while they climbed across
fallen beams, the spaces between filled with bricks and
God knew what else. A few beams, each almost a foot
thick, were supporting a partly scorched wall jutting from
the ruins like a protruding bone from a shredded limb
stump. Huge curls of wallpaper had peeled away from it in
charred tatters.

George paused in his climbing, which was hurting his
ribs, and was distracted by the wall for a moment. Bi-
zarrely, it was still upright and relatively unscathed,
though more solid structures around it had collapsed.
Three men were perched perilously atop debris lying
against the wall, busily heaving away large chunks of
rubble near what looked like the top of a door frame. The
house seemed to have collapsed in on itself, the worst
damage in the west wing, where fireman were still struggling to control the blaze.

George looked at the doorway. If there was a way into
the unseen remains of the house, piled up like a junk bin
behind the wall, this had to be it, he thought.

"Over here," Sergeant Medford said. George followed
him beyond the rescuers. Looking around, he guessed he
was in what had been a drawing room or dining room.
Enough of the bottom of the wing still stood that he saw
some charred, steaming remains of furniture, including
what he thought might once have been a grand piano.

In a cleared space by the piano he saw the second body.
It was wearing a navy blue, ankle-length dress with a high,
starched collar. The dress had a few frills, but seemed in
all to belong to someone with a serious view of life. Her
gray-tinged hair, undone and hanging in unruly strands,
and the soles of her brown patent-leather boots were
singed, but remarkably there was no other obvious sign of

her having been in a fire. George knew, though, that in a fire such as this, most of the victims died of smoke inhalation.

He approached slowly, forgetting where he was and what he had just been through, absorbed instead in defining and then resolving the problems the body presented. She was in a worse state than Scotch Angus. The whole top of the corpse was encrusted with brick dust, dirt, and dried blood. George circled the body as best he could, then stood over it. Medford remained several feet away and occupied himself lighting a cigarette, which he handed to George, then lit another for himself.

"Who was she? Anyone know?" George asked, without shifting his gaze. He blew out a stream of smoke, and for a moment it gathered like a mist above the corpse, twisting as it was caught in his flashlight beam. One of her knees was raised, and the dress thrown back to her waist, revealing a frilly camisole and dark underwear. She looked to be in her forties or fifties—it was hard to say, because three quarters of her face and some of her neck and left shoulder were missing.

"I'll have to check up on it when I get back to the station," Sergeant Medford replied. He glanced back, muttered "Bloody hell," and then faced George. "She's a right mess, ain't she?" He winced and turned away, spitting as he did so. "Gives me the willies every time I look at her."

"Take a look at the electoral rolls," George suggested.

Medford looked around, then shook his head slowly and said, "This was a nice-looking old house, you know that? Real Edwardian. You into architecture then, Taff?"

George didn't reply, returning and carefully kneeling beside the corpse, wincing at sharp stabbing pains from his ribs. Behind him he heard Fred Medford mutter, "It's a bloody shame, that's what it is."

41

There was no getting away from the fact. Something had made a right meal of this poor cow's face. From the left eye, the nose, and down to the collarbone, a piece of which gleamed as it was affixed by his flashlight, the flesh looked to have been gnawed away. Her one remaining eye stared sightlessly across the floor, where she lay on her cheek. It was impossible to say what her last expression might have been. There was only a mask of shredded flesh and gristle.

What had killed her? A wild dog? The bombing had certainly given rise to some roaming packs on occasion, left to fend for themselves after their owners were killed, their homes obliterated. If this had happened after the house was hit, there would have to have been more than one wild animal, surely, to do so much damage? What kind of animal would have the presence of mind to gorge itself on its prey in the middle of a raging fire? Let alone a pack of them, even if they were starving. Despite himself, George was unable to suppress a shudder. He put it down to his Chapel upbringing, but could not avoid the thought that for God to have allowed this to happen to someone, they must have done something seriously sinful.

He shook his head in a mixture of awe and horror, but was unable to completely take his eyes off the body. A professional instinct had kicked in, and he somehow managed to ignore his emotions and abstract the problem from its dreadful surroundings.

Maybe she was killed before the bomb hit? That gave the situation a different complexion. *How did it, or they, get inside the house in the first place?*

George shook his head, feeling suddenly weary. His side hurt, and he knew there wasn't much else he could learn here. He stumbled as he stood up, winced, and was caught by the sergeant. "Here, Taff, don't die on me now, will yer?"

"I'm okay," George said, waving Medford aside. He sat heavily on a tilted slab of concrete and stared at the body, catching his breath, trying to ignore the dull but persistent twinges of pain in his side.

Whatever killed her, no, George thought, *don't jump the gun here. Whatever* ate *her undoubtedly got at poor old Angus, too.* The wounds seemed too similar to ignore. *But why?* If the bombing and the fire had not driven the animals away, then it could only be because there was a lair nearby.

What am I thinking? he asked himself wryly, though feeling disgusted nonetheless at his woolly reasoning. *Ungodly wounds, creatures that aren't afraid of fire! Bloody Adolf's rattled my brains.* Still, the wounds on both bodies were quite extraordinary. George had never seen anything like them before, and he hoped he wouldn't be seeing any more.

"Here! I can see another one," a workmen by the wall shouted. "Looks like some stairs going down to a cellar." The man turned, urging others to join him in clearing the way. They dropped what they were doing and hurried over. George stood up, his muscles feeling stiffer by the minute, and hobbled to join them. He clumsily climbed up the rubble, pushing bricks and pipes aside, and grabbed one of the rescuers by the arm. "What is it?"

"A woman, by the looks of it. She's at the bottom of some stairs that look about as safe as a used rubber. Gawd knows how we're going to get down there. It'll take a while to get a block and tackle rigged up. She don't look too good."

George nodded in the direction of the dead woman. "If we're lucky, maybe she'll be able to tell us what happened to *her.*"

"You'll be lucky, squire. She's probably dead an' all. Ain't moving, anyroad."

The work progressed slowly, the opening carefully widened so that no loose debris would fall on the woman. She was lying on her back beneath a beam that had fallen across the stairs, but was braced by the stairwell so that its full weight could not crush her. A dreadful smell began to emanate from the hole as the men drew closer.

"Christ almighty!" one complained. "It wronks a bit down there, don't it?"

"Might be some ruptured gas lines," George said. The rescuer looked at George and then the hole. An off-duty fireman, drawing on a cigarette, wandered over to see if he could help.

"Put that thing out! There's a gas leak," the rescuer shouted at him.

The fireman quickly hurled away his cigarette and moved back a few feet. "Get up here and give us a hand, will you?"

About twenty minutes later they were ready to go down into the hole.

"Joined the brigade to be a bloody fireman, not a potholer," the fireman complained quietly as he slipped on a gas mask. "I bleeding well hope Hitler gets his nuts chopped off with a pair of rusty shears."

"Get this round you," one of the rescuers said and helped the fireman attach a rope under his arms so he could be lowered to the injured woman. They had stopped calling out to her. She was either dead or unconscious. Either way, it was wasted breath, for no answer came back.

George stood to one side, his injured ribs forcing him to become a bystander. Several men took a strand of the rope and swung the fireman into the hole, then slowly lowered him. A few moments later he tugged on the rope and was

44

hauled back up. He pulled off his gas mask and announced, "It's a right state down there. She's breathing, though."

"Anyone else with her?"

"Nope, just her by the looks of it."

An hour after that, they were maneuvering the unconscious woman out of the hole and strapping her to a stretcher in preparation for handing her down to waiting medics.

George had wandered away for a smoke and a belt from his hip flask and sat perched on a stump of a pillar some distance from the rescue, legs splayed as though watching the races at Ascot. Sergeant Medford made his way toward him, his face painted red from crusted plaster and brick dust. George handed him the flask. The sergeant took a long swig, gave it back, and accepted the already burning cigarette that George also handed him. He breathed deeply, inhaling the tobacco and exhaling a long jet. "How's your side?" he asked eventually.

"Okay," George replied. "Bit sore, but I've had worse in a rugger scrum."

"That's right," Medford said lightheartedly. "You Welsh blokes all sing dirty songs to each other in the showers, don't yer."

George didn't respond. Medford threw away the remains of the cigarette and, becoming serious, said, "You'd better come and take a look. That fireman found a cellar. You're gonna need to see it, Taff." He paused. "It ain't pretty, neither."

George wearily stood, and the two policemen ambled over to the gutted house. A ladder had been placed in the hole, and George peered down, gagging for a moment at the foul air that wafted into the night. "Jesus Christ!" he mumbled and attached his gas mask.

At the bottom of the ladder he cautiously adjusted his eyes to the dim light. Ahead of him was a brick wall that had partially collapsed. Lying in brick dust and splinters of brick was a small crowbar. George touched it, hefted its weight, as though it could tell him something. Behind the wall, George saw a doorway that had obviously been bricked up at some time and, beyond that, an old wooden door, now open, with several steps leading down into a murky, evil-smelling cellar. He heard Fred Medford reach the bottom of the ladder.

George knelt and examined the wall. From the looks of what still stood it was obviously a hurried job. The bricks had not been pointed, and the mortar had a damp, crumbly feel. This wall was new, or newish, anyway. *Now why would anyone want to brick up a cellar doorway?* he thought.

He paused by the door, smeared with encrusted mortar, and examined it more carefully. On the inside it was scoured with deep scratches about level with the door-knob, as though a big cat, housed in the cellar, had used it regularly to sharpen its claws. *What the hell did they have down here?* George wondered. Even through his incipient claustrophobia and the strong musty rubber smell of his gas mask, the stench was daunting, and he had to force himself to go farther. He stood at the bottom step by the doorway and swept the flashlight beam around the room. It reminded him of a nightmare he'd once had.

"My God," he murmured. Sergeant Medford's beam lit the room further.

It was a dark, damp place with deep shadows, about fifteen feet square, though the floor sloped backward from the stairs and the walls bellied out, with huge cracks splitting them like diseased, swollen skin. Overhead, two eighteen inch-thick pipes about two feet apart traversed the room, opposite, disappearing into large ragged holes in walls. The pipes had once been lagged, but what remained was shredded so badly it looked more like a spider's web. Along all the walls, in a band about five feet high, there were gouges and deep scratches. In a far corner, a steady dripping sound distracted George. He swung the flashlight beam over and saw a pile of chains. Moving closer, he saw a pair of steel cuffs attached to a length of chain links embedded in the wall. At least, one cuff was still in the wall. The other had been torn out. George could not ignore the general evidence pointing to some wild animal having been kept in here for a long time. With the door bricked up there was no way in or out. This cellar had been intended as *something's* tomb.

He followed Medford's flashlight beam as it focused on a three-foot-high pile of rotting refuse in the corner; a gelatinous pool of liquid had oozed from the rubbish and collected in a puddle. George realized at once that this was where the stench was coming from and gagged, reluctant to get closer. It was a smell he could no longer kid himself he did not recognize. Something had died in here, and not very recently.

George saw something move in the pile, and he started, then approached it cautiously, reluctant to discover more. He finally managed to make out what he was staring at. Buried amid the general rubbish were hundreds of bones, some still with remnants of flesh and gristle cling-ing to them. Only after a moment more did George recognize the rictus grins of several rotting animal heads entwined by squirming maggots. Before him were the remains of hundreds of small animals. Cats, rats, a couple of birds, all that was left of *something's* diet.

The awareness made him throw up a hand in disgust, as if to ward off the dreadful sight in the corner, and he

47

turned away, bile scorching his throat. *God damn it, I'm not going to throw up,* he thought. He took a moment to compose himself before he turned back for a last look. Then he quickly pushed past the waiting sergeant and hurried up the ladder.

He was drinking in the night air, gas mask in hand, when Medford rejoined him. "Holy Mother of Christ, Fred. What did they have down there?"

Sergeant Medford stared dumbly at the ground. George looked beyond him to where the half-eaten woman had been found, remembering the bricked-up cellar doorway. "What did that to her?" he muttered. "And where the hell is it now?"

FRIDAY

January 3, 1941

George accompanied the injured woman to the hospital and waited impatiently while the doctor, a harassed, gruff, red-faced middle-aged man with awry wispy silver hair, examined her in a curtained cubicle in the casualty department. The hallways were filled with the sounds of moaning and hushed voices, rubber shoes and trolley wheels squeaking along waxed linoleum floors, punctuated occasionally by sharp cries of pain. The green walls and the sharp tang of disinfectant unnerved George. It reminded him too much of another place an hour's car ride away—a hospital he felt guilty at not visiting more often. He dismissed the contrite thoughts, telling himself he had done what was necessary for his daughter, that he had a job that was too demanding, that he no longer had a wife to help him cope. . . .

The doctor pulled aside the curtain, and George saw the woman lying on a gurney. When asked, the doctor brusquely told George there was nothing else he could do for her at the moment.

The gurney was wheeled down a long echoing corridor

and George stood helplessly, watching her disappear from sight, wincing at the stabbing pains in his side. His arms hugged his body, and he felt a mounting frustration as his only likely witness slipped away from him.

A ward sister bustled into view, a dowager duchess surveying her realm, checking the patients and their charts in rows of camp beds crammed in the hallways. She spotted George, came over to where he was standing, and seeing the pinched, white expression on his face and his hands gripping his sides, in a no-nonsense voice ordered him back to casualty to have his ribs X-rayed and properly treated. George allowed himself to be led away by a nurse. He glimpsed the sister turn her attention to more pressing emergencies as rescuers continued to pull burned, crippled, and maimed from the wreckages, and they were sent up to overcrowded wards after stabilizing treatment in casualty. *The place is an organized madhouse,* George thought.

By noon Friday, he was thoroughly fed up with waiting and became more aggravated as he watched nurses and doctors rushing around while he sat by idly. Though the X rays were not back yet, he knew there wasn't much wrong with his side that a little rest and a hot bath wouldn't cure, and he began to feel like a malingerer; he had a job to do. He needed to find out about the condition of the woman they'd found. He needed to talk to her.

George finally found Detective Constable Williams drooping over a collapsible chair beside the injured woman's bed. The ward was filled with bandaged patients, some with limbs in traction, several of the more serious cases, like the woman, with curtains partitioning the bed from the rest of the room. The young policeman looked up, startled out of a doze, as George pulled aside the curtains.

"Watcha, Sarge. How you feeling?" Williams was a

good-natured, chunky-looking fellow in his early twenties. He slurred his words as though his tongue were a little too big for his mouth, and his nose, though healed now, had been broken in several places.

George nodded he was okay, his attention fixed on the woman in the bed. "She said anything yet?"

Williams rubbed his face with large hands, trying to wake up. "Been mumbling in her sleep a bit. Sounds like a foreigner to me."

George turned from the still form to Williams. "Herbert, I've got a couple of jobs for you when you leave here. See if you can find out if a local firm of builders did any work in that house recently. I want to talk to the blokes that did it."

"Sure, Sarge," Williams said a little uncertainly. "What kind of work? The inspector's been on at me about them burglaries—" Seeing a bad-tempered scowl appear on George's face, he added hastily, "Right, Sarge. Whatever you say."

As if speaking more to himself, George muttered, "The only reasons I can think of for bricking up a doorway is to keep something in, keep something out—or to hide something. The brickie might be able to give us a clue as to what that something was."

"Righto," the young DC agreed.

The woman on the bed began to moan quietly and move about as if in the throes of a nightmare.

"What's she saying?" George snapped, drawing closer to the bed.

"Don't ask me, I don't talk foreign. She's been doing that on and off since I got here."

"It's Hungarian," a woman's voice said. George turned and saw the nurse who had treated him at the bomb site standing by the partition curtain. She bustled over to the bed, checked the chart hung on a clipboard from the metal rail near the patient's feet, then took the woman's pulse.

"How are you feeling?" she asked George.

Momentarily caught off guard, he replied, "I'm okay." He wanted to get back to the woman on the bed. When the nurse did not say more he added, "Busy night," more as a way of getting her talking again. She nodded absentmindedly as she continued to stare at the watch pinned to the lapel of her uniform. The victim's restlessness subsided.

"Do you understand her?"

"Not really. She's slurring her words, delirious. Doesn't really make sense."

George placed a hand on one of her shoulders, smiling in his most boyish fashion. "What's she saying?" he asked softly. "Please."

She peeled off his hand with difficulty and backed away, eying George warily. He cocked his head to one side, his eyes gleaming. "You do speak Hungarian or whatever it is, right? It could be terribly important, Miss—?"

"Armstrong. *Mrs.* Vera Armstrong." Her voice hardened in the face of George's obduracy. "What she's saying is nonsense," she insisted.

George nodded agreement, arms crossed, waiting for more, wearing a look of avuncular patience.

Eventually, Nurse Armstrong said huffily, "It sounded like, 'It's loose' or 'It's free.' Something like that, anyway." Seeing the puzzlement on George's face, she added, almost spitefully, "See, I *told* you it didn't make sense." She rubbed her arm, obviously unsettled by him. "What do you expect from the poor woman after what she's just been through."

"That's it?"

A little abashed, the nurse went on, "She muttered something else. It sounded like, 'The Devil's creature. . . .'"

George's boyish look hardened, making the woman

53

fidget from the intensity of his gaze. Abruptly, he winked at her and said, "Thank you, Mrs. Armstrong. You're quite right. I appreciate your help though." Turning to Williams, he added, "Don't forget about that brickie when your relief comes, will you, Herbert?"

"Have a heart, Sarge. I haven't had any kip since yesterday morning."

As he left the patient's bedside, George glanced at Nurse Armstrong, raised his eyebrows knowingly, and said, "You're not the only one, you know. There's a war on, in case you hadn't noticed."

□　　□　　□

Ten minutes later, George made his way down to the pathology department in the basement of the hospital. He needed some serious answers about *what* had killed the older woman and Scotch Angus. Maybe the postmortem would give him some clues. *What the hell is going on?* he wondered angrily.

He was greeted by a lab assistant, busy typing an autopsy report when George entered the office. Around the walls, on shelves, were an assortment of developed human fetuses, from two months to full term, floating in bottles in a formaldehyde solution.

The assistant, a chestnut-haired, rat-faced man with a bulbous red nose, stopped typing and showed a yellow, gap-toothed grin when he noticed George. "Watcha, Taff," he said expansively. "And how're you this fine day?" He leaned back and pointed to a bottle on a shelf behind him containing a pink, bubbly-looking object. "Got a new one. Pink lung. Very rare, that, you know."

George grimaced. "You've got some disgusting habits, Eamon."

"Hear old Hitler gave you a bit of a smacking last night."

George ignored the jibe. "Where's Phelps? I need to talk to him."

"Ah, sure, things are bad when old friends don't have the time of day for each other, that they are. He's busy at the moment."

"Don't give me this load of old cobblers, you drunken Irish git. I need to see your boss. It's important."

"You'll be here about them two bodies, then, I'm t'inking." Eamon winced. "Right chewed up they was, by the looks of it."

"You should have seen them the way I did, boyo," George muttered, the images still firmly in his mind.

"Well, if you want to hang around a bit, I'll see what I can do. It's Old Spit-in-the-Sink's teaching day today. Got a bunch of first-year nurses in. Part of their course. Got to watch an autopsy, get the lay of the land, if you catch my drift." He winked slyly. "Phelpsy hates it. Got to be on his best behavior, of course. No drinking, no dirty jokes, no cigars. Still, he won't be long."

He rose from behind his desk and motioned for George to follow. "Watch this," he said, and led the way into the mortuary.

Inside the autopsy room, George saw a group of pale-faced, obviously intimidated young nurses trying not to show their nervousness. He stood to one side, away from them, while Eamon Keaveney bustled around making a big show of laying out the large, wicked-looking instruments and stainless-steel kidney bowls Dr. Phelps was going to use. Then he showed the nurses to a marble slab and suggested they sit there, so as to get the best view of the proceedings.

One or two looked decidedly green about the gills, George thought. He didn't blame them. The smell of the formaldehyde and disinfectant was nauseatingly over-whelming, and Eamon had a ghoulish sense of humor that bothered George sometimes; as for Phelps, he disliked nurses, and women in general.

Eamon returned, wheeling in a gurney. He stopped before the nurses and with a flourish whipped off the green sheet that covered the body.

The sight of the corpse was too much for a couple of nurses, who promptly passed out. Their friends went to help when a deep, fruity voice roared, "Leave 'em!"

A spade-bearded dark-faced man, wrinkles that looked more like crevices running from his eyes and mouth and across his forehead, stood at the entrance to the morgue and surveyed his newest class. He was wearing a leather apron and surgical gloves, his eyes beady and narrow as he advanced toward them almost menacingly.

"My name is Doctor Harold Phelps," he said challengingly. "This"—his arm swept about him—"is a mortuary—my do-main." He approached the operating table, where Eamon had shifted the body. "This is a corpse." He whirled around and stared at a girl trying to avoid being seen. She sat on one corner of the marble slab, gripping its edge with white hands, trying to stop herself from throwing up at the gruesome sight before her. "Ever seen a dead man before, girl?"

She shook her head, not trusting herself to speak, her eyes wide with distress.

"Well, take a good look. It's what you're all here for, isn't it?"

He proceeded to open up the corpse, slicing through the sternum with a scalpel, beginning a running commen-tary on what he was doing.

He turned to his assistant and held out a hand expect-antly. Eamon slapped a large pair of rib-cutters into them, then Phelps made a great display of cracking each rib, as though chopping holes in a mesh fence. Several more nurses were unable to contain themselves and ran from the room, weeping, while the remaining three held on valiantly, though a decidedly puce shade.

Phelps suddenly looked up from the cadaver and, picking a nurse at random before him, said, "Here, you girl, ever seen a liver after it's developed cirrhosis?"

The nurse glanced around wildly, hoping Phelps was speaking to someone else. "N-no, sir," she stammered, shaking her head.

"Catch!" The nurse instinctively went to grab what Phelps tossed toward her, realizing the moment she touched it what it was. She screamed in horror, then ran weeping from the room. When Phelps brandished a stainless-steel saw and announced, "We shall now move on to the cranium," her friends followed. "Class dismissed," Phelps roared after them with a malicious chuckle. "Damn petticoats," he muttered.

He wiped his chin with a shirt sleeve and, producing a bottle and a specimen glass from beneath the gurney, poured himself a stiff drink which he proceeded to guzzle, his eyes closed as if in ecstasy. Gasping for breath, he rummaged around in his waistcoat for a cigar stump and stuck it in his mouth.

"Quite a performance," George commented, as he emerged from the shadows.

"What the hell do you want?" Phelps said.

"Thought we ought to have a little chat about those two bodies brought in last night."

Phelps snorted with disgust, but his manner became less assertive. He knew exactly which corpses George was talking about. "You'll have my report in due time, Sergeant. Just wait like everybody else."

"What killed them?" George persisted.

Phelps paused. "In the man's case, amongst other things, severe trauma of the trachea and carotid artery."

Astonished, George said, "You mean he actually died from having his throat torn out?"

"That's an extremely crude way of putting it."

"What about the other one. The woman?"

"She's much harder. However, there's a skull fracture that suggests she suffered a severe blow, either from the bomb explosion or by hitting her head in some fashion, I'd guess."

"You sure about that?"

"Of course not, don't be ridiculous, you saw her, for Christ's sake. But if you want my opinion both victims were unconscious, if not dead, when they were bitten."

"That's definite then?"

Phelps sighed heavily. "There were no signs of a struggle on either of them, but there were puncture marks and gashes, possibly from claws, large canines—perhaps broken glass, I don't know . . ." He trailed off, sipping more scotch to hide his unease.

"What caused those wounds?"

"Some sort of animal . . . ?" Phelps shrugged.

"They couldn't have been freak injuries from the explosion, then?"

Phelps shrugged again and took his time lighting the cigar. He exhaled a large curtain of smoke between George and himself.

"So which is it?" George asked irritably. He rummaged under the gurney and came up with another specimen glass. He grabbed the bottle of scotch and poured himself a drink.

"Don't ask me," Phelps muttered helplessly. "What do I

know anymore?" He leaned back against a vacant operating table, nursing his drink.

George tossed back the scotch and placed his specimen glass next to Phelps's. "I need to know."

"If it was an animal, then it was at least the size of a medium-sized dog." Phelps hesitated, then continued, "But those aren't like any dog bites I've ever seen. I don't know what the hell they are."

George's voice was arctic. "What are you telling me? That after fourteen years as a pathologist you can't identify what type of animal made those teeth marks—or that it wasn't an animal?"

Phelps grabbed the bottle and poured himself another shot. "That's right," he said. His red-rimmed eyes bored into George's before he gulped down more scotch.

"What have you left out of that report? You know something you're not telling me, don't you?"

Phelps continued to stare at George, gripping the glass so tightly George thought it might shatter. "My advice to you, Detective Sergeant Llewellyn, is to contact the zoos, and if they can't help you, incinerate both those bodies and forget about them. They'll bring you nothing but trouble." He stood upright and reasserted some of his intimidating aura. "There's a war on, you know. Nobody gives a damn. Talk to Eamon, he'll give you all the paperwork you want," he muttered, walking away. "I'm too busy."

George stared after him for a moment. He'd known Phelps almost as long as he'd been a London policeman. Phelps had been a genuine hero, once upon a time, a survivor of an ill-fated army Arctic expedition. George couldn't quite understand what had happened to the man since then. What was Phelps hiding? He had seen something on those bodies and it had frightened him, George was sure. *Why?*

He leaned against the doorjamb of the outer office, watching Eamon assemble reports and photographs and slip them into a file folder.

George's hands covered Eamon's, squeezing them tightly against the folder. "I don't want *anything* to happen to those two bodies, you understand me, Eamon?"

Eamon winced, as much as George's intimidating manner as the iron grip crushing his fingers. "'Course, Mr. Llewellyn, you know me, right? Anything you say."

"Just remember," George warned. He made up his mind to go back to where the bodies were found and look around some more. An animal would leave some evidence of its presence, George was sure. All he had to do was find it.

□   □   □

It was growing dark as Nevil made his way over the mounds of rubble toward the common. He was certain unseen eyes followed his every move, and he hunched lower, bundling tighter in his arms more blankets, wrapped around tins of food he had scavenged from his meager kitchen resources, hoping to make the boy more comfortable while he worked out exactly what to do. His choices were so limited.

He stumbled down one of the hillocks of debris, heading toward the ruined house where he had carefully placed the boy. This was the second time today that he had been back to check up on the child, who had, for the most part, remained listless since his rescue from the devastation. Nevil at first worried that the boy had become so withdrawn he was beyond help. He had remained with him for most of last night, sleeping rough and fitfully, watching for any signs of recovery or further deterioration—a situation Nevil frankly dreaded—but gradually, after several hours of growing daylight, the child began to moan and writhe in pain when the daylight blistered his skin, and he made pitiful attempts to crawl away. Nevil had never seen anything like it. Once it had dawned on him what the problem was, he had wrapped the boy in more blankets and moved him to a corner, that, though damp, was shrouded in gloom.

The sudden shriek was riveting, a scream such as Nevil had not heard since his days in the trenches in France. It jerked him back to the present, causing an icy spasm in his stomach. His first reaction was to bolt, to get as far away as possible from the danger, but *something*, certainly not bravery, compelled him to investigate instead. The boy must be in trouble!

Nevil's weak flashlight beam flickered, its sickly yellow light barely illuminating the dank room he entered. Before he had a chance to look around and see what was amiss, something roared and bounded out of the darkness, slashing at his face with razorlike claws, its breath hot and fetid as it barreled Nevil against the wall, where he fell, breathless and dazed. He was overcome with terror and swung the blanket he was carrying as he crashed backward. In the darkness he couldn't make out more than shapes, but he heard the tins within the blanket connect solidly with the animal that attacked him. It howled with pain and jerked away, diving out the doorway into the freezing night, leaving Nevil alone and shaking. His face was bleeding, and when his hand came away stained with blood he wet himself, crouching in a ball in the dirt, arms raised in false protection above his head, whimpering, waiting for the animal to return and deliver a final blow. . . .

Nevil was suddenly eleven years old again, feeling the

sore coldness of wet underpants, hearing the dreadful screech of his mother threatening to cut "it" off, brandishing a butcher's knife in her rage, if he didn't stop wetting himself. Nevil recalled, as if it were yesterday, being forced to wear his stained, stinking short pants to school the next morning as a punishment. The other kids formed a circle around him in the playground, though he tried to hide from them, tormenting him with chorused singsong rhymes as sharp as blades. It was, Nevil thought, no more than he deserved. *I'm a wicked, ungrateful child; Mother was right.*

Nevil returned to consciousness. He felt the hard coldness of the gritty floor beneath his cheek, numbing his face and side, and gradually heard again the whistling of the wind through the wreckage. He had passed out for a few moments. Realizing he could not stay where he was, and relieved that he was still alive, he cautiously examined his surroundings, feeling the grit of the wrecked house pinch his hands, hearing the rush of air as he came to fully, his hearing by now fully restored.

The flashlight lay where it had fallen, its beam struggling to bring light to a meager few feet before it.

In the corner from whence the creature had charged, caught in the shaft of light, Nevil saw the remains of an infant. He went to investigate, convinced he was seeing something else, making sense of the dreadful injuries almost as an afterthought.

Stumbling outside, he fell to his knees by the entrance, retching at the image of the half-chewed baby seared into his memory.

Wiping his mouth with a sleeve, his hands shaking almost uncontrollably, Nevil forced himself to sidle back into the room. He hadn't seen the boy in there! Had the animal attacked and killed him, like the baby, dragged him away somewhere to devour at its leisure? The thought tormented Nevil; that he could be responsible for the child's death through his own fears—it was too much to bear.

Nevil's every nerve screamed that he should run far, far away, but he retrieved the flashlight and, avoiding the dreadful sight in the corner, carefully examined the rest of the room. The boy was gone. Nevil could only hope that *somehow* the child had managed to get away.

Nevil sank to the floor, his back scraping against the rough brickwork, the flashlight dropping from his limp fingers and extinguishing itself as it hit the floor with a clatter. What was he going to do? He was getting deeper and deeper into this thing the more he tried to stay above it. If the police found out he had found a child, not reported it, and the child turned up dead or injured somewhere . . . "Oh God," Nevil moaned.

He managed to get to his feet, though he was groggy and shivering. Forgetting to retrieve his flashlight, wanting only to get away, he stumbled into the darkness of the ruins.

He was near the foot of the hillock separating the ruins from the street when the sound of falling masonry warned him something was nearby—the creature had come back for him!

Nevil scooted over to a pile of rubble near the shell of a bomb-blasted house and held his breath to hear better. He cautiously peered around. The sound of movement in front of him grew louder and mingled in his ears with the rapid throbbing of his pulse. Whatever it was had deliberately come between Nevil and his route of safety.

The darkness made identifying shapes difficult, and for a moment Nevil thought, from the sounds he heard, there were *two* of them out there after him.

Then he caught a glimpse of movement and fur, and hurled a piece of brick in the creature's direction. The brick bounced harmlessly on other masonry. Whatever it was out there snarled and scampered away.

Breathing a sigh of relief, Nevil resumed his cautious journey toward the safety of the street.

Once again the sound of something moving pulled him up short. Christ! It was back and coming to get him for sure this time. Nevil groped for another rock, and settled into a new hiding place, fear drying his mouth and making him shiver. This time, the noises revealed a man stumbling toward Nevil's hiding place.

Nevil was tempted to call out a warning that there was some sort of creature loose, but instead held his tongue, waiting for the newcomer to reveal himself. He was, after all, heading away from the direction in which the animal had fled.

Then, to Nevil's dread, he saw who the newcomer was, recognized the face as that of a man he had come to fear above all others. For stumbling toward him, though oblivious to Nevil's presence, was Detective Sergeant George Llewellyn.

And in that moment of recognition, Nevil knew exactly what kind of creature had attacked him and was now stalking the ruins!

SATURDAY

January 4, 1941

George finally arrived back at the station house at about ten Saturday morning. An echoing babble from the foyer greeted him as he opened the front door.

The lobby, with its posters and tiled lime-green walls, was not much warmer than outside, though the lack of an icy wind was a blessing. A gaggle of people gathered around the front desk, acting aggressively petulant in their efforts to catch the attention of Station Sergeant Medford, who was meticulously dealing with them one at a time.

He looked up as George went by and called out, "Oi, Taffy, the guv'nor wants to see you, soon as you like." An elderly lady pulled at the sergeant's arm to get attention. "Just wait a minute, madam," he snapped. "DC Williams says he needs to see you as well," he called over her shoulder.

"Jesus Christ," George complained. "Take one day off and all hell breaks loose. Tell Herbert I'll see him in the canteen."

66

"Now madam," said the sergeant, returning his attention to the old lady. "What's your problem?"

"There's this thing, see, and I don't know what to do about it. Thursday, it was. My old man goes out back to the khazi with his *Sporting Life* like he always does after supper. Next thing I knows, there's this bloody great bang. Frightened me witless, it did. I goes rushing out, don't I, and there he is, bold as you like, sitting on the pot, chain in his hand, trousers round his ankles, khazi blown to hell. 'I only flushed it the once,' he says, like it's his fault, silly old fool. Then he tries to stand up and finds he's stuck in the seat, ain't he, with a Jerry bomb that ain't gorn off sticking out the ground next to him."

"What's the point of all this, missus?"

"Still there."

"What? Your husband?"

"*No,* the bleeding bomb. You'd best send someone round like . . ."

The woman's voice faded as George climbed the stairs to the second floor, reached the chief inspector's office, and knocked on the door. "Come," a wheezy voice called. George entered. The uniformed inspector, ensconced behind a scarred wooden desk, was animatedly talking into a telephone. He waved George into a seat and continued nodding and repeating variations on, "Yes, sir, I quite agree. No, sir, very difficult."

The inspector was a rotund man with permanently flushed features that were accentuated by blue veins visible in his cheeks. He breathed heavily, as though about to suffer an asthma attack, and had to be two years over retirement by now, George reckoned. It was only the war and a shortage of experienced manpower that had kept him in the Job.

At length the inspector hung up, then dabbed at his face with a handkerchief.

"You wanted to see me, guv?"

"Yes, George. How you feeling now? Not too banged up, I trust."

"Fine, thanks."

"Good. I'm starting to get some flack about those two bodies you found Thursday. We need to sort this out smartish. What's the latest?"

"My bet is there's a wild dog roaming around. That's what the pathologist thinks anyway."

The inspector doodled. "What about this missing kid you're working on?"

"Frank Isley's boy, you mean?"

"Don't think there's a connection, do you?"

"No, guv," George said, with more certainty than he felt. "It's the third time in eighteen months. Lad's a bit of a tearaway, if you ask me. Then what do you expect with a father like that?"

Finally, as though discussing something distastefully personal, the inspector said, "These chewed-up bodies are a bad business, George. I want you to get in touch with all the local zoos, wild animal dealers, the RSPCA area inspector, air-raid wardens, you know the drill. Animals orphaned by the bombings are our responsibility first, you know."

"That's just what we need, guv," George complained. "Bloody Jerry's causing havoc, everyone and his mother's on the fiddle, and I'm stuck being dog catcher."

"I'll tell Fred Medford to make an announcement at morning muster, get the uniform lads to keep their eyes peeled, but you'll have to deal with it."

George sighed in resignation. "I know, guv. I got

Herbert Williams checking out private labs as well. Leave it to me."

"Good man," the inspector said expansively. He looked up from his paperwork as George was by the door and added, "How's the kiddie?" It was more a pro forma remark than a genuine inquiry, and its insensitivity angered George.

"Fine," he replied tightly.

"Good, good," the inspector muttered, his head already buried in forms and reports.

□   □   □

An hour later, George and DC Williams braced themselves against a damp, bone-freezing wind as they walked down an east London side road called Owlswick Street. They passed anonymous, identical-looking doorways that led to two-up and two-down boxlike homes, the outside facades chipped, glossy red brick.

A red double-decker bus groaned past them, its engine laboring as it headed for central London. Bombs or no bombs, the buses kept running. It was a fact of London life that still amazed George. After months of raging fires and high-explosive destruction, people still showed up in the mornings at bus stops waiting for the number nine to take them to work as usual. Somehow, the buses always seemed to turn up, if a little behind schedule.

"What's the address again?" George asked Williams.

"Number seventy-two."

"Would be down the other end of the street, wouldn't it."

As the policemen strode past, George glanced at the house numbers. A grey fedora pulled well over his forehead barely protected him from the bracing wind. Fifteen, seventeen, nineteen . . .

Ten minutes later, they arrived at 72 Owlswick Street.

Their continued knocking was finally answered by a series of bangs and clumps inside, then a woman's deep voice yelled, "'Old on, I can 'ear yer. There's no need to bang the bloody door down." George continued to knock. "*Je-sus* Christ! Keep yer hair on. I'll give you a piece of my mind, I will . . ."

The door was jerked open by a large-breasted, middle-aged woman, her plain face showing weariness and suspicion, a fuzz of mustache on her upper lip. She had fair hair coiled tightly into a bun, and wore a faded, flower-patterned pinafore over a gray sacklike dress. A steel brace and surgical boot were just visible on her left leg.

"Whatcha want?" she said.

"Does an Ernest Richard Didcot live here?"

"What of it?"

"You Mrs. Didcot?"

"I ain't got no money, so you can just bugger off." She looked at George more carefully.

He said, "All I want's ten minutes of your time."

"*He* looks like a bailiff to me." She pointed at Williams. "But you—I know your sort. You're after something. Well, I ain't interested, can't afford it, so hop it. I'm sleeping—or trying to," she added pointedly. She tried to shut the door, but George leaned against it, preventing her. He gave her his warmest smile.

"We'd really like to speak to him."

The woman laughed nastily. "You and a million others. Who wants to know?"

George flashed his warrant card. The woman snorted. "I shoulda known."

"Where's he at, then, Mrs. Didcot?"

"In the bleeding army," the woman cackled. "Got his call-up papers near a year ago, didn't he, and that's the last me or the kids has seen or 'eard of him since. Good riddance if you ask me." She made to close the door again and George stuck his foot in the way this time.

"It's arseholes out here. What say we have a nice cuppa, missus?" George blew into gloved hands, ignoring her efforts to shut the door. Mrs. Didcot decided to acquiesce.

"What's your name, love?" Williams asked as they traipsed into the tiny kitchen, the woman's rolling gait clumping stiffly before them.

"Peggy."

As she put on the kettle to boil she asked, "What's this all about then?"

George didn't answer for a moment, gazing around the kitchen instead. There was a strong smell of stale food and perspiration. It was a cluttered, small space, dominated by a large butcher's-block table that had seen much better days. She thumped down the teapot before the policemen and while the tea was steeping, rummaged around in a cupboard above the sink and produced two chipped coronation mugs. She limped over to the table with them and poured the tea.

"Ain't got no more milk nor sugar," she announced, flopping down in the spare chair by the wall.

The policemen nodded their understanding. After the cold outside the tea was welcome.

"So what did Ernie do for a living then, missus?" George asked.

"Little as possible, lazy sod."

"You work yourself, do you?"

"In the kitchens, Lyons. Been there, what? Must be nigh on ten year now."

"Kids?"

"Three boys and two girls. But they's in the country wiv their granny."

"Good idea."

"They wants to come home, though, bless 'em. The little 'un, Sarah . . ." Catching herself, she stopped talking, waiting for the policemen to explain what they were doing there.

"Jobber, then, was he? Part-time work an' all that?"

"Could say that."

"So who did he work for just before he got called up?"

"Flannigan and Sons, mostly." George and Williams exchanged glances. Several hours canvassing local construction firms by DC Williams was finally paying off.

"Builders, right?"

"Yeah, that's right. 'Ere, what's this all in aid of?"

George sipped his tea and gazed around the room again. Eventually he said, "Did Ernie ever mention a job he did at the big house on the common?"

"You mean the one what burned down the other day?"

"That's the one."

"Did he ever! Spent near a week in there, what was it? Month after the war began, I reckon. Bloody weird if you ask me. He had to brick up a doorway down in the basement, he told me."

She stopped talking.

"Go on, missus," Williams said eagerly.

She peered at the two policemen. "What's this all about?"

"It's all right, he ain't done nothing illegal that I know about, anyway," George answered. "So, tell me, he talk to you about it any?"

"Little bit, didn't he, when he was drunk. Place gave him the willies. He reckoned they 'ad something down in the basement. . . ."

"What do you mean, 'something'?"

"Animal or something," the woman muttered, a little frightened by George's hard manner. "Didn't want to bloody find out, did he? Mind our own business, we do, round 'ere."

"What was it that upset him, do you think?"

"He could hear this howling sometimes. Said it used to chill his blood, it did. He told the old biddies about it, but they said it was a neighbor's dog what wandered round the grounds sometimes."

"But he didn't believe them?"

"Well, I wouldn't say that, exactly, 'cos he was dead careful coming home of a night, I can tell yer that fer nothing. Only reason he did the job in the first place was he did this deal wiv the ladies, like. They gives Flannigans the old 'eave 'o and hires Ernie, who was going to do the job anyway, right? Paid him two hundred nicker, too."

"Lot of money."

"Yeah," she said cynically. "Me and the kids didn't get to see much of it, though. Pissed it all up against a wall, didn't he? Big man round the boozer . . ." She stopped talking, her disgust choking off anything else she was about to say.

"These old dears got a name, then?"

"Ain't got the faintest. Don't want to know, do I? Not exactly my class of people, if you knows what I mean. Bloody foreigners or something, weren't they?"

"Right," George said, standing up. Williams gulped down the rest of his tea and stood with him. "You've been real helpful, missus."

"Yeah, ta for the tea," Williams added.

"You remember anything else about Ernie and that house, you come round the station and let me know, right?"

"Sure," the woman said, struggling to rise.

"You stay there, we'll see ourselves out," George said, patting her shoulder.

Outside, George and Williams began the long walk back up Owlswick Street.

"What we got then, Herbert?" George said, somewhat rhetorically. "Fred Medford's lads say the house was owned by a Robert Henderson. Flannigan reckons he was hired and fired by a woman named Camilla Stepan. So who is she, eh, Herbert? Where does she fit into the picture?"

"Maybe she's the dead one, or the one in hospital."

"A good point, Herbert, and if she ain't either, who the hell is she? And what did they kept in that damn cellar!"

"You think we've got a new Jack the Ripper or something then, Sarge? The Hound of Smiths Common, like."

George stopped walking. Williams, who had been joking, turned to face his sergeant, his grin fading. "I bloody well hope not, Herbert, for all our sakes. A wild animal's bad enough, but just the thought that there might be some lunatic out there doing that . . ." He left the rest of his thoughts unvoiced, the nightmarish images overwhelming him for a moment. More forcefully, he added, "Right, Herbert. I'm going back to the station. You're off to Regent's Park and then a trip in the country to Whipsnade Zoo." He grinned suddenly, disarming Williams. "Don't forget your nuts for the monkeys, will you?"

Williams grinned back. "I never forget me nuts, Sarge. Take 'em everywhere I go."

"Go on with you, you cheeky sod. And no hanging around after, chatting up the land girls in the local. I want to know what made those puncture marks as soon as possible, right?"

"Right," Williams agreed.

□   □   □

The ungainly, boxlike red double-decker bus crept along Whitechapel High Street, bringing Nevil ever closer to his home. He had spent the day fruitlessly looking for the boy, feeling more afraid with each passing hour. What had that monster done with the child?

"Why did I have to get involved?" Nevil moaned aloud. Several passengers in the bus stared at him, seeing, he was sure, a broken-down, middle-aged man talking softly to himself. A crazy man! A man who could hurt children . . . Nevil cursed at drawing attention to himself when he least wanted it, and hunched lower in his seat. He should have just left the child where he had found him. The Mad Arab's message was obvious now. Nevil had been warned about this mess but he had chosen to ignore it.

"Smiths Common," the conductor yelled, as the bus ground to a halt.

Startled out of his preoccupation, Nevil abruptly stood and carefully made his way to the rear platform.

"Bloody gypos are back," one woman complained to her companion as she looked out the window.

"Where? So they are," came the surprised reply. "Well, there's a turnup. Dirty, thieving little buggers."

"Nazi bloody spies, more like," someone else commented, as Nevil stepped off the bus. "They should do something about them. There's no one safe in their homes. . . ."

The bus chugged away, its engine drowning the rest of the conversation.

The sparse common, with its clumps of bushes and brambles around the edges, had been churned up by half

75

a dozen once-gaily-painted caravans and aging, skeletal-looking shire horses, presently tethered to several lines staked into the earth, leather nose buckets filled with oats plopped on the ground for easy grazing.

The caravans, parked about three quarters of a mile from the road's edge and looking like fairground stalls that were past their prime, were gathered in a rough semicircle, the center of which was marked by a large smoking bonfire. Clotheslines stretched from poles to caravan eaves, sagging with washing, while screaming kids ran wild, chasing one another, joined by yelping, half-starved-looking dogs.

Nevil had never really been bothered by the Gypsies, particularly since his time in the Greek islands. The gypsies, after all, were guardians of a Truth of which many were not even aware, let along their pursuing it as he now did. *But they do make the place look a mess, nevertheless,* he thought, as he turned into Sebastopol Street. In the distance, tugs on the River Thames hooted at each other like angry swans.

Nevil let himself into his house and put on the kettle to make some tea. Then he retired to his front room, where he took down his copy of the *I Ching*.

Carefully, he cast the yarrow sticks, reading the hexagrams they disclosed as he silently asked the question: *What should I do?*

The answer was not reassuring. The first hexagram was The Strength of the Dragon: Use this time to develop your inner strength. Consult with those wiser and more knowledgeable, it said.

But there were moving lines that changed the hexagram into another, gave a suggestion for the future.

The Sun: Search out evil, it said, and expose it.

□   □   □

"Mr. Stimpson? Are you there?" a woman's voice called. Nevil winced from his aches and pains as he sat up on the sofa. The knocking at his front door continued. "You all right?" the voice called again.

He shivered from the cold and, glancing around, saw the fire had almost gone out. He dropped some more coal on the embers, then hastily shoved his blankets under the sofa.

Eventually, he called back, "Um, coming, wait a moment."

He felt like he'd been hit by a bus. What time is it? he wondered. In the corner the grandfather clock showed 5:30 P.M. He vigorously rubbed the sleep from his face.

Standing at the door, with the mien of avenging Jehovah's Witnesses, were two women and the local vicar, Reverend Bullfinch, a mousy-looking man thinner and shorter than Nevil.

Nevil peered at them, holding the door as though to shield himself in some way.

"May we come in?" a beanpole-like, pinch-faced woman demanded, her breath steaming in the cold.

"Uh—what's it about? I was taking a nap, actually."

"Could we discuss this indoors? It's awfully chilly out here," the vicar said. He stamped his feet to emphasize his point.

It seemed Nevil had no choice. He invited them into the parlor and then bustled in the kitchen, using the opportunity of brewing up the last of his monthly tea ration to collect his thoughts. How to get rid of these people quickly? It wasn't often he had a visit from the self-appointed stewards of their community. Not since his mother had died, in fact. What on earth did they want?

He carried the rattling tea tray, with its riches of rare goods, back into the parlor and the quartet spent five minutes in inanities. "I'm afraid I've run out of biscuits. Bread and Marmite, perhaps?" A frown from the vicar prompted Nevil to add, "N-No, of course not. M-Milk? Sugar? How many lumps?" Daintily poised fingers used his mother's silver tongs to plop sugar lumps into bone china teacups. "It's so cold this time of year . . ." he ventured, then stopped. The situation was absurd.

He retreated to the wooden chair by the window table, putting on his spectacles, stirring his tea for a distraction while he waited. "I-It's nice to see you after all this time, Mrs. Tunbridge. H-How are you these days?" he stuttered. She was obviously the engine of this visit.

"Stop stammering, boy, speak up," he recalled a housemaster at school scolding him. *"Only guilty people stammer, Stimpson. Not guilty about something, are you?" "N-no sir."*

Cup and saucer balanced precariously in one hand, the vicar ensconced himself in Nevil's favorite high-backed chair. Mrs. Tunbridge said, "We'll come right to the point, Mr. Stimpson—Nevil," she added uncomfortably. "Reverend and Mrs. Bullfinch and I are collecting signatures for a petition to get rid of those dirty ruffians and their brood camped illegally on the common. Knowing your mother as well as I did, we decided it was only right that we call on you and get your support. I'm certain she would have agreed with us. She was always such a *staunch* pillar of our little community."

"That's right," the amply endowed Mrs. Bullfinch echoed, while her husband nodded sagely. *It's like looking at Jack Spratt and his wife,* Nevil thought, moving his gaze from one to the other.

He had always hated Mrs. Tunbridge, even as a teen-ager. Bossy, fastidious, never a good word to say about anyone. *She's probably right about Mum though,* Nevil thought. *She'd disliked the Gypsies right enough.*

"Um, I don't know what we can do, really," he said, with a sickly smile.

"There's plenty we can do," Mrs. Tunbridge snapped. "Don't be so defeatist, Nevil. You don't mind if I call you that? Where's your war spirit? Wouldn't do to have Mr. Churchill go round saying things like that, would it?"

"No, no, of course not."

"Health hazard," Mrs. Bullfinch volunteered. "That'll fix their nonsense." The vicar again nodded agreement, though he would not look at Nevil directly, staring instead at his teacup.

"All this awful trouble that's been going on around here. It's all their fault, you know. It's bad enough with the Nazis"—she pronounced it "narzies" like Churchill,—"but those wretched Gypsies are simply too much for a body to bear, don't you agree? They're a godless bunch. Lazy, smelly, filth everywhere—filthy kids getting up to filthy mischief, juvenile delinquents. But what can you expect when the women *sell* themselves so, going door to door like that, disgraceful; and God knows what the men get up to all day."

"Bunch of thieves, the lot of 'em," Mrs. Bullfinch commented.

"Um, I suppose . . ." Nevil mumbled.

"Wouldn't be no trouble if it weren't for those women," Mrs. Tunbridge went on.

"What women?" Nevil asked, loosing the thread of her tirade.

"You know."

Nevil shook his head.

"Those crazy women, who lived all alone in that big house . . ."

"What about them?"

"See, I told you nobody knew," Mrs. Tunbridge said to the others triumphantly. Turning to Nevil she went on, "This is all their fault. Foreigners, you see, can't trust any of them, can you? They should intern the lot, if you ask me."

"Always been Gypsies coming here, as long as I can remember."

"Ah, well that's where you're wrong," Mrs. Tunbridge said. "You were probably in *foreign parts*,"—she made it sound like a visit to a Soho brothel—"but about ten years ago my William, bless his soul—"

"Amen," echoed Mrs. Bullfinch.

"—he and some of the other men around here got together with the police and run 'em off. Didn't have no more trouble 'til those women started helping them, a year or so later, letting them camp near their house, giving them things, encouraging them and such."

"That's right. They'll steal anything that's not nailed down."

"And their sympathies, at this awful time, are perhaps a little suspect too," Reverend Bullfinch volunteered, though he shut up at a glare from his wife.

"You think they're German spies or something?" Nevil asked, somewhat shocked, both at the idea and the statement.

"Can't be too careful, can you, these days? I mean," Mrs. Tunbridge went on, "we could all be murdered in our beds one night."

"Best safe than sorry, that's what I always say," Mrs. Bullfinch added.

"So," Mrs. Tunbridge continued, producing a long sheet

of yellow paper, "first off we're collecting signatures." She rose and crossed to the table, plunking down the paper and pen expectantly. The sheet Nevil noticed, was nearly full with two columns of illegible handwriting. "We've even got one of those *Labour* councilors said he'd help us if we get enough people, said he'd present it at the next council meeting."

"D-Do you think it wise, at the moment I mean," Nevil began, searching desperately for a way to avoid signing.

"Why ever not?" Mrs. Turnbridge said indignantly. She stared at him like a governess dealing with a recalcitrant charge. "Um," Nevil added hastily, "don't they have enough to deal with at the moment, the authorities I mean, what with all the people needing help because of the bombings."

"It's *precisely* because of all that *we* have to do something. It's our civic duty. Our bit for the war effort. Fifth columnists are dangerous. They ought to be locked up."

Nevil knew full well that most of the foreigners and the Gypsies were refugees from Hitler. They had probably more reason than most for being against him. However, admitting defeat, Nevil said wearily, "You're right, of course." He just wanted to be rid of these people. "When is the next council meeting?"

"Thursday. Would you be able to help us collect more signatures?"

This was too much. Grabbing the pen he scrawled his name and address on the sheet and handed them back. "No, no, I can't, I'm sorry . . ." He tried to think of reasons but needn't have bothered. His signature was all they really seemed to want.

Mrs. Turnbridge collected the pen and paper and then faced the other two, who rose from their seats.

"Well, thank you *so* much for your time," she said coldly, and marched from the room.

Nevil hurriedly rose and tried to beat her to the front door. He failed and was forced to open it while she stood frowning, impatient at being kept waiting, as though Nevil was an inept servant.

As he stood by the door watching them walk down the short pathway, he heard Mrs. Turnbridge say, "Such a *strange* little man. Went a bit funny after the last lot, if you know what I mean. Reads tea leaves and things for a living, you know, from what *I* hear. Probably part Gypsy himself if the truth were known."

The diminutive vicar, sandwiched between the women, turned briefly to look at Nevil, though his cow-shaped wife grabbed his arm and pulled him along.

"Knew his mother, poor woman," added Mrs. Turnbridge. "Such a trial for her . . ."

And then they were gone, leaving Nevil shivering.

□   □   □

By six o'clock Saturday evening, George had finished his briefing of the local RSPCA inspector. He had also drawn a blank at the few private wild-animal dealers still in business, and was contemplating the problems he'd cause if he was forced to call out the army from Woolwich Arsenal or St. John's Wood barracks. "Not yet, anyway," he decided. That was a decision of last resort.

George was also hoping that DC Williams would be able to talk a volunteer from the zoos into helping them. With luck, and George certainly hadn't had much recently, whatever the hell this animal was would be taken care of by the experts, and he could get back to being a real policeman again. George was certain that somehow the two women who had lived in the big house on the common were a part of the answer as to what was going on. All his instincts told him it had to do with whatever it was they'd kept in that bloody cellar. Meanwhile, uniformed bobbies had been told to keep an eye out for stray dogs or anything unusual—in these anarchic times a ridiculous instruction, George thought. There was not much else he could do.

He tried to catch up on his mounting paperwork, but found himself uncomfortably distracted by thoughts of his child. Such thoughts fueled George's already mounting frustration with his case load. He became unreasonably angry, pressing so hard on the paper he was using that twice he had to unbend the nib on his Waterman, gouging several sheets and blotting others with splotches of ink, forcing him to redo at least an hour's work.

George had not even thought of his daughter, Wendy, for a couple of months. It was just too painful an experience to keep repeating. He told himself there was no need to feel guilty about his little girl, that he should just let things be. It was that drunken slut Gwenyth's fault. Yet the urge to acknowledge his offspring's existence, however flawed that existence might now be, to once more reassure himself of his ultimate legitimacy through her, became more compelling as the day wore into evening. The feelings lurked in the background all the while he tried to attend to his duties, though he ignored the feelings as best he could.

He supposed his unbidden thoughts about his daughter must have something to do with surviving the bomb blast, while at the same time being painfully reminded of his mortality.

Eventually, he managed to calm himself and finish his reports. Then at 7:30 P.M., all hell let lose.

George had heard the yelling and shouting from the

front lobby growing louder and was contemplating going downstairs to see what was happening when Sergeant Medford stuck his head around the door and said curtly, "Get your skates on, George. There's a riot brewing!"

"Do what?"

But Medford was already heading back downstairs.

Somewhat perplexed, George nevertheless responded to Medford's call for help and was donning his overcoat on the run by the time he joined the sergeant in the rear parking lot. Medford was supervising the boarding of a busload of bobbies. "Quick as you like, lads, don't hang about," he urged them. Once filled, the rickety blue single-decker quickly made its way through the east London streets.

As the bus clattered along Whitechapel Road, George cornered Medford and asked for an explanation.

"All I know is, Taff, we got some frantic phone calls saying the people in Sebastopol Street are getting ready to string somebody up." He surveyed the parallel rows of seated, uniformed policemen with their high collars, then looked back at George. "They've found another one all chewed up. Apparently this one's a nipper."

George smashed the seat in front with a fist and shouted, "Damn it! What the hell's going on, Fred?"

"Don't ask me, George. I just work here, don't I?"

□   □   □

They reached the junction of Sebastopol Street and Whitechapel Road, and the bus disgorged a corps of policemen, George bringing up the rear.

The asthmatic-looking, tubby chief inspector was already directing men into a line, facing an obviously angry, yelling mob of local residents. Someone gave the order, "Draw truncheons!"

"You'd better take a look at the body, George," Medford suggested. He looked around and, sizing up the situation, added, "We're all right here for the moment."

George made his way over to the inspector, and a flabby, resentful-looking middle-aged copper was detailed to guide him.

There was something about the street that nagged at George, something familiar, though he couldn't remember what. All the jowly, pasty-faced copper said was, "Over 'ere," and lumbered toward the river end of the cul-de-sac, where the houses had been pummeled into debris, what remained looking like a surrealist painting, buildings at crazy angles, gaping holes, walls ready to collapse at any moment. They clambered over several hillocks of rubble, and then George paused, surveying the devastation, trying to orient himself, catching his breath. He suddenly realized he was only a quarter mile, as the crow flew, from where the other two bodies had been found. He'd been over this ground the other night.

"Down there," the policeman said. He pointed toward a small knot of officers, identifiable in the dark by their luminescent arm bands, gathered by a cordoned-off area on the outskirts of the common.

George made his way down and was greeted by a couple of somber nods from assembled policemen. He made his way past them and headed toward the shell of a house, obviously the center of attention.

"Anyone inside?" he asked the nearest uniformed copper.

"No, Sarge."

"You been in?"

The young policeman shook his head. George took a moment to address what he was looking at.

The front half of the house had been blown away, though the back rooms were still intact. Removing a long, rubber-covered flashlight from his trenchcoat pocket he shone the thin blue light into the interior of the house and followed its beam. His mouth was dry, and the threads of anxiety that had been slowly tying themselves together in his gut all afternoon yanked suddenly into a knot.

His imagination began to race in gruesome directions, fueled by what he had already seen. He knew blokes in the RAF Bomber Command whose job was to pick up the pieces when a Lancaster or Wellington made a crash-landing, bagging bits, identifying what they could of burned remains. Blokes they had been drinking with, only hours before . . .

Taking a deep breath, George forced himself to breach the dark maw of the back of the house. In one corner by the entrance someone had been violently sick.

About a quarter of the head and shoulders of what had been a six-month-old infant had been shredded on a diagonal from left to right. George took one look, then found he couldn't breathe, and he stumbled as he quickly turned away, flashbacks of standing over his own child overwhelming him for a moment. He crouched down until he mastered himself.

Still crouching, he inched toward the body. He pushed himself to examine it carefully. Tears stung his eyes, and he blinked them away, tentatively reaching out a hand and touching a chubby, ice-cold foot.

Abruptly, he stood up and yelled, "Get a fucking blanket in here!"

A moment later the young policeman on duty outside rushed in, trying to avoid looking at the body.

"Why hasn't she been covered up?"

"Sorry, Sarge," the policeman said. He could hardly admit that no one wanted to get near the corpse if they could help it. This was the stuff of nightmares. "The medics is ready to take it to hospital, Sarge," he added, in a whisper usually reserved for church. "The photographer's been and gorn. They found a flashlight. Looks like someone might have been in here. Afterward, I mean."

Or during, George thought. He nodded, unable to trust his voice not to crack.

Outside, he breathed in the cold night air, his face still flushed with anger as his other feelings subsided. When the young PC came out, George draped an arm across his shoulders and said quietly, "I want to see the forensics lads as soon as they get here. *Nobody* goes in or out. Got that? Get them to go over every inch of this place. And don't let them give you any bother." Without waiting for a reply, he strode away.

Rejoining Medford and the other coppers, a scene of "controlled" chaos confronted George. The riot was pretty tame in comparison to what he remembered they could be like, when he was a child in a mining village just outside Swansea from people as frustrated and angry with their lot as he; there was more yelling and irate hot air, than anything else. Nevertheless, some teenage lads were beginning to gang together and head for the Gypsy encampment intent on a punch-up. The inspector ordered policemen to form a ragged barrier across the road to block them. The adults joined in now and were hurling verbal abuse at the police and shaking fists at the Gypsies. A group of Romany men, armed with clubs and pickax handles, had formed up about twenty feet behind a restraining police line, shouting back.

George's frustration broke as a bore of anger surged through him.

He stormed over to the knot of locals being urged on by the shrill voices of several women and stopped a foot away from a man he recognized and took to be one of the ringleaders. George towered over the man intimidatingly.

"Clear off, Frank," he said to the bloke, who had a mass of fair curly hair and arms like Popeye. "You got more than enough to take care of on your own doorstep at the moment, what with your son roaming around at all hours. Know what I mean? This is nothing to do with you."

"Who's gonna be bloody next!" a woman in the back screeched. "Ain't we got enough to cope with already? It's them buggers fault."

"Who rang your bell, missus? Shut your row." George surveyed the crowd with the disgust of a drill instructor facing new recruits. "This is none of your business. There's nothing you can do, except go home. I'm giving you all three minutes to disperse, then we're gonna nick the lot of you."

He stared down at the stubbled face and narrowed eyes before him, and added more quietly, "Sod off, Frank, you've made your point. I've got work to do. Nobody's doing *nothing* on my manor, you hear me?"

"Get rid of them buggers then, George. Send 'em back to Kent. Back to where they come from, for all I care. What they doing here in the first place? Weren't no trouble round here till them gypos arrived. My kid *seen* 'em this time. Either you run 'em in, or we're gonna take care of it."

"You listening to me? I'm the one responsible round here—not you."

George turned and signaled to Sergeant Medford, who took several paces toward the crowd. His men followed suit, truncheons at the ready.

"They don't give a toss about us!" a woman yelled. "My home's been blown up, my kids is wandering the streets getting up to Gawd knows what 'cos I'm too busy trying to find us somewhere to kip for the night . . ."

"You want someone to do something, go down the Town Hall."

"What's left of it, you mean," someone grumbled.

"You must be joking—them useless buggers."

"Leave these people alone and clear off." George glanced at his watch and then looked up. "You've got one minute, Frank. Get rid of 'em, boyo, or it's you I'll nick first. Then you can kiss your license goodbye."

The truncheon-wielding policemen closed ranks and made ready to launch into the increasingly hostile crowd. For a moment it seemed as though the riot would ignite, then the man called Frank mumbled a curse, but turned and belligerently shouldered his way back through the crowd. "You're all a bloody fifth-columnist's dream," George shouted at them. "You should be ashamed of yourselves."

"Don't call *me* no bleeding Nazi!" a wizened old man yelled, waving a stout bottle in the air. "I've voted Labour all me life."

"Shut your face, Gran'pa, before I run you in for drunk and disorderly. And that goes for the rest of you. This is your last warning, clear off out of it—*now*."

In the face of obdurate policemen, the resolve of the crowd weakened. The bobbies moved forward, in control once more, shooing the people away from the common. The chief inspector mopped his face with a handkerchief

and emerged from the ranks of his men, obviously relieved.

Frank's right about one thing though, George thought, as he
relinquished control of the situation to his superior: *What
are* them gypos doing back here?

George felt a hand on his shoulder. Fred Medford's
surly fat constable took a step back in surprise as George
whirled to face him. "What?"

"There's a witness over 'ere, when you're finished being
a bloody 'ero."

"Eh?"

"Found the little bugger, like Frank said. Saw who done
it, didn't he."

□   □   □

Just as he was about to enter The Wolf and Lamb, the
door to the pub opened. George said to the publican,
"Right, Frank, where is he?"

"Upstairs. The missus put him in the kitchen, 'cause it's
warmest."

"The medics seen him yet?"

"Yeah. He's all right, but you can't be long, mind."

George walked through the nearly deserted saloon bar,
went behind the counter, and made his way upstairs to the
living quarters of the publican and his wife, where a knot
of concerned local women were gathered in the hallway
and the front room. After a brief conversation with the
publican's wife, George went to the kitchen.

The boy was about twelve or so, dirt smudged on his
face despite an attempt to clean him up a little. A blanket
had been draped over his shoulders, and a large mug of
tea plonked before him on the table. He had his hands

cupped around it, but was staring at the wisps of curling steam. In the background was an oceanlike susurration of conversation from the adults gathered outside. Someone unseen said, "It's them bleeding Germans done this, you mark my words. . . ."

"Hello, Andy bach," George said quietly. "Remember me? I'm a pal of your dad. Come to help you." He moved from the doorway. A voice behind him whispered, "Take it easy, George," as he entered the room. George closed the door, muting the clatter outside.

Cautiously, he pulled out a chair near the boy and asked, "Do you mind?" There was no reply.

"Is it Andy or Andrew?"

He waited a moment and then sat down. "My name's George." Still no response. Despite himself, George shivered as the child's apparent withdrawal from reality recalled for a painful moment his own child's condition. "I'm going to catch him, you know. I'm like the mounties. You know about them, don't yer? Always get my man, that's me."

For the first time, the boy acknowledged George's existence by raising his eyes, though his head was still bowed. The expanse of white eyeball spooked George. The boy looked possessed, his hair spiky and unruly, his eyes edged red from weeping. Then George noticed the terror in them.

He's still not sure what he's seen, George thought.

"You didn't do anything bad, you know. It's my job to see that brave lads like you stick around to help us win this war. Like Simon Templar—the Saint, you know. You like him?"

The boy nodded almost imperceptibly. His eyes were feral, like a cave dweller wary of predators. Then the look passed, and George saw the little boy emerge again, cowering, shivering.

George lit a cigarette and leaned back on the table. "What do you think he'd do then, old Simon? I reckon he'd jump in his Hispano Suiza and follow the villains."

The boy didn't reply, but George noticed he was paying attention still. "Do you think your mum's cross with you, because you were playing where you shouldn't?"

After a moment, the boy gave a hesitant duck of his head.

"She isn't, you know. She just told me."

The pale face gazed up at George, the bottom lip quivering.

"I reckon you spotted a German spy, didn't you, and you followed him. I bet you could tell me what he looks like, right?"

The boy's lip quivered more violently and he sniffed, bringing up the blanket to cover the bottom half of his face until only his red-rimmed eyes were visible.

"What did you see, lad?" George asked gently.

Still no response. George restrained his impatience with difficulty and added, "Did he see you?"

Hesitatingly, the boy shook his head.

"He speak to you?"

Another shake of the head.

"How far away from him were you? Top of the mounds overlooking the common, I bet."

"Yeah . . ." the boy whispered.

Carefully, as though defusing a bomb, George asked, "You ever seen him before, Andy?"

"Yeah," came a whisper, so soft George had to strain to understand the words. "He lives round here, I think." The boy cringed in the blanket.

Then, in a sudden flash George recalled why Sebastopol

Street was familiar to him. "He won't hurt you, bach. You think old Simon Templar would let a villain get one of the good guys? 'Course not. Same with me, bach. Nobody's going to hurt you or your mum and dad while I'm around, see?"

There was something about the edge in George's otherwise soft tone of voice that seemed to calm the child a little; the absolute certainty, perhaps. If George said it would be so . . .

"So you followed this German spy up through the bombed-out houses onto the common. . . . What did you see, old son? It would really help if you'd tell me."

Falteringly, the boy added, "He went into the house, late last night it was. I heard this animal howling, like some big dog or something." The boy shuddered at the memory. "I hid and, like, kind of fell asleep. Then when I woke up I got scared, staying out, like, wiv me mum an' all, and went down to have a look-see, maybe hide there for a bit until I figured stuff out . . ."

"Take your time, lad . . ."

". . . and I saw something in the corner . . ." The boy exploded into tears. The door flew open and the publican's wife burst in, engulfing the child in hugs and hysterically whispered soothing noises.

Outside, George found himself squinting from determination. This was going to stop. Right now!

He beckoned to DC Williams, standing around chatting with a group of idle policemen, and when he had sauntered over, said, "Get the kid to take a gander at some pictures, take down his statement. There was a case I was involved with a few years ago, the Devonport kid. Make a point of showing him the suspect pictures from that, 'specially the ones of a toe-rag called Nevil Stimpson." He gazed down Sebastopol Street toward the river. "I want this bastard, Herbert. I want him badly."

□   □   □

Detective Constable Herbert Williams had spent a lot of time wandering the streets of the East End recently, late at night, in search of what, he wasn't quite sure—answers, he supposed, not only to DS Llewellyn's problems, but questions of his own. Local coppers, especially those on the beat, knew just about everybody in their district; and yet finding information about the two sisters who had lived in the big house on the common was proving remarkably difficult.

Williams glanced at his watch: eleven-thirty. Across the road a streetwalker in a heavy fur coat was lounging in a doorway dragging on a cigarette, the tip glowing in the gloom like a red eye. *It's a cold night for it,* Williams thought.

Occasionally buses and taxis went by, everyone passing through, no one stopping. A couple of airmen boisterously walked up to the whore. She straightened, a wolf scenting fresh meat.

"Whatcha, sweetie. Fancy a good time, then?" She had a voice like fingernails on a blackboard. Williams had half a mind to run her in, just so that he had *something* to show for an otherwise totally wasted evening. The airmen dickered and joked with her about her price. *She's old enough to be their mother,* Williams thought in disgust, turning away. When he turned back she was laughing raucously, skipping down the street between the airmen, arms around their waists, leaving Williams to a deserted dark street.

Why did no one know anything about these two sisters? Williams wondered, once again worrying at the problem of the bombed house and its evil cellar. He pulled up the collar on his overcoat and, hunching against the cold, walked slowly toward Whitechapel Road in the wake of the whore and her clients.

More and more, it seemed to Williams, the Stepan sisters had deliberately isolated themselves. The question was: Why? The answer continually led him back to something they wanted to keep secret.

Williams reached the main road, relieved at seeing a little more life, though the dim lights and brutal winter weather seemed to have kept most sensible people indoors. He walked another half mile, heading east, passing sandbagged buildings and a blue police call box.

His hand was throbbing from a damn animal that had bitten him last night, and his patience was wearing thin. For Williams that was a sure sign it was time to jack it in for the night.

Though Herbert Williams never thought consciously in these terms, his bulky build and amateur boxing abilities allowed him to give most people a lot of leeway, because if ever he lost his temper, which he did rarely, he knew he could pummel the shit out of them with his callused, ham-sized fists. But outside the ring the urge simply never came upon him. His dad, who was also his trainer, was always telling him to work on his "killer instinct," that he could be another Primo Carnera if he wanted to be, but Herbert had no desire to test himself with any serious boxing. Besides, he had only to look at his dad to see how punchy you could get if you didn't watch yourself. Herbert didn't want to end up with ears like cauliflowers and his nose spread across his face, slurring his speech like a drunk from too many shots in the head.

He paused by a bus stop, deciding to catch the bus home.

He could have moved into the police station house if he'd wanted, but his mum and dad insisted he stay with them as long as he liked, and frankly, Herbert liked having his mum cook for him, and do his laundry, and all the other things most of the blokes in the section house had to do for themselves. And he got along with his dad okay, too—most of the time, anyway. He was lucky, he knew.

He peered up and down the street, waiting for the bus. The bombing had screwed up all the timetables, of course, but one would be along when it could.

Engrossed in his thoughts, it took a moment for the screams to register. They were faint, carried on the crystal-cold night air. Startled, he looked around, wondering first where they were coming from, and second, what was going on.

He moved in what he thought was the right direction and realized he was heading toward the bomb-damaged houses backing onto the common.

Another scream, suddenly truncated, forced him into a trot. No point running like a lunatic if you didn't know where you were going.

Then he thought, "*Oh Christ, it's another kiddie!*" and as the realization sank in he broke into an earnest run, heading for Maple Terrace where he had decided the sounds were coming from.

He compelled himself to slow down and look around. He couldn't find his bloody whistle! He yelled out, "Hang on. This is the police," feeling like a fool. His shout was answered by the wailing sounds of the air-raid sirens going off again. "Sod off, Adolf," he said to himself. "Not bloody now!"

Williams was breathing hard when he finally spotted several people congregating outside the front of a semi-detached house. A woman was banging on the window, yelling something unintelligible, while two men were shouting, "Dora, you all right?" and pounding on the door. Several neighbors had gathered in the street and were calling out half-hearted instructions.

"Stand aside," Williams said to them as he arrived. To one of the men by the door he asked, "What's going on?"

"Gawd knows," a middle-aged, potbellied bloke replied. He looked glad someone else was ready to take responsibility. "We lives next door." He pointed several houses away. "Just getting ready for bed when we hears these screams . . ."

"Who lives here?" As he spoke, Williams made his way to the front window, though the blackout curtains obscured any possibility of seeing in.

"Widow, with a young 'un. Name's Dora Smith. Works down the depot." He watched Williams test the front door and said, "We tried that. It's locked."

"Is there a back entrance?"

"Through my house is best," the bloke said.

"What's your name?"

"Tom Ringwald."

"Right, Tom, you come with me. The rest of you, get down the shelter, smartish. Them buggers'll be overhead in a minute." The spectators needed little encouragement. One woman hung back, and said, "Will she be all right? I'll stay if you want. . . ." but Tom shook his head and muttered, "You get down the shelter, gel. We're all right here. See to them others." Then he turned his attention back to DC Williams and quickly led the way.

The wailing sirens continued, a counterpoint to the droning rumble of aircraft engines, growing louder as they came in from the east. Already, though in the distance, Williams could feel the vibrating detonations of firebombs.

The two men entered Tom Ringwald's house and ran through to the kitchen. Ringwald opened the back door, and they descended to a postage-stamp garden, the lawn dug over and newly planted with vegetable and herb patches.

They climbed a wooden slatted fence and made their way over the rubble to Dora Smith's backyard.

Williams paused. "You stay here," he warned Ringwald and then cautiously moved forward. He had a bad feeling about all this.

The night was suddenly illuminated by the nearby explosion of a bomb, making both men duck, flames and debris spurting into the air with a roar. The thunder of ack-ack fire grew louder in the response.

Dora Smith's kitchen door was wide open, though no light spilled out. Williams glanced into the night sky, shredded by sweeping searchlight beams, then screwing up his courage took out his flashlight and shone it into the dark interior. Another crash, so close it sounded overhead, made pots and china rattle. Then the windows cracked and shattered. Williams ducked, no longer certain whether it was safer outside or in.

"Dora Smith? You okay? This is the police. Can you hear me? You hurt?"

There was no answer, although it was hard to hear with the racket going on outside. Williams couldn't stop shaking.

He crouched by the doorway beside an overturned table until the first wave of bombers began to pass overhead, moving south along the river toward the Houses of Parliament and the West End.

The kitchen was a wreck. Crockery lay smashed on the floor, there were spears and rough diamonds of shattered glass everywhere, and the overturned kitchen table had been wrenched to one side of the hallway entrance, as though futilely set as a barrier.

There wasn't much of a gap, but *something* had pushed past. Williams was edging his way through when a noise from behind caused him to jerk around, his flashlight raised like a club.

Tom Ringwald appeared in the doorway looking disheveled and dirty. Williams swore nastily, then more calmly ordered, "Keep your bloody head down. Stay here!" and waved Ringwald to a crouch.

The baritone thrum of the second wave of bombers grew louder, accompanied by the whistles of more falling bombs. Their blasts rattled the house, showering Williams in dirt and plaster.

He edged along the short hallway, peering through the motes of dust swirling in the blue flashlight beam, but could see nothing out of the ordinary. He pushed aside a door to his left and peeked into the front room. It was empty, though several chairs were overturned and a ripped shawl was lying near the doorway.

He started up the stairs, wincing at every loud creak and groan as he shifted his weight from step to step.

On the top landing he paused and listened. He thought he could hear a snuffling sound from one of the rooms, though he wasn't sure because of the racket outside. It was enough of an unnatural sound to make him shudder. "Dora?" he called again.

He moved toward the sound, noticing the door was ajar. He edged it open with his foot, peering cautiously into a bedroom. A terrible stench wafted toward him. . . .

Ducking back, Williams felt his heart pounding. *Oh my God* he thought. *There's a bloody animal in there!*

He switched off the flashlight, drew his truncheon, and, swallowing hard, edged inside. It was a small room, no more than nine feet square or so, dominated by an old, sagging double bed, the light from outside almost blacked out by heavy curtains. On the floor nearest him by the head of the bed, Williams saw a hunched figure.

"Oi, you!" he yelled. The figure didn't move nor acknowledge he was there. It was grunting quietly, too engrossed in what it was doing.

Glancing around to make sure there was nothing else waiting to attack him, Williams moved rapidly toward it, not knowing quite what he intended to do, but having to do something quickly. As he neared the figure the stench became overwhelming. He switched on the flashlight and was confronted with the back of something.

As the beam spilled across the figure it whirled around, hair flying in long strands, arms outstretched, claws clearly visible, sharp, crooked teeth catching a beam of light for a moment as it snarled. Something it had been holding thumped onto the floor, and to his horror Williams realized the thing—whatever it was—was crouching in a slowly spreading pool of blood.

The creature launched itself at the policeman, hair and claws flailing. Instinctively, Williams swayed to one side and swung the flashlight to defend himself. He felt it land solidly on a shoulder, and the animal howled with pain, but kept on moving, making for the stairs.

A bomb exploded a street away, and the house shook violently, the air filled with the deafening roar of erupting TNT, airplane engines, and ack-ack gunfire.

Recovering his wits, Williams took off after the creature, determined to stop it, taking the stairs two at a time. Halfway down he tripped and pitched forward, managing to curl himself into a ball just before he hit the first step, tumbling heavily to the floor. A sharp pain lanced through his shoulder. In the background, through the nausea that washed over him, he heard Tom Ringwald yell, "What the hell . . ." then scream with terror.

It took a moment for the pain to pass before Williams could again stand. He lurched toward the kitchen, his left arm numb and useless, seeing the back door gaping open, the scene beyond like something from hell. Flames roared into the night sky from burning buildings, and in the flickering light he saw Tom Ringwald picking himself up. He had obviously fallen backward as the animal had burst upon him. The light from the fires was strong enough to show the smudges of footprints leading out the door.

Williams hurried back upstairs. He found Dora Smith almost catatonic with fear, crouching out of sight by the far side of the bed. He approached her gingerly.

More bombs rained own. His adrenalin fading, Williams felt his fear of dying in an explosion gain hold. Not knowing what else to do, he knelt beside her, tearing off the eiderdown and sheets from the bed. He quickly wrapped them around himself and the woman, then put his good arm about her protectively. She was twitching in spasms, her muscles stiff, her skin ice cold. The sounds of destruction outside were deafening. He covered their heads, then forced her to lie flat, pushing her as far under the bed as he could.

Another series of bombs whistled down. Williams knew from the sounds that this time they'd had it. . . .

□　　□　　□

An hour and a half later the all clear sounded as George hurriedly made his way toward Maple Terrace. He parked the Austin and began walking. As he turned into the street, an ambulance raced past, filling the crisp night air with clanging alarm bells. The skyline glowed orange from burning buildings, the spire of the small, medieval church of St. Thomas near the end of the street cutting a black cruciform shape against the fiery smoke.

As he walked farther down Maple Terrace, George heard the sounds of pick and shovel, the nerveracking clatter of pneumatic drills, the thudding of fire pumps, men shouting. Everywhere there was the acrid smell of burning. People wandered in a daze, gazing at what had just happened, the homeless salvaging precious belongings from drenched, steaming sites despite efforts to keep them back. Older people were sitting spread-legged on the pavement, awaiting help, bewildered by the wreckage of their homes. George spotted an elderly couple, both blood-spattered, walking aimlessly through the scene, supporting each other.

Around George the crash of falling masonry was almost deafening. Houses in all directions were vigorously ablaze, many perilously close to collapsing. Frontages bellied out at dangerous angles, and as George passed several infernos, showers of sparks rained down, in places melting the macadam, buckling the pavement. Behind him, uniformed policeman and ARP wardens continued to rope off the street as too dangerous to pass through. Beyond, fireman were busy playing jets of water on flames that licked through doorways and windows, maintaining their raging rigor with dumb insolence.

George saw the ambulance pause as burning rubble crashed into the street, then the driver gunned the engine and drove straight through, bouncing the vehicle over obstacles she couldn't drive around, and through several sheets of flame that suddenly leapt at her. The smell of burning rubber wafted toward George as tires started to melt.

A mongrel dog slouched past, its tongue lolling out the

side of its mouth, its fur singed and matted, its tail curled between its legs nearly level with its belly. A man dashed by, urging along his wife, who was sobbing as she ran.

George spotted a copper taking a break, his tin hat at a jaunty angle as he smoked a cigarette, deep in conversation with a civilian. It took George a moment to recognize Fred Medford out of uniform.

The bobby spotted George approaching and tossed away his fag, straightening his posture and giving Medford a sign.

"How is he?" George asked, as he reached the two men.

"Lucky," Medford said. "If that bugger fell down a hole he'd come up clutching gold. Bomb took out the back garden, ripped off the bloody roof and half the back of the house, but nary a scratch on him."

"Jesus," George muttered. He glanced around. "Where is he now?"

"Inside." Medford nodded toward the house in front of them. "Refused to go to hospital 'til you got here. He's right shook up, I can tell yer. The woman's already gone, but you ain't going to get much out of her for the moment. I think she's lost it."

Gazing around, George said, "Can't imagine why, can you?"

"This way, then." Medford nodded to the uniform to carry on and led George into the house.

They found Herbert Williams sitting on the settee, looking pale, his face pinched with pain.

"Watcha, Sarge," he managed.

"You stay there, son," George said. "No need to get up." He looked over the young policeman and went on, "You should be in hospital."

"Naw, not me, Sarge. Takes more than Hitler to knock me out."

"That's the spirit, lad," Medford commented. He glanced out the open doorway as someone shouted at him. "Be right there," he yelled back. "See you in a minute, George," he added, and disappeared.

"Right, Herbert. What happened?"

It took Williams several moments of alternately squinting, wincing, and shaking his head, as though arguing silently with himself before he eventually said, "I seen him, Sarge."

"Go on," George said quietly. "Take your time."

Williams shook his head again and gagged for a second. "Least, I think it's a him. He had its *arm*, for Christ's sake. . . ."

George had never before seen a look of such wretched incredulity on a man's face. It was unnerving. He looked away, making a business of taking out and lighting up a cigarette. "Where?" he finally asked.

"Upstairs. Not there now, thank Gawd. They took it away when they come for the woman. Just the blood. I didn't think anything so small would have that much . . ." Again he broke off, unable to complete his thoughts.

"All right, Herbert," George said, blowing out a stream of smoke. "Let's get it over with and then we can both sod off home."

Williams straightened his shoulders. "Yeah, 'course, Sarge."

"You heard these screams, right? Come round here with a neighbor, left the poor bugger downstairs."

"Yeah," Williams whispered. "How is he?"

George shook his head. "Sorry, Herbert. House fell on top of him. You know him?"

"No."

George waited.

"I went upstairs," Williams finally said, "and went into

the bedroom, like. Didn't see her 'cause she was hiding. I thought, at first like, it was that animal we've been after . . ."

Again he broke off, but mastered himself. "But it wasn't—at least, it's no animal I ever seen before. I mean, it looked like a big monkey at first, I mean, really big, come up to my chest, I suppose. I couldn't see much of its face, 'cause there was all this hair, that was matted and such— and talk about stink! Christ, you never smelled nothing like this, Sarge. It was like something had died.

"Anyway, I yelled at it, but nothing happened until I shone me flashlight on it. Then it jumped up and went for me. I give it a belt and went after it, but I stumbled on the bloody stairs, didn't I?

"When I went back, I saw what it had been doing." He swallowed hard. "I first saw it, like, crouching in a pool of blood, that was, you know, still spreading."

He broke off, and pointed toward the shattered kitchen. "Somewhere under that lot are its footprints."

George pursed his lips. That would be how this case was progressing. On his way in, he'd seen the back of the house, or what was left of it. There was no way he'd be able to dig down and still find a print. Nevertheless, he determined he would take another look tomorrow if he got the chance.

"From what I can gather," Williams went on, "it come in through the kitchen, and she stuck a table in the way, but it got past. It must have gone for her and caught her shawl, which is why it was all ripped up. Then it come up the stairs after her and managed to snatch the baby. She went potty, of course, which was them screams I heard. God knows what happened next, but she just lost it, ended up crouching the other side of the bed. This . . . this *thing*, Sarge, it killed her kid. Took it from her and bit it in the throat. It had bit its arm off and was chewing on it when I come through the door. . . ."

"Jesus H. Christ!"

Williams looked up from his crouching position on the sofa, straightening and tightly gripping George's arm with his good hand. "This thing ain't animal nor human, Sarge. I've seen it. It was . . ." He shook his head in frustration. "It looks like a human, but it ain't—I dunno how to describe it . . . like some kind of werewolf or something." He gave up and let go of George's arm, embarrassed at his desperate flight of fancy.

"That's enough for now, lad. You go to hospital, get yourself fixed up, and I'll see you in the morning." George rose and placed a hand placatingly on Williams's shoulder. The young detective nodded, engrossed in his thoughts, then looked up. "There's something I've been thinking about. When I first come in, it didn't pay me no attention, even when I shouted. When it saw the flashlight, it turned on me like a bleeding lunatic." He paused, then said, "I think it's deaf. That's why it can eat during the bombing and not get frightened."

George's grip tightened. "By God, I think you're right, Herbert."

"And another thing, Sarge. I don't think it killed them first two victims, at least, like the doc says, they wasn't conscious when it come upon them and finished them off. It really ain't big enough to go after an adult—"

"—so it's going after the kids because they're easy meat," George finished for him.

"That's what I think. This thing's got a taste for us." He shuddered. "Just the thought of being injured in one of these raids is bad enough; but having this thing come up and start gnawing on you while you're trapped. Jesus!"

George's voice hardened. "You keep this to yourself,

106

Herbert. Tell Fred Medford if you like, but that's it. Nobody else. You understand me?"

Williams ducked his head again. "Sure, Sarge. I understand."

More sympathetically, George added, "I knew you would, lad. You're a good copper, Herbert. What you did here took some balls, let me tell you. Wouldn't be surprised if you didn't get a medal or something."

"Yeah?"

"Definitely."

SUNDAY

January 5, 1941

G eorge stared at himself in the bathroom mirror, lathering the shaving soap with the stumpy brush, then painting the foam across his face. The red-rimmed eyes that gazed back had dark bags, and there were gray streaks in the bushy mustache. For a moment, he saw his father, and the sudden recognition startled George.

He supposed his thoughts were prompted by the letter he had received from his Auntie Mabel yesterday. "Your father's been took poorly," it said. "I didn't want to bother you before . . ."

George knew what was expected of him. He should have been making plans to return to Swansea as soon as possible. The arrival of the letter meant his father was probably dying. But George could not find the filial affection he was supposed to feel.

"Sod you, you evil bastard!" he said into the mirror and then looked away, wiping his face.

The day had dawned icy and fresh, and a cold draft gusted into the tiled, linoleum-covered bathroom through warps in the framework of the narrow, frosted second-floor window. A damp patch was growing on the peeling white ceiling in the corner behind him, George noticed, like a dark cloud gathering. He'd have to do something about that.

He remembered as a lad watching his da' shave with a cutthroat razor on a Saturday night. In his collarless shirtsleeves, old man Llewellyn would stand by the kitchen sink, a mirror propped against the taps, stropping the razor on a thick leather belt with steady, rhythmic strokes—the same belt he often used to punish George and his brother. Then he would take his time spreading the lather, testing the sharpness of the razor's edge, stropping once more, painstakingly scraping away several days' stubble.

George turned his thoughts away from home. Well, not home for many years; perhaps, he thought, never home really because of that sadistic bugger. Never a haven, like other homes. Arthur, older than George by four years, had gone into the army in 1917, just in time for the bloody futility of Passachendale Ridge, and returned transformed—half blind, bitter, and unemployable. George, meanwhile, had labored away his adolescence in the pits. His mam died in the flu epidemic of 1919, when he was sixteen. He'd left the mines, and home, soon after, and had not returned for over twenty years.

The pipes moaned and burped as the old couple downstairs got ready for their weekly visit to church, something else George no longer bothered with, not since his wife . . .

He spat toothpaste into the sink and rinsed his mouth. The bumps and thumps of the water pipes were aggravating the hell out of him this morning.

The PM's personal private secretary had telephoned the chief inspector from Downing Street late last night to find out exactly what was going on. Disturbing reports, he said, had begun appearing in the newspapers. "Mr. Churchill is *most* concerned at the low morale in the district." The inspector had passed along the message. "Which means," he had added at the end of it, "that I'm ticked off too, George."

"You and me both, guv," George had said. "My bet is still on some animal or other. Trouble is, it could be anywhere in all that bloody chaos out there. Don't worry, we'll get it soon enough."

"Make damn sure you do. This is a bad business, George, nasty. Get it sorted."

Nasty doesn't come close, George thought.

The locals were quick enough to complain when things went wrong, but East Enders prided themselves on taking care of their own problems, be they murderous lunatics or Gypsy interlopers. As a result, the police had been able to find out precious little so far.

Over a drink in the boozer last night before the air raid, DC Williams had told George the zoos couldn't help much either—or wouldn't, anyway. The teeth marks could not be identified, and they were too short-staffed to go into it any further. The director of Regent's Park had said bluntly their best bet was the army. Find whatever it was and shoot it. Whipsnade Zoo had been as useless, and anyway, was too far from London.

Why me? George thought bitterly. Things were going from bad to worse. He was beginning to feel scared of the dark, a feeling he'd banished since childhood, and admitting even that much to himself wasn't easy.

□   □   □

George and Sergeant Medford arrived at St. Mathew's Hospital at eight fifteen. They climbed the sandbagged stone steps leading to the barricaded main entrance and, once inside, were reminded of their school days. The Victorian building had a familiar wide echoing entry lobby, sweeping stairs to the upper two floors, and the patrician scope of a barely clinging bygone era.

At the front desk, the policemen introduced themselves and asked for Vera Armstrong. Ten minutes later, obviously weary after finishing a night shift, she sat with the two men in the dining room, while around them other nurses and white-coated doctors finished meager breakfasts.

"We need an interpreter," George said, after the introductions were out of the way. "I was hoping you might do it for us."

"What's the language?"

"Gypsy—I don't know." He looked down, chagrined. "I'm sorry," he began, then smiled ruefully. "I'm not exactly top-hole at the moment. That's no excuse, I know . . ." He let his apology hang with embarrassment.

Her hard look softened. She had a pert face, though her fatigue had given her a slight double chin. "I've heard what's going on," she said. Her eyes carefully searched his face. As if making a decision against her better judgment, she added, "I doubt I'll be of much help—I really only speak French and Hungarian, and both of those are pretty rusty."

"You seemed to be doing all right the other night, as I recall."

"Probably use a nurse, anyway," Medford commented.

"We have to interview one of the Gypsies. Mother of a kiddie that . . . well, anyway. The kiddie died, see, Friday night we think, but we're not certain."

"I shouldn't think she's in a state to tell you much, then."

Sergeant Medford took over the conversation, and George found himself distracted by Vera Armstrong, imagining her as she would have been a couple of years ago, before the war, a pretty suburban housewife, probably, from Richmond or Edgware or somewhere. Quiet, but with some steel in her, he judged.

"What?" George said, annoyed his reverie had been interrupted.

"I said, are you fit, then? She's just going upstairs to fetch her coat."

"Right."

In the car, while George drove, Sergeant Medford tried to put Vera Armstrong at ease. "How long you been a nurse, luv?"

"Six years." She leaned forward onto the front passenger seat. "What about you?"

"In the force, you mean? Twenty year now."

"And you, Mr. Llewellyn?"

"Detective Sergeant," he corrected her. "Twelve years here, and five in Cardiff."

"I thought I detected a bit of an accent. Do you ever go back?"

"No," he said, and concentrated on driving.

"You married then, Vera?" Medford asked, giving George a dirty look. *Behave yourself,* it said.

She was silent for a while, then said quietly, "He was a pilot, at Biggin Hill."

"Ah, one of the 'Few,'" Medford said lightly.

"Depends on how you look at it, I suppose," she said morosely.

"Get yourself a nice Yank, that's my advice, when them buggers finally get their finger out and join in."

□　　□　　□

At nine-thirty, while most of the station force was helping to clear up the previous night's bomb damage, George, Sergeant Medford, Nurse Armstrong, and four uniformed policemen entered the Romany encampment. In the distance, several fires still burned in the shells of houses, and occasionally ambulances and fire engines raced by on the main road, alarm bells clanging.

The campsite looked a wreck, George thought with disgust. The police stood for a moment, waiting for someone to emerge from a caravan and silence the yapping dogs, straining at leashes, their front legs pawing the air in frustrated attempts to leap free, their barks turning to snarls as the policemen neared. The ragamuffin horses reacted skittishly, snorting, pawing the already churned earth, and nickering. A smoldering bonfire spread like a gray skin disease in the center of the parked caravans.

"Which one is it?" George asked Sergeant Medford.

"Only know her first name, Taff. Magda something or other."

"Big help you are," George muttered. With a signal, he dispersed the uniforms through the campsite.

"I'd just curb that damn temper of yours if I were you, George Llewellyn," Medford said. "You're like a bear with a sore head these last few days. I've got enough to deal with here without you giving me aggravation as well."

They were interrupted by several Romany men emerging from behind caravans sporting logs like cudgels.

"There'll be no need of *that*," Medford said, pointing to their clubs. "Now just behave yourselves. Who's in charge here?"

The men did not seem impressed with the warning, and eyed the policemen with unmasked dislike.

"Come on, let's be havin' you, we ain't got all bloody day. Who's the head gypo around here?"

One of the men insolently indicated a caravan at the far end of the circle. They fanned out behind the policemen, not so much menacing as ready to finish anything the coppers wanted to start. George and Sergeant Medford made their way to a gaudy, but now weatherbeaten red-and-gold–painted caravan with scalloped eaves, and a shaggy, mud-caked pinto munching oats beside it.

A moment later a hunched old lady quickly shut the door behind her and stood, hands on hips, looking down. She wore a hand-decorated red shawl around her shoulders over a green blouse and ankle-length skirt. The peacock effect disappeared, however, the closer George drew to her, for the clothes were worn and patched, the skirt almost threadbare in places. *These people are little more than tinkers,* he thought disgustedly.

"You in charge here, missus?" George asked.

"What do you want?"

"We have reason to believe that one of your people can help us with our inquiries," he went on officiously. "We also have reason to believe that a dead baby found Friday last belongs to a woman here."

The old lady's face was like old tan leather. She stared at George, seeing beyond the Romany men watching, fidgeting, ready to act on a sign from her should she need help.

She climbed down and walked toward another caravan. As she approached, she called, "Magda, Gus, the rozzers are here." She had a strong Scottish accent that seemed to belie George's concept of what Gypsies should sound like. Somehow, he always expected them to be foreign, not

British. But he realized it was their culture that set them apart, not how they looked or sounded.

There was no answer from inside, but the old lady strode up to the door and, barely knocking, went inside. She emerged a moment later and beckoned to the policemen. George, Fred Medford, and Nurse Armstrong followed.

The caravan was dimly lit, and it took a moment for George to see that a woman was curled up in bed.

"Does she speak English?" he asked. A man, whom George had not noticed before, leaned forward from the shadows by the head of the bed. The old lady said sharply. "What do you think?"

"Who's he?"

Before the man could reply, the old lady said, "His name's Gus. He's her husband. He doesnay talk much, specially to coppers."

"This lady's a nurse," Sergeant Medford said, indicating Vera Armstrong. "We'd like her to examine the woman."

"Don't need fancy nurses," the old lady snapped. "Take care of our own, we do. I've got all the trainin' that's needed round here."

Nurse Armstrong drew a deep breath, and George saw she was about to start trouble. Quickly, he asked the old Gypsy woman, "Can she talk to us or not?"

Nurse Armstrong glared at George, then moved to the woman's bedside, brushing Gus's knees out of the way.

He rose from his chair into the light, moving to push her back, a thin fellow with a mass of curly black hair and a white scar snaking across his lips. George grabbed the man's arm, his grip tight. "I'd keep my hands to myself, were I you," he cautioned. For a moment, George flashed back ten years to another young man in another gypsy caravan. He felt the tension in the young Romany's muscles and readied himself for a struggle. A nod from the old lady was enough to dissuade the young man from making further trouble; he relaxed.

George turned to the old woman. "Don't I know you?"

"No," she said. "I'd remember *you*."

George wasn't so certain. He sat on the bottom of the bed as there were no other seats. If it mattered it would come back to him. Instead, he watched Vera Armstrong. She examined the woman briefly and said to the old lady, "What have you given her?"

"Something to quiet her. A herbal."

Nurse Armstrong turned to George and said, "You won't get much sense out of her for a while. She's been sedated."

"You got a license to practice medicine?" George asked the old Gypsy woman.

"I can tell ye anything ye want to know."

"Is that right? It *is* her baby we found then?"

Gus seemed suddenly cowed by the statement and nodded from his chair, staring at the floor.

"She was outside doing some laundry," the old lady said. "Friday afternoon. That was when she noticed the child was missing. She'd been asleep in her pram."

"You mean someone took her?"

"Not exactly."

"What *do* you mean, missus?" There was no response. "And no one saw anything, I suppose?"

Fred Medford looked ready to intervene, but he caught Vera Armstrong's eyes and shook his head, straightening his posture instead.

"If they had've done, do you think you'd be here now?"

"Any ideas?"

"None you'd want to hear."

George breathed a sigh of restraint, then abruptly stood.

118

"Right, Fred, I've had enough of this nonsense. Get the lads to search the place. Make it thorough."

"You got no right," the old lady said, standing in his way.

"I've got every right, missus." George withdrew a folded sheet of paper from within his coat pocket and waved it at her. "This is a search warrant, duly signed by a magistrate and being lawfully executed. I don't give a damn what happens to you lot. I want to know what's going on; I've a good mind to run the whole lot of you in as accessories to murder. I've done it before, I can do it again. Now, what's it to be?"

The silent battle of wills strained the atmosphere in the room. Eventually, the old lady pursed her lips as though sucking lemon and, turning, muttered something to Gus, who quickly scampered from the room.

"Where's he off to?" Fred Medford said.

"Go and have a quick look, will you?" George suggested, still not taking his eyes from the Gypsy woman. When he had gone, George looked at Vera Armstrong sitting quietly beside the patient, watching him. He wondered what she thought of him after that performance—her opinion seemed important, suddenly—and then he silently chastised himself for being distracted. He took his time lighting a cigarette and offered one to the old lady.

"Now then," he said calmly, "let's have it from the beginning, shall we? Full names, times, the lot."

□   □   □

Fred Medford and George strolled down the ruined high street. Nurse Armstrong had been thanked and sent home, though she protested she had done little to be thanked for. George had shaken her hand and looking her in the eyes said he'd be in touch, though quite what he meant by that he did not know. He supposed he would like to see her again. She interested him.

"What do you reckon?"

Angrily, George said, "Load of rubbish. I'm bloody certain I know that old cow from somewhere."

They passed a series of bomb-damaged shops with hand-painted signs in the window like BUSINESS AS USUAL and UP YOURS ADOLF. A café with ruined glass frontage was nevertheless doing business on the pavement, bacon and eggs and sausages sizzling in large frying pans on Primus stoves. Two cooks in grease-spattered aprons were bustling around as though nothing much had happened.

While George bought a bacon sandwich and sipped a cup of hot, strong tea, Sergeant Medford surveyed the damaged street and commented, "Funny bloody war, ain't it. Changes you, like, when you don't expect it to. Too much to deal with, these days. People don't like that. Can't say's I blame 'em, to be honest."

"Nasty, bach, if you ask me."

"I dunno, it's like too ordinary somehow. Not what we was expecting anyhow. I mean, that's what's so scary I suppose. That something so ordinary can be so bloody nasty."

"Them Tories made a right balls-up, as usual," George said. "And now we got to deal with it, as usual. Bloody coffins like they expected the whole population killed, and nowhere to house nor feed the poor buggers what ain't."

"What was it old Churchill said a couple of months ago? 'There's more agreement round here than among the authorities.'"

"We're in worse shape than I thought, then," George replied. He lit a cigarette.

The two policemen walked farther, passing shopkeepers and residents busily brushing shards of glass and other rubble into the gutter in neat piles. A woman stood in their way, oblivious, hands on hips, staring at what was left of her fish and chip shop after shrapnel had come through the roof and wrecked the inside. "That's a downright shame," one of the café cooks called out to her.

She turned and yelled, "Here, who are you sympathizing with? That was our shrapnel, that was!"

"No accounting for some, is there?" Medford said to George with a smile as they strode past. "Heard about Herbert Williams and the monkey then?"

George's moroseness gave way to curiosity. He shook his head.

"Found this monkey in the ruins, didn't they, the other night. You know he's running around like a blue-arsed fly looking for this animal we're after, right?

"Anyway," Medford continued, "he's chatting up these WVS bints who are dragging this mobile canteen out of a bomb hole in the street when they finds this monkey under a slab. As he's the only copper around, some officious twit of an air-raid warden comes up to him and says, 'An animal what's injured in an air raid belongs to the police. You're it.'"

"So what does Herbert do?"

"Well, he was stumped, poor bugger. He finally gets one of the WVSes to give it a cup of tea—'Shock case,' he says."

"Get away."

"Straight up, George," Medford said, chuckling. "That ain't the half of it. The warden gets out his pen and starts a file called Monkey and insists, seeing as how it's a shock case, that they wrap it in blankets and lie it down.

"So young Herbert looks at the poor little thing lying there shivering, and says to the WVS, 'Maybe he'd like some hot milk,' so they all look at each other, then finally someone goes off and gets some. Herbert takes the milk and gives a sip of it to the monkey, right, who sort of shakes his head as if to say, 'What the hell happened?' then takes the tin cup from Herbert and drains the lot. 'There you are, you see,' Herbert says, 'he's right as rain.'

"And he was dead right, cause the little bugger turned round and bit him."

"You're pulling my leg."

"Eventually, the zoo sends over this little ambulance, I swear to God, and takes it away for rest and recuperation."

For the first time in what seemed weeks, George found himself laughing. It freed him for a while from the oppressiveness of the day.

"Come on, it's Sunday. I'll buy you a quick one," he said.

"After we see young Williams if you like," Medford said. "One of the lads told me he's hopping up and down on one leg waiting to see us. Says he's found something."

"Not more monkeys, I hope."

"Probably a gorilla. You ever met his dad?"

Both men chuckled as they renewed their strides.

□   □   □

"This is Mrs. Tanner," DC Williams said to the two sergeants. They were in the front room of her house, next door to a local post office-cum-general stationer's store. It was a dark room, the wallpaper a faded art deco. A large, rounded wooden radio stood on the mantel piece next to a huge mirror. At the other end, a clock noisily ticked away the minutes beside a photograph of a mustachioed sardonic-looking policeman. Thick lace curtains obscured the windows.

As the two sergeants entered the front room behind Herbert Williams, a rotund woman in her sixties, seated in an armchair by a crackling wood fire, looked up at them and smiled broadly, struggling to rise.

"Well, I never," she said, giving up and sitting down again heavily, with a wince of pain. "Hello George, Fred. How's tricks?"

"Well, I'll be! It's Ethel Tanner," George said. "I thought you were up north somewhere."

"Naw, I come back down with Sid—what? Must be two, three year ago now. He died about eighteen months back, and I been running the post office out front, or what's left of it now, anyway, ever since."

Medford grinned at her, taking in the heavy bandages wrapped around her tree-trunk legs jutting from beneath a worn patterned pinafore. "How you been, Ethel?"

"Fair to middlin', Fred."

DC Williams looked confused. Taking pity on him, Sergeant Medford explained, "Ethel used to work down the station a few years back. In the filing room."

"More than a few," Ethel Tanner commented. "You wasn't much older than this laddie here. Just made sergeant, both of yers, as I recall."

"I thought they was born sergeants," Williams muttered.

"None of us was ever *that* young, Ethel." Medford grinned at Williams, noticing his bandaged left hand. The grin became wider as he glanced over at George.

"I told you, son," George said to Williams, "never go nowhere without your nuts. See what happens."

"Very funny," Williams said, ignoring his hand in favor of nursing his injured shoulder.

"What you doing here, darlin'?" Medford said to Ethel Tanner. "Everybody else I know has buggered off out of it."

"Fred Medford," she said. "Mind your language. And on a Sunday an' all."

"Sorry, Ethel."

She indicated a sofa across from her for the policemen to sit in. "It's my 'ome, ain't it? Mine and Sid's.

"So, George," she went on, examining the two sergeants sitting side by side, "you've put on a bit of weight at last. Down the boozer too much by the looks of it. Still trying to charm the knickers off the ladies with that little-boy act of yours?"

"Naw, not me, Ethel. I give all that up. There's a war on, you know."

"Right," she said laughing. Medford and Williams smiled along with her.

"So how is it, since you got back, you never come round to say hello, then?"

"And what would your dear lady wife think of that, George Llewellyn?"

He looked away. What should have been a joke instead chilled the atmosphere. One look at Fred Medford's almost ghostly shake of his head, and Mrs. Tanner realized she had said the wrong thing. George replied breezily, "What about a cup of tea then, Ethel?"

"'Course George. Excuse if I don't get up, but my arthritis is playing havoc with my legs at the moment. Ask this nice young man, here."

"Yeah, of course," Williams volunteered, and disappeared into the kitchen.

"Seen the papers this morning?" she asked.

The two policemen shook their heads.

"You should." She handed George a copy of the *News of the World,* a Sunday rag George didn't usually bother with. "Page five," she suggested.

The headline read, "Nazi Werewolf Terrorizes East

End." The story was about as accurate as the headline, but it made the most of the trouble between the locals and the Gypsies, and the dead Gypsy baby. *Thank God they haven't found out about the fourth one yet,* George thought. The newspaper speculated on whether it was all a diabolical German plot, whereby a psychotic lunatic had been parachuted into the city and let loose to terrorize the inhabitants.

George showed the piece to Fred Medford. "You should know better than to believe this load of old rubbish," he said to Mrs. Tanner. "It's worse than that one about them Jerries dropping plague rats on us."

"Oh, so that's what them little parachutes was for," Medford said.

"Get away with you, you foolish man!"

DC Williams, returning with the teas, overhead Medford and was suddenly caught by a violent coughing fit, nearly spilling the contents of the tray he was carrying. He hastily put it down and hid behind a large handkerchief until he had recovered his composure.

"You can be mother," Mrs. Tanner joked to him as he set about pouring milk into each cup. "So, what you come round for, George?"

"Herbert?"

"Yeah, right, sorry, Sarge. Mrs. Tanner here knew the old biddies what lived in that big house on the common."

"You mean them two weirdos?"

"Them's the ones," George answered, suddenly all business.

"Well, I can't tell you much, really. Kept themselves to themselves, they did. Some chauffeur or something used to come round the post office once a month like and pick up any letters for 'em. Bills mostly, from what I could tell. I really knew the bloke and his family what used to live there before them. From what I gather, these two sisters was looking after the place for him. House sitting, or something, I suppose you'd call it. Stepan, their name was, as I recall. Immigrants I think."

"His name wasn't Henderson, was it?"

"That's right," she said. "Mr. Robert. Right gentleman he was—a bit of a lad before he got married, if you get my drift, though not a patch on his younger brother."

George and Fred nodded they understood.

"Yeah," Mrs. Tanner continued, wincing slightly as she shifted position. "Packed up with his wife and kids and everybody and went orf to Cape Town or something, if I remember right. About fifteen years ago now, it must be."

"What about the two women. Anything unusual you can remember about them?"

"Well, as I say, George, no one really seen too much of them. At one time, blimey, must have been ten, twelve year ago at least, they used to have lots of parties, you know, posh like, but then they stopped and sort of locked themselves away." She paused, and added, "It was about then them gypsies started coming round here again, an' all."

"Got to be more than that," George complained. "How come you know all this then, Ethel?"

"Get away with you, George," Mrs. Tanner said, rocking forward on the chair. "Fancy you asking me a question like that. I'm surprised at yer. People come in the shop, tell me stuff, you pick up bits and pieces here and there, you know."

George nodded.

"What happened to poor old Sid, then?" Fred Medford asked.

"Ticker give out on him. Didn't feel nothing, so they tell me."

In memory of her husband, a silence descended on the room for a moment, as both men conjured up memories of ex-Police Constable Sidney Tanner. It was broken by Williams slurping his tea and spilling it on the notebook resting in his lap. He looked around, guilty at disturbing what seemed to have become a hallowed moment for the three old friends.

"Lot of it about at the moment," Medford commented.

"Anything else?" George said, almost pleading with her.

"Well," she began, dragging out the word as she searched her memory, "as I say, this ain't gospel, but I heard one of them was a musician or something. Used to give piano lessons, any rate. I suppose the other one looked after the house."

"You hear any funny stories, like? Strange pets, stuff like that?" Medford suggested.

"Always stories about foreigners round here, ain't there? I mean, they're different. They smell funny. Never cottoned much to that sort of rubbish meself though, you know that. You should've heard Sid going on about that Oswald Mosley feller and his gang of brownshirt louts, wandering the streets, stirring up trouble. Gawd strewth!"

"Allright Ethel. You've been really helpful, I mean it," George said, glancing at his watch and standing up. He seemed suddenly withdrawn. He looked down at Fred Medford, still seated on the sofa, and said, "I gotta go. If I'm going out to Epping Forest this afternoon I'd better get my skates on."

Medford raised his eyebrows in surprise, but said nothing.

"Keep well, girl."

"You too, George. Come back, have a natter. I'll be here. About all I can do these days, anyway."

Medford said, "I'll hang on here for a bit."

"Yeah, right, good idea," George said, adding, "You done well, Herbert."

He buttoned up his overcoat and let himself out into the chilly January air.

□　　□　　□

Stiff from his sleepless nights on the floor of the ruined house and the bomb blast only days before, Nevil shuffled with an arthritic gait through the ruined landscape toward the back of his house.

His mind reeled with panic. *"You've really done it this time,"* a devilish voice within him gloated.

"But I haven't done anything," he silently argued with himself.

"They'll still blame you, though."

"It just isn't fair," Nevil thought.

Hidden nearby, a gang of kids were yelling with abandon, accompanied by the tinkle of smashed glass and the hollow clangs of metal clouting metal. Nevil topped the rise of a man-made hillock of debris that descended to Sebastopol Street and was jerked from his anxiety by a rock that bounced toward him, quickly followed by several others. "Here, watch it!" he shouted in warning. The kids took no notice, laughing and shouting back at him, mocking is limping walk. "Stimpo the gimpo," they catcalled in chorus. Several more rocks bounced perilously close. It was all suddenly too much for him.

He stood, head bowed, swaying, a verbal storm growing to a thunder in his mind, until the ache of it was so bad he thought he must pass out. He held his head in his hands, shaking it from side to side, feeling nauseous, a low, keening moan escaping despite himself, half expecting a blow round the side of his head. His mother had favored the left ear. . . .

Several rocks bounced close by. Fearful of attracting more attention Nevil hurried away.

He halted by the back fence of his house and warily looked around for policemen. There were none that he could see, so they probably weren't watching his home yet. It had only to be a matter of time before that bastard sergeant latched onto him. If they could prove it was his flashlight he'd dropped. . . . He really ought to go round the station and get it sorted out.

Knowing my luck, he thought, *they'll lock me up and throw away the key. Or maybe they'll let me go and tell the locals all sorts of lies as usual so they can tear me apart.*

He slipped over his slatted wooden fence and then into the kitchen. He was exhausted after two days of roaming the ruins fruitlessly looking for the boy, a wary eye out for the creature—he couldn't yet bring himself to name it—that attacked him the other night. He entertained fantasies of killing it; saving the child, being a real hero for once.

It had all happened so quickly, Nevil thought. A blur of shadows, flashing teeth, lots of hair—and those claws—like knives!

He reached a hand to his face and fingered the deep scratches. He tried not to think about the house, the assault, but his mind kept shifting back to an image of the baby. As if death were not enough, this one was horrifying in its betrayal of innocence. *We don't care what kind of a world we've made for our children,* Nevil thought.

His queasiness passed, and he hauled himself up the stairs by the banisters.

He looked around his dingy, ill-lit bedroom wondering how much longer he had before they came for him. Feeling exhausted, he lay back on the bed, closing his eyes, basking in the protection, however temporary, of his home. Yet his inner turmoil did not subside.

As Nevil sank into an uneasy doze, from the dark recesses of his memory hulking shapes formed in his mind's eye—specters he thought he had banished, once again freed to torment him.

The shadows coalesced into a familiar face, white as flour, on the opposite side of a shellhole in no-mans-land, transfixing Nevil with a blank, yet somehow accusing stare. Someone was again yelling angrily at him, but thankfully he couldn't make sense of the words.

He clutched his tin helmet and Enfield rifle as shells slithered above his head and exploded, part of a demonic symphony laced by the gurgling stutter of machine-gun fire and high-pitched screams.

Nevil and eight other British Tommies had made the German forward lines that afternoon and then been forced to take cover as the main British assault force withdrew, leaving Nevil and the eight men isolated, surrounded by fifty yards of darkness and desolation raked by sporadic gun- and shellfire from both sides.

A flare whooshed into the night sky, exploding in blinding brilliance and then, somehow suspended, hung like a sun, illuminating the ghastly scene. The corpse, splayed against the shellhole, had begun to putrefy. An inquisitive worm peered out at Nevil from an eye socket. Another shell exploded nearby, sending up a gout of frozen earth that rained down like sleet. The ground vibrated with the shock.

Nevil cautiously poked his head over the top. The landscape was a frozen muddy termite nest of ramparts hiding trenches, barbed wire coils, shellholes, dead and wounded. In the foremost German trench, now abandoned, six of the stranded Tommies were hunched in a dugout, pinned down by the shelling and lighter but equally deadly fire from a gradually advancing Hun platoon, determined to regain what they had lost.

As the flare sputtered and faded, not twenty yards from his position Nevil saw Lance Corporal Atkins, hanging on barbed wire, alternately moaning and then hoarsely pleading for help. His only answer now was machine-gun fire that ripped over Nevil's position and gouged the earth near Atkins, but never quite reached him.

The artillery shelling continued, softening up the Huns for a renewed push at dawn. With luck, Nevil thought, perhaps he could just wait it out where he was. But for the men still crouched in the dugout, it was only a matter of time before they were killed by one of their own shells or the advancing Huns.

Two men from the dugout had already tried to crawl over to rescue Atkins, but had been cut down like fairground ducks. The others were angrily calling out to Nevil to try, cursing his cowardice; he was the closest. . . .

He awoke in a cold sweat, his breathing shallow and rapid, wondering for a moment where he was, then remembering. Still keeping a blanket around his shoulders, he rose and crossed to the bathroom.

Once he had shaved and bathed he felt a little more resolute and went downstairs to his living room.

He reached up to a high shelf and carefully removed a lacquered box, returning with it a moment later to the table by the window. He removed a cloth-covered pack of Tarot cards, pushing the books on his table to one side to make space. He shuffled the cards awkwardly, hesitated, and remembered as he reached forward that he should use his left hand.

He made three piles to the left, then reconstituted the deck. He chose a card at random. It was the Hierophant.

Placing it face up in the center of the table, he stared at it grim-faced. The Hierophant was ruled by Taurus, his star sign. He traced the detail in the card with a finger. *The four guardians at the altar are the different aspects of being,* he recalled: fire, earth, air, and water. *The Hierophant has combined all these elements in himself. But to become the Awakened One, he must fight the strong need to conform, to have the approval of others.*

Quickly, he dealt the rest of the cards. Then, with stiff, clawlike fingers he followed the hidden meanings before him.

The first card was laid across the Significator, four others dealt to the cardinal points, north, south, east, and west. To his right he lay down four more cards from south to north.

He pointed to the King of Cups reversed. *This represents the influences set against me. A man of violence, injustice.* He paused. *The policeman,* he thought, with dread. He had been right all along. The cards did not lie; he examined them further. There were four cards of the Major Arcana here. That suggested powerful outside forces controlling his life. The outcome of all this might well be entirely out of his hands.

He stared at the cards, trying to make sense of what he saw. *This one,* he thought, an index finger dangling over the fourth card, *the Star reversed, means doubt, pessimism, stubbornness. But she is also Mother nature, representing perpetual renewal and creation.*

This one, he thought, moving on to another card, *represents what I feel about the matter: Judgment, awakening, a change in how I think.*

Nevil looked up, seeking a sign in the faces of the gargoyles leering down at him from the pelmets, but finding none.

He continued to appraise the meanings of the cards, finally reaching the tenth one. *This represents the sum of the others.*

Before him lay the Tower. Lightning was striking, destroying the roof, while flames licked from the windows. Two figures were falling head down. He knew exactly what it meant: the overthrow of selfish ambition.

His eyes glazed as they moved from card to card. *The crown of materialistic thought has been struck by the lightning of the righteous spirit. The man and woman will be dashed on the rocks of hard truth below them.*

"Except the Lord build the house, they labor in vain that build it," Nevil muttered. Before him was the card of conflict, of unforeseen catastrophes, bringing enlightenment in their wake. Whatever was to be destroyed in his life was for a reason: to purify him. Somehow, understanding did not help.

They were cards of transition. But into what?

He swept up the cards, wrapped them, and carefully put them back in their container. There was nothing more he could do but wait. Bowing his head, he lay it on the table and stared blankly out of the window at the red-tinged evening sky, almost hoping the bombers would return and put him out of his misery.

□   □   □

The Green Line single-decker bus that took George out to Epping Forest labored up and down the hilly roads of north London like an exhausted animal.

George was too preoccupied to really notice the irregular changing of passengers around him as people stepped off, others stepped on, and the bus lurched forward from a stop with a mechanical groan. The newcomers walked down the central aisle balancing like drunks in church, searching for seats before they tripped and made fools of themselves.

Despite himself, George was thinking about the past. It did no good whatsoever to dwell on these things, but the inactivity of the long journey—and his destination—acted as triggers, plunging him once again into situations he had tried hard to forget for so many years.

Sunday was always a strange nonday; a day, George had learned as a child, for family and worship; but for George, Sundays had always been the epitome of boredom and wet empty streets, relieved, now he was an adult and when he wasn't on duty, by a visit down to the pub lunchtime and again in the evening, with a snooze after lunch.

He sometimes wondered what things would have been like if he and Gwenyth had managed to stay together, but was unable to make the imaginative leap today. Family, to George, still meant home with his parents, not a life shackled to Gwenyth.

His father had disliked Gwenyth and had called George a fool for having to marry her; but what did a rebellious eighteen-year-old know? It still irked George that his da' had been right.

"Knocked her up, and now you got to pay for your pleasure, bach. That's how they get yer. They're all whores, don't you know that yet? Now you'll learn—the *hard* way." And then he had laughed. It was the last time George had spoken to his father face to face.

You needed to see the world through a lifetime of bruising frustration to fully understand what his da' had been getting at, George was sure. As he had grown older and dealt with his own disappointments, George thought he understood his father a little better, though he would not forgive him.

George could not really say why exactly, but he still felt that when he was a child his father had taken something from him and never returned it, or perhaps kept something from him he should have had but didn't, though George could not say precisely what "it" might have been. He thought he knew how to put right his father's mistakes; yet Gwenyth had not been as conscientious a homemaker as his mam, their early attempts at "family" life bankrupted by her constant complaints, her tears, her reluctance in just about everything. "But what about *me*," she would wail, as his mother never had.

As boys, George and Arthur would usually have finished their supper by the time their da' came home from the pits. Once his bulk was through the front door, casting a dark shadow throughout the house, George's mam would absentmindedly stroke his hair, then leave the brothers to their own devices. She would bustle around, checking on the meal, drawing hot water for a bath, which the Old Man would take in a large iron tub in the front room before a crackling fire. Cleaned and dried, George's da' would then sit to supper on his own, knife and fork clenched upright in his hands like sentries while he noisily chewed his food open-mouthed, his dark hair slick and parted in the middle, the sides and back of his head shaved so close he looked like a medieval monk. Then it was down to the local until closing time.

George's mam had once got hold of a copy of *Peter Pan* to read to the boys at bedtime. She'd made friends with a peddler who roamed the hills and valleys sharpening knives and scissors, mending pots and pans, and he'd bring her little extras as a surprise, stay for a mug of tea or maybe a bowl of soup while his da' was down the pits, laughing and joking and calling her "missus" in a mischievous way, making her blush at comments pitched low and conspiratorial that young George never understood and which made him angry at being so deliberately left out of the adults' world. He'd play with wooden soldiers on a corner of the kitchen table, pretending he didn't care, wasn't interested in their grown-up talk. The peddler would often busy himself, rummaging in his rucksack for herbs and potions that he helped George's mam apply to visible bruises and the occasional black eye. George sometimes caught, but did not understand, the strange beady-eyed look on the blue-veined, ruddy face of the wild-bearded man as he scrutinized Mrs. Llewellyn. It made George even more jealous. He vowed to tell his da' on more than one occasion, though he never did.

Like his da', George had not liked the peddler, though he had enjoyed the attention his mam would give him after Jones the Knife had gone, the stories she would tell or read to him. Unlike his older brother, George had not been taken with books; they needed too much effort, especially when you could be outside playing instead. For a long time, George had secretly shared his father's loud and often expressed opinion that books were a waste of time. "Only *one* good book," his da' would bellow at George's mam, though for an equally long time George had never been certain exactly what book his da' was referring to. "What you want to go reading this rubbish for, woman?" Old Man Llewellyn would bellow, cursorily examining what she was currently enjoying. "Waste of bloody time. Get ideas above your station, for what? Me and my house not good enough for you, is it? Rather be traipsing round the damn countryside with that bloody tinker instead."

Once, after a brutal argument between them about the peddler, as George now remembered it anyway, his da' had snatched up the book his mam had been reading and ripped pages from it, hurling them onto the fire, yelling all the while, "No more, woman! This is the end of it," while his mam sat hunched in her knitting chair, withdrawn and weeping.

George, in all honesty, didn't care one way or the other about books. He had been a poor student, more concerned with playing rugger and soccer, hanging out with a gang of other grubby prepubescents who roamed the mottled yellow-green grassy slopes overshadowed by black mounds of slag, growing inch by inch, year by year.

George's wife, Gwenyth, was the instrument of his leaving Cardiff and moving to London with Wendy, their daughter. It was to be a new beginning for them. After five years of being married to a beat copper, Gwenyth was clear about her dislike for police work and its hours, but in those days, as George had so often and heatedly pointed out, it was a job with security and a future at a time when most other men were cursed with poverty and unemployment—indeed, they had banded together thousands strong and marched south from Jarrow in the north of England demanding work; but to what real avail? George thought. Here they were, nineteen bloody forty-one, and the working classes were still cannon fodder for the rich mine owners and factory owners, and the squires and upper bloody classes.

He'd spent a year in a stiff-collared uniform on the beat in London, having rejoined the police, the Met this time, before getting his transfer to the Criminal Investigation Division and finally passing his sergeant's exam. Gwenyth refused to sleep with him for a fortnight after he told her. *Twelve years,* George thought. He'd been a man to watch in those days, a rising star, one of the youngest sergeants on the Job at the time; but she'd dragged him down, and he'd watched as it all drifted away. *Like pissing in the wind,* he thought, *it all comes back to you in the end.*

"As ye reap . . ." he recalled his father so often gloating.

When George had come home from the pub after a duty shift and a quick drink with the lads, there had rarely been a meal waiting for him. Gwenyth, George quickly learned, was not as willing to please nor as meek-mannered as his mam, and disappointment and frustration slowly rotted both sides of the marriage bed. Her pregnancy, which had entrapped him somehow, "miscarried" and they were stuck with each other. Then along came Wendy, the light of his life. Despite the worsening fights, some of them physical, George and Gwenyth had managed to carve out a neutral, if loveless existence until Wendy was ten. . . .

George looked around the bus, more to distract himself from thoughts and feelings he did not want to experience again. Damn it, it was to save himself from such torments that he had tried to forget about all this. His daughter was taken care of, he'd done his duty by her as a parent, which was more than that bloody cow Gwenyth had ever done. It had been blow after blow, George remembered, despite himself; his baby in the hospital, his wife gone when George and Fred Medford had finally returned to George's home that night. "Try to forgive me," she had written to him, in a note left on the mantelpiece. "I can't do it any longer." Even now, after five years, the anger still burned within him when he thought about it, the rage at her betrayal. "Do what?" he still asked himself, though not really caring about the answer any longer.

This trip is a mistake, George thought. But it was too late now, he had come too far.

At four o'clock, he descended from the bus and was left

standing by the square stone pillars of a gatehouse while the bus labored away, its rear quickly obscured by sooty, steaming exhaust clouds. Brick walls with shattered glass embedded atop them stretched away in both directions, enclosing the grounds before him. A discreet brass plaque on one of the pillars announced the Essex County Hospital Authority, Mary Kitteridge Home. Guarding the entrance were heavy wooden gates, stiff on their hinges as George pushed them apart and began the long quarter-mile walk down the graveled driveway through the countrified grounds to the main building. It loomed larger, uncomfortably reminding him of the exterior of Wormwood Scrubs prison, with its stacked rows of barred windows and anonymous yet imposing presence. There were few other houses nearby, as if the site for the home had been chosen for its isolation.

At the main door, George rang the bell and waited in the cold for an answer. It was some time in coming, and he had to ring several more times. Eventually, he found himself facing a frumpy girl in her late teens, her lips a little too thick and her chin dotted with acne, a cigarette dangling from one corner of her mouth. She squinted from the smoke, looking weary. Her oversized yellow cardigan was speckled with small cigarette burns and smears of ash, and beneath it she wore a one-piece, shapeless dress that reached her ankles.

"Yeah?" she asked, in a harsh, bored voice. She lounged against the doorpost, blocking the way, her bosoms heaving beneath the cardigan as she dragged on the cigarette and blew smoke at him.

George contained his aggravation at her insolence. "I'm here to see Wendy Llewellyn."

The girl seemed of a mind to send him away, but said, "You are . . . ?"

"Her father."

After giving George a closer examination she mumbled, "Better come in, I suppose." It was plain she regarded him as a disruption of her routine. "Visiting hours is nearly over. Three 'til . . ."

"I know the hours," George snapped. "It's not the first time I've been here."

"I ain't never seen you before," she replied huffily. "And I've been here eighteen months. You'll have to wait in there while I tell Matron. Doctor's not here till tomorrow."

She led him into a small room off the main entrance hall that reminded George of a dentist's waiting room. He sat down and began scanning a copy of the *Picture Post*. He skimmed an article about King George and Queen Elizabeth narrowly escaping a German bombing raid on Buckingham Palace, shaking his head at the strained everyman comparisons between the suffering of the Royal Family, now united in a common bond with the working-class victims of London's East End—obviously the reason the piece had not been censored.

George tossed aside the magazine and wandered over to the window where he peered at the lawns and the poplar trees, standing like centurions in neat lines.

The home was chilly, so he kept on his overcoat, though he removed his hat. The place reeked of polish and disinfectant, and, partly from boredom and partly to disguise the unpleasant sterile smell, he lit up a Woodbine, blowing tobacco smoke at the ceiling.

He was stubbing out his second cigarette when shuffling footsteps announced the girl's return. *"She looks like one of the damn patients,"* George thought, eyeing her slovenly appearance and unwashed, dark-rooted straw-colored hair, inert as a beaded curtain.

"This way," she said, in a surlier manner than before.

George was sure she had been coerced into accompanying him. "Matron's busy. Says she'll see you later, if you want."

They walked down a corridor that echoed with their footsteps. Somewhere in the house a child screamed, accompanied by loud rapid banging. An adult's voice suddenly rose in volume to match it, though George could not make out what was being said. The girl didn't seem to notice.

She paused by an entrance and, producing a set of keys from a chain beneath her cardigan, unlocked a heavy wooden door. "Through here," she said, stepping back to allow him to precede her.

They entered a ward lined with cots and beds both sides of the room. Even though he had seen it before, George could not suppress the revulsion that shook his shoulders.

That the patients here were human, possessed souls trapped in warped and twisted shells of flesh, he could not deny. He was confronted with society's throwaways, the genetic mistakes. He forced himself to remember their humanity as he strode through the room toward the opposite doorway. The attendant paused by a table and chair in the center of the room and stubbed out her butt in a tinfoil ashtray, glancing at a crossword puzzle she had obviously been playing with before George's arrival.

The ward was eerily quiet, broken only by occasional snuffles, coughs, and moans. Those patients who could, followed his progress with their eyes, though many were flat on their backs, unable to move, and in a couple of cases, belted into their beds. It was impossible to speculate on their ages, anything from two years to late teens, for few resembled what is regarded as "normal."

A child with a head the size of a beachball, wobbling dangerously on a stick-thin neck, tried to sit up and see the newcomer more clearly. In the next bed, another sprayed drool from its toothless mouth, tongueless moaning sounds emerging as it twitched its body alarmingly with each effort to get attention.

George turned away and faced instead what he presumed was an infant, its hands and feet sprouting from shoulders and thighs instead of at the ends of arms and legs. As he looked it turned its face away, and to his horror he realized the wrinkled face had a concave back of the head.

In the far corner, another, looking like a white china doll with blond hair and wide blue eyes, was strapped down securely, but was nevertheless rocking and straining at its bonds, growling with frustration as it tried to bite fingers it could not reach. Here, something that was more insect-like than human; there, an indescribable mass of melting flesh, urinating on itself as George passed.

Then they were through to the other corridor, the girl apparently unaffected by the monsters they had just left behind. George's mouth was dry, his heart beating rapidly. *What kind of sissy are you?* he scolded himself. *You've seen worse than this, and recently, too.* But it was one thing when the victim was dead; you could tell yourself it was just a mangled, empty shell. It was another when you knew that something was inside that wracked, twisted body; impossible not to imagine, for a horrifying moment, what it must be like to look out at the world knowing that God had cursed you. The anger, the frustration . . .

They passed several more wards that could be viewed from the corridor through glass windows set into the doors, and eventually arrived at a door, which the attendant unlocked. "She's in here."

The room George paid handsomly for to keep his daughter out of the main ward was about ten feet square, and chilly, with a bed and a chair by a barred window, the walls plain white and in need of repainting. She was seated in the chair, an overgrown child now fifteen, covered from neck to foot with a grey, institutional blanket.

The hysterical screaming started up again, the echo of it fleeing through the corridors.

George drew a deep breath and walked over to the figure. "Hello, *caraed*," he said.

Wendy made no sign that anyone had invaded her little universe, continuing to stare out the window. It had been the coma, of course. Four weeks of a deathlike limbo after . . .

He banished the thought from his mind. What's done was done. There could be no going back; no "If only . . ."

She looks so normal, he thought, feeling his chest constrict.

He knelt beside her, taking up a limp, icy hand in his own. He squeezed, hoping she might acknowledge his presence in some way, a return squeeze, a movement of a finger, something anyway, to hang on to, to believe in.

Gently, he rubbed warmth into the hand, staring at the blank, expressionless face, wondering where she was, what underworld she was roaming, searching for an exit.

He cradled her unresisting head to his chest as he murmured, "I'm so sorry," over and over into her long dark hair. He raised his face to the ceiling, trying to regain control, wondering what he was doing here, what it would gain him.

Composing himself, he moved over another chair from behind the door and, sitting beside her, busied himself combing her hair from her face with his hands. As he always did, he began talking to her. Anything and every-thing, it didn't matter, pouring out his heartaches and triumphs, apologizing for not coming more often. The sound of his voice would be enough, he hoped. One day, perhaps, things would be all right again. He would be forgiven. He tried rubbing more life into her hands as he spoke. One day . . .

□   □   □

The Home Service radio broadcast of hymns of the St. Martin's-in-the-Field choir had a soothing effect on Nevil's ragged nerves. Later, after the amusing ITMA show, Eric Blair, better known by his pen name George Orwell, was due to give a talk that Nevil was looking forward to hearing, despite what Nevil considered Orwell's rather adolescent socialist leanings; that would be followed by a Mozart piano concerto from the Albert Hall with Arthur Rubinstein as the soloist accompanied by a war-thinned Royal Philharmonic. Nevil was determined to take his mind off his worries tonight.

Thus, while humming along to "Oh, Jerusalem," Nevil spread before him the local Sunday newspaper, keen to see if anyone had found the child yet.

Unlike the *News of the World*'s Nazi werewolf story, the local paper more or less reported the facts, what little there were of them anyway: three bodies with strikingly similar horrible wounds, victims of a roaming wild animal, found at different times and places, the first two discovered in or nearby the ruins of a house owned by two sisters named Stepan; the dreadful cellar where it was thought they may have caged the wild animal responsible . . .

It was then that the awful, obvious truth struck Nevil so forcefully he uttered a cry and dropped the paper.

Click, click, click, like the tumblers of a lock it all snapped into place. *How could I have been so stupid!* he berated himself, pounding his thigh with a clenched fist, then biting the knuckles, his eyes wide with revelation. *Oh my God—of course!* That's what she had been hinting at—was it only three days ago? It seemed a lifetime.

Nevil rose and hurried to the window table, careless of the books and papers he cursorily examined, then tossed aside. Where was it?

He paused in his frantic, fruitless searching, calming himself. "More haste, less speed," he muttered, glancing around the room. The hymns ended and the week's featured vicar's sermon began. Shutting out the plumy, stridently hollow-sounding radio voice, Nevil stood rooted to the spot, his eyes taking in the familiarity of the room. *Where the hell did I put it?*

He *knew* he had last seen it on the table. . . . Rushing upstairs, he quickly searched his tiny bedroom, then in growing desperation, the bathroom and finally the kitchen, rooting through the rubbish bin, but finding only disgusting detritus.

His despair mounted, almost in proportion to his empty-handed failure. He cast his mind back to Thursday afternoon, then he remembered: The night of the bombing, the night she had first given him the journal, he had gone to her house to *return* it, unread. *That* was where he had lost it! Somewhere in the ruins of her house.

Nevil sat heavily on a kitchen chair, as though deflated of purpose, Thursday's events replaying themselves like a mescaline trip. He vividly recalled her gestures, her voice.

"Thy brother's blood crieth unto me from the ground . . ." declared the radio preacher, " . . . and the Lord set a mark upon Cain . . ."

For a moment, Nevil was certain the voice was speaking directly to him. "I have set before you life and death, blessing and cursing: therefore choose life, that both thou and thy seed may live. . . ."

Nevil would have no peace until he found the journal.

What he suspected now was so appalling. . . . no wonder she had chosen him! To whom else but a student of the occult could she have unburdened herself, in however allusory a manner? Who was he kidding? He wasn't important—didn't count—*that's* why she had told him.

She had sat before him, the harsh hint of a Slavic accent still reverberating in her spoken English, a vaguely guttural intonation, while he affected his most attentive expression, even though his thoughts had begun to wander. Why hadn't he paid more attention? She had a friend, she had told him, who had been having nightmares about being attacked by an inhuman beast.

"My friend has been cursed," she declared. Nevil hadn't treated her confession with any seriousness then—what else had he missed by condescending to her? "It has made her sick beyond any doctor's help. You are our last hope. How can she remove it? How can she atone for her terrible sins?" She had been earnest, and her seriousness had disconcerted Nevil with its intensity.

"I have this awful premonition of disaster, Mr. Stimpson. You must help my friend. I don't know what to do."

Feeling more like a psychiatrist than an interpreter of occult sign, Nevil had said, "Tell me about—your 'friend' and her problem," his skepticism clearly evident.

She spoke softly, hesitantly, when finally she replied. "I don't know how to begin."

Nevil leaned back in his chair, affecting the nonchalance of an indulgent schoolmaster, waiting for her to continue.

"Do you believe in evil spirits, Mr. Stimpson? In possession?"

"Yes," he said, though in all honesty it was the theory he was discussing, not, as Miss Stepan was suggesting, fact. "The church says so, doesn't it?"

"Are you a religious man; do you believe in God?"

Nevil paused. It dawned on him that by implication she was actually asking him if he believed in the Devil. "There are more things in heaven and earth, Horatio, than are dreamt of in your philosophy," he said, quoting *Hamlet* as a glib way of avoiding her question, a thin, fixed smile on his face.

"Where I come from, as a child," she began, "there were many stories, old wives' tales I suppose you'd call them. Stories meant to frighten children, make you behave when you were naughty. My friend told me such a story. . . ."

"You wicked little bastard. You can't be no child of mine," Nevil heard a voice scream down the years, heard the click of the lock in the understairs closet, trapping him, drowning him in darkness. *"If you don't behave yourself I'll get a policeman, and he'll come and lock you up worse than this, I can promise you!"* In his head, Nevil relived his mother's rage. He quivered with shame and guilt, even as he sat quietly half-listening to Camilla Stepan. He couldn't recall what he had done to spark such rage in his mother, only the leaden feelings of worthlessness. For a while, he was certain she had been possessed by some wicked spirit, an ogre perhaps, that hated children, ate them if they misbehaved. . . . *Can a person be possessed, she asks,* thought Nevil.

He was suddenly aware the room had gone quiet, that the woman had stopped speaking. "I'm s-sorry," he stammered, his face flushing from the lingering feelings that still clung to him, had haunted him for so long. "P-please, go on. What about your dream—er, I mean your friend's dream?"

"My friend," she emphasized, "has had it on and off since the war started. She caged a monster, because she couldn't bring herself to kill it outright. So she decided to starve it to death, instead. Now she is terrified it will get loose. That's what she dreams about, that the creature will get loose. Can't you see it in the cards?" She gestured at the Tarot cards spread on the table between them.

"I need to see her to tell that. But I can see that you are troubled—about your friend, no doubt—and you have been for some time. The cards indicate it will end soon."

"For us all I hope," she whispered. She rummaged in her coat sleeve for a handkerchief and noisily blew her nose. She straightened her posture in the chair, as though getting a grip finally, her voice harder than it had been. "She deserves to be cursed—she's been very wicked. . . . " She hesitated, then continued, "She's being punished, for doing too much—but not enough. It's evil, you see, possessed, and even though my friend wanted to kill it she could not. She even tried to poison it a few years ago, but it wouldn't die as we all hoped it would.

"My grandmother told me when I was a little girl—only *something silver*"—those had been her exact words, Nevil now recalled—"only something *silver* can destroy a creature like that. It's no longer human, you see. . . . "

She choked on her embarrassment, falling silent.

Feeling increasingly uncomfortable at the way she had abandoned manners and convention, Nevil gathered up the Tarot cards and gazed out of the window, allowing her time to regain her composure. He stared at the ruins of Sebastopol Street for a while, then moved his gaze to the astrological charts before him on the table, one of a child and another of a woman. Except, with hindsight, he realized it might not be a child—but this *thing* she had been telling him about, a demon that ate human flesh—some sort of *werewolf*—they had caged for nearly a decade.

Nevil shook his head, rather as a gesture of unwillingness to hear more than in direct answer to anything she had said to him. He turned once again to the desolate view outside. *It looks like snow,* he thought.

□　　□　　□

For a couple of hours now, unable to face his cold, miserable home tonight, George had been napping in a hard wooden chair set by the curtained-off bedside of the woman they had pulled from the wreckage. He alternately dozed and then jerked awake when a noise filtered through, hoping always it was the injured woman coming awake, not someone passing by.

She lay quietly. Dormant, George thought. No more restlessness, according to the nursing staff. *Who are you?* he wondered.

Williams and Fred Medford's lads had spent the last three days digging around, listening to gossip, rumor, innuendo, questioning everything and everyone, getting nowhere fast. It was as if these women had appeared out of thin air. Which was absurd, George decided. You don't live in this part of town for years without somebody knowing something about you. *Somebody, somewhere,* knew this woman's story. She had to be someone's wife, girl-friend, employer. . . .

"You should go home, get some proper rest," a woman's voice said.

George blinked himself awake again and turned to see Vera Armstrong checking the chart by the bottom of the bed.

"How is she?" he asked.

"She's dying, I'm afraid."

"Taking her secrets to the grave," George murmured bitterly. "What did you keep in that cellar, damn it?"

"What did you say?" Nurse Armstrong asked.

"Sorry. I was thinking aloud. You're right. This ain't getting the baby washed, as my mam used to say."

He expected her to bustle off to her next patient, but instead she remained, watching him as he eased the cricks in his neck and back, and sat up straighter in the chair.

"You look exhausted. Why are you here?"

George shook his head. "It seemed . . . I don't know, the only place left to go at the moment."

They both knew, however, that wasn't his only reason. An awkward silence fell between them as they ran out of words. Eventually, Nurse Armstrong said, "You're a dangerous man, George Llewellyn, but I don't think you're anything near the hard case you make yourself out to be."

"Maybe," he said, and bounced his eyebrows. Despite herself, Vera Armstrong gave a weary chuckle. "God, I feel stiff." George stretched and stood up, wincing at a stabbing pain in his ribs. "You still on duty?"

"Actually, I finished half an hour ago, but we've been so busy tonight I've just got to my rounds. Why?"

"Thought you might want an escort home. Who knows what's lurking out there these days? We could have a chat on the way, see if we can find somewhere to have a drink or something. . . . "

She stared at him for a moment, then said, "All right," in what George thought was a dubious tone. He felt like saying, *Don't do me any favors here,* but instead, replied, "Good."

"About twenty minutes," she said. "I'll meet you at the main entrance."

As he made his way downstairs, George thought, *You're too old for this nonsense.* Nevertheless, he felt excited at again spending some time alone with a woman. It had been a long time since he'd felt like this on such a casual acquaintance, and it seemed somehow inappropriate. Not that this was a date, of course. Nothing like it.

They walked round-shouldered, side by side, George

conscious of her scent and the gap between them as they occasionally brushed shoulders, then pulled apart in quiet embarrassment. It had rained since he had last been outside, and the pavements glistened and squelched beneath their shoes. A cold wind had picked up, gusting through their clothes and chilling them both. It bent the thin, leafless branches of sporadically placed trees planted in islands of earth amid the flagstones.

"Brass monkeys weather tonight, isn't it?" George said. He shuddered within his overcoat as the arctic wind hit them full blast again.

"It's the damp that gets me," she said. "I'm still not used to it."

"Where're you from, then?"

"Hungary, a long time ago anyway. My father was an undersecretary at the Hungarian embassy in London. We came here when I was eight. He died about twelve years ago. My mother decided to stay, and I ended up getting a job nursing to help support us."

"That's why you speak so many languages, I suppose."

"I've always had an ear for them. Not that I do anything with it these days."

"Where are we going, by the way?"

"I thought you were walking me home?"

"I am."

She chuckled. "What do you want, Sergeant?"

"It's George."

"All right." She brushed auburn hair out of her face and tucked it beneath her scarf, drawing her cape closer. George was tempted to put an arm around her shoulders, more for warmth than anything else, he told himself, though he resisted the urge. She seemed to sense what was going through his mind though, and slipped an arm through his, huddling against him as they continued to walk.

"You don't live in the nurses' quarters, then?"

"Why do you say that?"

He turned to a side street they had passed and said, "I thought they were down there."

"They are. But as it happens I don't live there. Anyway, you obviously want to ask me something, so we might as well have it out, don't you think?"

George vigorously slapped his gloved hands together to warm them, feeling suddenly seal-like and foolish. "Whatever you say, miss."

She smiled and pushed him at arm's length. "It's Mrs., remember?"

"I got an idea," George said. "An after-hours place. Bit cramped, but musicians and theatricals use it after they've finished work." He glanced at his watch. It was just gone midnight. Place wouldn't be too busy just yet, so they might get a quiet table.

The weather made conversation difficult, the cold beginning to numb George's face and lips, dew freezing slightly on his bushy mustache. He wiped it away with a free hand, thinking, *I should be home in bed, not freezing my arse off trying to chat up some bint.*

They hailed the next passing black taxi, and George gave the driver an address in Whitechapel. It let them off in a dark street, filled with anonymous closed doors. George approached a green one and knocked hard. A moment later it opened a crack, a pair of eyes looked out, and a voice said, "Who's there?" then the door opened wider as the man behind it added, "Well, well, well. George Llewellyn as I live and breathe. Ain't seen you for a while. Where you been hiding yourself then, sport?"

"Work, you know, Charlie."

"Better come in, hadn't you, before you freeze your bloody goolies off." He suddenly noticed Vera Armstrong and hastily added, "Beg pardon, miss. Didn't see you standing there. Mind your head, George," he went on, as the policeman ducked under the lintel.

They made their way along a thin passageway and down a coiled, rickety set of stairs to the basement of the building, Charlie leading the way, George bringing up the rear. "This is a friend of mine, Vera Armstrong."

Charlie turned to face George over her shoulder, and commented, "Very nice. Getting some taste in your old age, I see."

"Don't embarrass me now, Charlie."

"What, me, George? Perish the thought. What'll happen to my license renewal if I was to do that? Don't want to upset the local constabulary now, do I?"

The warmth from the club wafted toward them, thawing them out, and when they finally entered the dimly lit main room, a cheery glow emanated from a blazing wood fire. The low ceiling was thick with wine-bottle corks, somehow defying gravity, while unoccupied rustic tables and chairs were spread throughout the cramped-looking room.

The first thing they noticed was a man wearing a woman's dress, seated at a far table engaged in an obviously amusing conversation as he shared a bottle of wine with a heavyset older woman. In a corner, a skeletally thin bloke was hunched over an upright piano, strands of blond hair hanging curtainlike before his face, a half-finished pint of black market gin standing open on the piano top, large spider fingers roaming the keys as he quietly segued from "Ghost of a Chance" to "Creole Love Call."

The transvestite looked up and beamed George a smile,

which he returned. Charlie seated George and Vera Armstrong at a table in an alcove near the fireplace, then produced two menus.

"Just tea, mate," George said, looking to see if Nurse Armstrong approved. She nodded agreement.

"'Course. Anything for you, George. You know that."

"You smarmy bugger. What are you after?"

"Well, as a matter of fact, like I said, my license renewal's up before the beak in a month. Thought you might be able to help me out. . . . " He glanced at Nurse Armstrong and said, "It ain't important. We'll talk about it some other time."

"Good idea," George said with a wink.

When the owner left, Nurse Armstrong leaned across the table and whispered, "How do you know *him*?" surreptitiously indicating the man in the dress.

"That's Harvey. He's an accountant, good one actually, so I'm told. Totally harmless, and before you ask, he's not a nancy-boy, even though I know he looks like a raving queen. He's married with three kids. Gawd knows why he does it. Usually, it's only when his old lady gives him a hard time. Thought he'd given it up."

"Actually, I was rather admiring his dress. He's got good taste."

"Oh, Harvey's a piece of work, all right. Marvelous painter, believe it or not."

"Pictures, you mean?"

"Well, he charges too much to do houses."

"So you have got a sense of humor after all."

"Not been too much to laugh about recently."

She leaned her elbows on the table and poured the tea Charlie had brought them. "No, I suppose not. How's it going?"

"All right," George muttered. "Why don't you tell me some more about yourself. How did you get married?"

"Church, vicar, the usual."

"That's not what I meant."

She chuckled. "I know. He used to visit a friend of his I was looking after. Mosquito pilot who broke both his legs when he crash-landed. Things are only made of wood. It caught fire and the poor chap was quite badly burned. Shipped him off to the burns unit in East Grinstead a couple of months after Robert and I met. Robert, that's my husband—was my husband—used to visit him all the time. Read to him and stuff. He played cricket for Cambridge and then Lancashire before the war; until he joined the RAF anyway. Gung-ho to get into the fight. He was at the head of the queue."

"What did he fly?"

"Hurricanes, mainly. What about you?"

"What about me?"

"I take it you're not married. You don't have the look."

"Married blokes have a look, do they?"

"Oh, yes."

George paused, peering into his teacup as if seeking guidance. "I was, for a while."

"Any kids?"

George grew visibly more uncomfortable. "Little girl."

"Who looks after her?"

"Well, she ain't that little any more."

"You don't like talking about yourself much, do you?"

"I thought I was the copper round here."

"Am I being too nosey?"

George shook his head. "No. I'm sorry." He sipped his tea, more to have an excuse to stop talking for a moment. Replacing the cup carefully, he asked, "You said she was dying. What from?"

"Who? Oh, the woman in the ward, you mean? They ran a batch of tests on her. I shouldn't be telling you this, but she's in the advanced stages of syphilis."

"You're pulling my leg!"

"It's nothing to joke about. She just seems to have given up."

"Jesus Christ," he muttered. He began to assimilate this unexpected piece of information. It went some way toward explaining why at least one of the sisters had secreted herself away for all these years. The upper classes at play, he thought cynically. Tea and crumpets with the vicar wasn't the half of it.

It was a moment before he realized Vera Armstrong had said something to him. "Tell me about your daughter," she asked him again.

George sighed deeply. "When she was ten, she had an accident. A bad one."

"How awful. What happened?"

"Her mother used to drink, and we fought a lot. We had a nasty row that night. I lost my temper and, er, walked out. When I got back I found Wendy unconscious on the floor and Gwenyth drunk in bed. Doctor I know came round, we took her to hospital."

"Where is she now?"

"Hospital, out near Epping Forest. Been there five years."

"I'm sure it's still very painful for you."

"Yes, it is." Glancing at his watch he went on, "Look, I don't mean to be rude, but I've got an early start tomorrow. We'd better go."

Somewhat bewildered, Nurse Armstrong rose with him and put on her coat while George left money on the table. Before Charlie objected George gave him a look that said,

Shut up! and taking Vera Armstrong by the arm, led her upstairs and back into the cold.

They stood on the pavement in silence, waiting for a cab to hail. As George flagged one down, he turned to her and, holding her elbow, asked, "Would you like to do this again some time?"

She didn't reply, turning her back on him as she climbed into the cab, settling into the seat. Still averting her face she rubbed a clear patch in the steamed-up side window, as though busying herself while she found the words to politely reject him. George breathed deeply and hunched into his coat, readying himself to hear aloud what he already knew she was about to say.

"I thought you were the type of bloke who'd ask me home to see his etchings."

George was taken by surprise. *This is ridiculous,* he thought. He chuckled and said, "I haven't shown anyone my etchings for a long time." He reached for her hand. "In dangerous times live dangerously, eh?"

He gave the cabbie his address, then sat back, enjoying the closeness, the fragile intimacy, the tingle of anticipation—the fact that something in his life was finally going right for a change.

◦   ◦   ◦

The dark shadows of the ruins loomed ghoulishly above Nevil as he crawled around the rubble, whimpering softly, a flashlight awkwardly tucked under his chin, certain he would be discovered at any minute. The search was a hopeless task, he knew, especially in the dark. The moon was constantly shaded by unseen clouds.

He had found the twisted frame of his bicycle, and then tried to work out from it in widening circles. After an hour he was sore, frozen, and more frustrated than when he had begun.

Nevil was distracted by the sound of tumbling rubble. He peered into the bleary dark, unable to pinpoint where the sound had come from. He held his breath, hoping to hear better. The sound was closer this time. He spun in the direction it came from, still on his knees. The peculiar thought struck him that it was a rather fitting position in which to end his life.

After several moments he realized the sounds had stopped. He was overwhelmed with the feeling of being watched, tracked—hunted.

The werewolf was out there, biding its time.

Eventually Nevil forced himself to stand and look around. He probed with the flashlight, hoping the beam might scare it away or at least make it think twice about getting near him. Such creatures were of the night, shunning exposure, he recalled.

Despite his fears, he ventured toward where he thought the sounds had come from. He rounded a bend and was confronted by the barely upright skeletal limbs of structures that might once have been houses. As soon as he saw the dark bundle by one wall, hidden partially from view, he knew the creature was nearby. Dreading what he would find, he neared the bundle, his worst fears confirmed as he crouched and turned it over revealing a boy of about twelve.

Blood still oozed from the shredded flesh, dripping onto Nevil's hands. The sensation, perhaps more than the realization that he was the first on the scene of another child murder, caused him to jerk away, rubbing off the sticky wetness on his coat. Then, as if in a nightmare, he clearly heard the loud sounds of someone clambering over the rubble, saw the beam of a flashlight sweep the area, and, before he could duck away, pin him to the spot, revealing him kneeling bloody-handed beside the creatures's latest victim.

"Oi, you!" a gruff voice yelled. "Don't you bleedin' move, you evil bastard." Then, worst of all, Nevil heard the shrill blasts of a police whistle summoning help.

He rose to a predatory crouch, his eyes wide with terror, his arms before him futilely warding off the sight of the advancing policeman, a truncheon drawn menacingly. Nevil's bloodstained hands clawed at the air in desperation: It was the end of him for sure! Years of suppressed rage at the injustice of life welled up in him with volcanic fury.

A keening moan escaped from him, growing into a primal cry of survival. He launched himself through the shadow-filled night, colliding with the surprised policeman, Nevil's tackle crashing them both to the ground. The plainclothes copper groaned as his head bashed against a brick.

His arms like windmill sails, Nevil made a gurgling noise as he thrashed around atop the policeman like a man in a seizure, while the dazed copper struggled feebly to free himself from the onslaught. Nevil groped for a weapon, a stone, anything, and his right hand closed on a piece of masonry. He gripped it tightly and brought it down on the policeman's unprotected head, missing, and hitting his shoulder instead. The policeman cried out and jerked his body as though electrocuted. He twisted and bucked while Nevil grimly held on, trying to rain more blows under the copper's upraised arm, which protected his exposed head, grappling at the same time to catch hold of the Nevil's wrist, groaning with the agony of movement.

An image came to Nevil, amid the red swirling mist that had enveloped him, of riding on the back of an enraged demon, its leathery, taloned wings flapping wildly, while Nevil hung on to the taut reins, too terrified of letting go to consider what might happen next. He looked down and saw only a vast ocean of molten fire, at the same time feeling the bucking demon finally dislodge him. He slipped, tumbling helplessly into the inferno below. . . .

The jabs of bashing against hard-angled debris brought Nevil back to himself. Thrown free of the policeman, he glanced up to see the copper rising like a groggy, revenge-filled bear, clutching at his shoulder, his face twisted in pain and rage.

Nevil swung his right fist with all his might, drawing confidence from the unusually solid feel of it, catching the policeman on the side of the head. A lance of pain shot though Nevil's arm as his fist connected with a strange clunking sound, then the policeman dropped to the ground as though poleaxed.

Shocked at his own success, it was a moment before Nevil realized he was still holding the rock. He stared at the injured copper, blood streaming from a gash near his temple, then the rock in his hand, hurling it away, crying aloud at the realization of the awful thing he had just done. He crouched over the injured man, relieved to discover he wasn't dead.

Exhausted, Nevil collapsed onto his haunches, catching his breath in rasping gasps, feeling like David, staring almost in awe at the Goliath lying before him. Nevil still tingled from the ebbing power that had surged through him, not knowing how his paralyzing terror at being found by the policeman as he crouched over the child's body had turned into such an explosion of action. It was so out of character. Nevil raised a hand to his cheek, touching the ragged, pitted parallel lines where the creature had scratched him.

What did the books say? He tried to recall. *If you're injured by a werewolf and survive, you'll turn into one yourself when the full moon rises.*

Collapsing backward, his pulse pounding loudly in his ears, no longer able to tell whether the loud rasping wheeze he heard was his own or the injured policeman's, he stared into the night sky, losing himself in its star-spackled vastness. The moon hung in the heavens, its bloated whiteness obscured by veiling clouds, sailing past like ships of the line, the icy breeze chilling Nevil into the present. He examined himself quickly: He hadn't changed externally *this time; Perhaps it takes a while for the full extent of the metamorphosis to catch hold?* Nevil wondered. He stared again at his skin, searching for signs of coarse hair or longer nails, finding none yet, though in the dark it was hard to be sure.

He had to get away. He scurried back from the prone form of the policeman as if it were contagious. Already he fancied he heard approaching reinforcements. He dare not stay longer, but where to go? His life had gone so appallingly wrong. He hadn't even found what he'd come here for.

As Nevil considered the journal, a thought, like a shaft of hope, pierced the Stygian gloom, and he hastened back to where he had left the wreckage of his bicycle. He stumbled over rubble, weeping at his desperate fate and clumsy efforts, wiping his face with a coat sleeve as he dropped to his knees, searching the buckled frame. It looked like something from a surrealist's painting, its wheels and spokes bent at right angles to each other. Where was the saddlebag? He couldn't find it! He remembered exactly now what he had done with the journal. He'd put it securely in his saddlebag.

Oh God, please, he thought as he crawled around, squinting to try and make out moonlit shapes. He peered molelike before him, his breath steaming as it emerged in ragged gasps, finally spotting a broken leather strap, barely visible beneath a mound of debris.

He scrambled over to it and tore at the earth, heaving away stones and bricks until the saddlebag was free. The leather was ripped and twisted, but in one piece. Nevil scrabbled to unbuckle the retaining straps and saw the book, still nestled where he had left it.

Clutching the saddlebag to his chest, he glanced around, not knowing where to turn, where to hide; spotting a likely direction, he hurriedly limped away.

He had always feared that something like this would happen to him one day: that from out of the darkness an inhuman creature would come for him, intent on hurting *him*, crippling *him*, just like his parents had threatened it would if he misbehaved.

His worst childhood nightmares, born of that black, understairs closet, had finally come true.

□   □   □

From his hiding place near the shell of the Stepan sisters' house in the rubbled wasteland, Nevil watched the activity in the Gypsy encampment below through a pair of old binoculars. The sharp chill in the air felt like a meat locker, but still he remained, shivering, protected by a meager blanket and a thermos of hot tea he'd brought with him from home, where he'd stopped only long enough to gather some things. He was on the run now. He'd probably killed a policeman. His best hope was that the chaos of the bombing would help him until he figured out what to do—much as he thought it must be helping the werewolf—and at the same time the bombing might also hinder the manhunt that was sure to be launched when they found the policeman. More for his own sake than the copper's, Nevil prayed the man didn't die. Then he heard the bombers approaching.

Despite the virulence of the night's bombing, the spectacular pyrotechnics kept him rooted to the spot. There was nowhere to run to, anyway.

In the confusion of the aftermath Nevil crept from his hiding place, skulking in the night, sneaking around the edge of the common, drawing closer to the caravans. The Gypsies were all indoors or down in air-raid shelters, so the camp appeared deserted.

He crouched out of sight. A wave of panic paralyzed him for a moment. What was he going to do?

Closing his eyes, he forced himself to stop gasping, his body tingling with expectation and anxiety. The journal was tucked safely inside his army greatcoat, and despite his desire to read further than he had, he knew now was neither the time nor the place. The last entry, dated only a week ago, and several others going back much further, had made reference to a Gypsy woman called Mother Celina. What the relationship was, Nevil as yet had no idea; but he knew he had to find out—his life could well depend on it.

As he cringed behind a caravan the door opened and a man jumped to the ground, purposefully striding away. "Fix him good for me, Gus," he heard an old lady call out. "That evil bastard deserves everything he gets for what he's done to us." Nevil scuttled under the wagon bed, hiding deeper in the shadows. From his limited vantage point he saw an old Gypsy woman's ankle-length green dress and heavy brogues, saw her looking at the fires from the bombing blazing around them, giving the night an angry pink tinge. In the distance fire engines and ambulances raced by, alarm bells clanging, while snatches of shouting voices drifted toward them. The cold wind also carried sparks like fireflies. Nevil crept along the ground, feeling safe beneath the wagon, when he heard her say, "What the hell do *you* want?"

Nevil glanced around, trying to see who she was addressing. Was there a new danger he had missed? In a terrible flash of comprehension he realized she was talking to him!

Shamefacedly, he crawled from under the wagon and slowly stood upright. She was standing, hands on hips, waiting for him, squinting to make him out in the firelit darkness.

His voice shaking, Nevil said, "Something awful's happened."

She examined him closely as if making a momentous decision, then said, "You'd best come inside for a bit then, hadn't ye?"

Nevil scurried past her into the caravan. She smiled to herself in the darkness and followed him indoors.

□   □   □

Treating him as though he were in shock from the bombing, the Gypsies wrapped Nevil in a blanket and forced on him a hot herbal tea laced with gin. He lay on the old Gypsy woman's bed shivering and sweating as though in the grip of malarial fever.

The old Gypsy woman—Mother Celina, someone called her—quickly silenced the angry clamor of those who gathered in her caravan, wanting to know how long the Englishman was going to stay with them, what he was doing there in the first place. In a strong voice, she ordered them all to be quiet. "He's harmless enough,"

Nevil heard her pronounce. "He can be a help to us, trust me."

His nausea came swimming back. With an effort, he got to a sitting position on the sagging bed and bent his head below his knees. Gradually, it passed. The next room was cordoned off by a red blanket, but he could hear the low mutterings of conversation.

He looked around the dingy, ill-lit bedroom wondering how long he had been there. The tea and the sweaty, smoke-filled warmth of the caravan made him drowsy. He lay back on the bed again, closing his eyes, basking in the protection, however temporary. Yet his inner turmoil did not really subside. What was he doing here? Hiding? Because of Camilla Stepan's journal? It was foolish—but where else could he turn for help? "Nowhere," he answered himself.

He dozed off, suffering nightmares, old and new, awaking in a cold sweat, wondering for a moment where he was. Keeping a blanket around his shoulders, he rose and crossed to the partition. He listened by the curtain for a moment, then cautiously peered around one edge.

In the next room, a group of fifteen or twenty Gypsies, mainly women and children, were packed where they could find space around the small living room. Their shadows, cast by the swinging storm lanterns, writhed across walls and bric-a-brac. Faced with so many females, Nevil felt somehow outnumbered, threatened, as though he was about to be punished for ogling the women in the ladies' loo. He drew the blanket tighter and crouched into a corner, hidden by the gently swinging curtain, feeling invisible.

"What should we do, you asks?" Mother Celina cackled. "What indeed. This *Vargamor* is our curse. If we do not stop it, it will kill again. Already it has taken Magda's youngest. More will follow. I helped where I should not have—" She broke off speaking for a moment, staring at the curtained window.

"Not many of you, perhaps only the old ones here, remember Mother Isabelle. She was the one who taught me my skills, just as I teach Sylvia here. When I was a girl, perhaps twelve or so, we visited fisherfolk up in the Highlands of Scotland—a cold dour place, like its people. Mother Isabelle had been wintering there on and off for years, and her mother and grandmother before her, though this was my first visit. It was one of those places, like here, where we had a friend who would help us out, let us fix our wagons, rest our ponies, heal our sicknesses."

She surveyed the faces around her, her gaze for a moment falling in Nevil's direction as he hid in the corner, as though she could see through the cloth partition, then moving on. He had the feeling that somehow Mother Celina was talking directly to him, knew he was there.

"We were in our wagon beside an old crofter's cottage, built against a dune that led down to a gray ocean crashing on the pebble beach, whipped by a cold wind. The closest home was near a mile away.

"We were the first of our people to arrive, and while I sat huddled on the seat, Mother Isabelle yelled out to the crofters that we had arrived. Instead of a greeting, though, from inside the cottage I could hear exclamations and shouts, as though a fight was going on.

"I looked to Mother Isabelle, startled, when out of the house ran a small boy, perhaps eight or nine, like you—" she pointed a gnarled finger at a boy who, suddenly frightened at being singled out, curled beside his mother and older sister.

"He was chased by this woman, built like a fat old horse,

166

carrying a thick piece of dead tree branch. Catching hold of his shirttail, she struck him across the shoulders with a resounding thwack.

"'What has he done?' I whispered to Mother Isabelle. The fat lady must have heard me, for she screamed, 'Done? Done? Nothing! That's why I beat him. For doing nothing! And you'll be next, by God, if you're as lazy as he!' She flailed him once again with the branch. 'Lazy, good-for-nothing . . . ' emphasizing each word with a blow.

"'Hold your *huish* now, Mary Campbell,' said Mother Isabelle. 'There's no cause to go on so. I have his medicine, as I promised. I came as soon as I could.'

"The woman let go the squirming child, who instantly took off.

"A little later, he came up to the wagon as I was busy sorting medicines and herbals and with a beckoning finger indicated I should go with him. He glanced around as though approaching me would be his death, signing frantically when I did not move.

"'Come, please,' he begged.

"Mother Isabelle was in the croft with the fat harridan, so I decided to go. In that way we have as young 'uns of learning truths without understanding, I thought my newfound healing skills might be of help. And I admit my curiosity had got the better of me."

The faces stared up at Mother Celina as she spoke.

"'Why does she treat you so harshly?' I asked the boy as we trudged through crusted gorse.

"'She says my da' was a demon and I spend all my time talking with evil spirits. But for you and your mam I would have been beaten again. She hurts me terribly sometimes.'

"'She's not my mam. She's just Mother Isabelle. Everyone knows her. My mam and da' are gone.'

"'My mam is a spirit, too. Now you and Mother Isabelle have come that fat cow's days of beating me are over. Today was the last time.' His young face seemed so determined it was hard for me not to believe he meant what he said. I imagined he was planning to run away, perhaps hide in our wagon when we left.

"He paused, hearing something I could not, then added, 'I must go now. My mam is calling.'

"Night was falling like gray ash, and although I had intended returning to the croft I decided instead to follow and see where he went.

"I walked over dunes that overlooked the dark mass of the seashore, coming eventually upon a small copse of trees growing halfway up a cliff path. Cautiously, I crept through the trees, drawing close to a pond in the center of a clearing.

"By now a pale moon was rising above the tree line, throwing the scene into silver and black. Despite the biting wind and the chill of the November evening, I fancied I could smell the scent of unseen plants huddled, like myself, by the base of a tree.

"Before me facing the pond stood the boy, who began to recite an incantation. All I could really hear was the rising and falling of his voice, not the words.

"The wind and the darkness and the strange subdued sounds frightened me, and I found myself sweating and shivering at the same time. I was so concerned with my own fears that I lost sight of the child."

Mother Celina peered around the room, as though seeing it for the first time, her gaze finally alighting once again on where Nevil was hiding. "I was terrified. I didn't know what to do for the best.

"When I collected myself enough to look for him again he had gone.

"In his place was a strange, undulating bulge in the earth that swayed to and fro, gaining in size until it was at least seven or eight feet tall. It writhed in my direction, vibrating, humming. Around it, whirling ever faster, was a bluish light.

"I stepped back in alarm, cracking a twig and stumbling. When I looked up, advancing upon me were the yellow eyes and low, menacing growls of a wolf, its teeth flashing as it sniffed the sea breeze on the night air. I ran blindly, heading for the croft, desperately calling for help.

"I must have fallen, for the next thing I remember is being on the pebble beach, being tended to by Mother Isabelle.

"We reached the door of the croft and from inside could hear growls and wheezing, the crash of overturning furniture. Then all fell suddenly quiet, except for the sound of crunching, as though some creature was feeding.

"Mother Isabelle clutched at me, then banged on the door calling, 'Mary Campbell, Mary Campbell.' She pushed me behind her then, when no answer was forthcoming, forced the door full open, so that the eerie light of the night spilled through.

"The gnawing sound stopped.

"Before us, on the floor, lay the half-eaten remains of the fat woman. Crouching in the corner, at first only its yellow eyes visible, was a bristling wolf, ready to spring at our throats.

"Mother Isabelle shouted a command, using sharp throaty sounds I did not recognize, and, to my horror, in place of the creature stood the boy, his hands and face smeared with blood, his eyes wide and gleaming, his white teeth still bared to us in a hideously triumphant grin.

"He ran past us into the night, and to this day his fading howls and shrieks chill my blood as I recall them."

Outside the caravan, a dog started baying as the air-raid sirens went off again and the drone of another wave of aircraft engines grew louder, insistent as a throbbing toothache.

Mother Celina bowed her head. "It must stop," she muttered tiredly. Then the caravan shuddered as the bombs began falling.

MONDAY

January 6, 1941

I n his dreams that night, George found himself wandering an alien landscape of bitter memories. All around him the terrain was gray and he trudged up and down the bleak slag heaps of his childhood, as though in a black desert, while the sun traversed the paper-white sky and daylight was gradually replaced by the cold, silver light of a full moon.

He saw a figure in the distance and hurried toward it, but tripped, falling face down. The black dust, instead of cushioning him, parted beneath his weight, and he tumbled headlong into a pit, falling faster and faster. . . .

He did not recall hitting bottom, but when he sat up, to his horror he found himself in the basement of the house on the common, the pile of animal corpses somehow reanimating themselves from the gelatinous goo they had disintegrated into and slithering across the floor toward him. Worse, as he moved to get out of their way, he felt chains, heavy as lead, shackling his legs to the wall, restricting his movements, rubbing painfully, forcing him into the path of the slimy things that crept up on him.

A noise caused him to glance up: a key turning in a lock. He cried out from pain as he was struck by lances of light from beyond the doorway, ducking his head; it was hard to make out the silhouetted figure that approached him, but it seemed to be the same one he had seen earlier in the distance on the slag heaps. Her hands were filled with metal dishes of bread and milk. He lunged toward her, but the chains jerked him back. She screamed and threw the metal plates toward him, then hastily retreated. The milk spread on the floor, turning slowly yellow, then blood red.

George found himself scrabbling for the food on the cold concrete, but instead of bread, he realized with abhorrence he was hungrily chewing on a human leg. In disgust, he threw it on top of the writhing pile, his hunger unabated.

Another figure loomed, its shadow filling George with dread. He knew without looking it was his father, come to punish him. Though he should have fought back, George's instincts were to cower instead as his father picked up the discarded leg and began to beat him with it.

When next George looked up, he saw his father had hunched down before him and was chewing on the discarded limb. He now saw where it had come from.

His father was crouched over the figure of George's mam, wrestling with her other still-attached leg, while she passively allowed him to devour her, waving George away with a smile, propped against the wall as she nursed a child, rocking and crooning to it. His father turned and snarled, and George saw he had developed long teeth and glittering, slitted yellow eyes. . . .

With a cry that awoke him, George opened his eyes, his heart pounding, taking a moment before he recognized his bedroom, bathed in the shadows of night. "It's just a nightmare, that's all," he told himself. It took a few moments to calm down, and he wiped away beads of sweat that trickled down his face and neck. The smell of sex lingered thickly in the warmth of the bed sheets. He listened, but heard only the even breathing of Vera Armstrong sleeping peacefully beside him and the ticking of his alarm clock on the bedside table. Four fifteen.

George closed his eyes again and slowly returned to sleep, determined not to be tormented by something as ethereal as a dream, consciously thinking about the woman curled on her side next to him, remembering what it had been like to make love with her.

As sleep overtook him once more, it wasn't Vera's face he stared into, however, but Gwenyth's. She lay passively beneath him while George pounded away, feeling with each thrust of his hips that he was punishing her in some way for all the frustrations and lies and tricks, for her unwillingness, her taunts—and *there*, he thrust heavily against her. She smiled up, challenge in her eyes, and *there* again, nothing sexual about the situation, but a desire to punish her, to stab her with himself, as he had seen his da' punish his mam. Suddenly nauseated, George rolled off her while she taunted him to continue, to make her *feel* something. As he looked around the room he saw Vera Armstrong watching him from the bottom of the bed, her hand covering her mouth, her eyes wide with disbelief.

"Help me," he pleaded. She shook her head, still staring at him. His body itched, and when he rubbed himself he saw he had fur instead of skin. Irrational anger flooded through him—he gnashed his teeth, saliva dripping from the corners of his numb lips, then lunged toward her.

"Animal," she cried, stepping backward. *"You're an animal!"*

His hands found her throat and he began to squeeze, forcing back her head, growling with hunger and expectation, lowering his teeth to bite the pale, exposed skin, the arteries throbbing visibly; only it wasn't Vera Armstrong he was attacking, but Wendy, his daughter. . . .

"Oh, God," he thought. *"It's me!"*

□   □   □

Nevil awoke on the floor of Mother Celina's caravan with a start, knocking aside the eiderdown quilt, sitting up suddenly and looking around for the beast he had been dreaming was about to eat him alive.

She walked over from the table and handed him a tin mug of steaming black tea, which he sipped, pulling a face at the bitter, sugarless taste.

"You can't stay here," she said. "You're not welcome. Outsiders always bring us trouble. I should have sent you away last night, like they wanted. Don't know why I didn't, 'cept you looked so pathetic."

Still groggy from sleep, Nevil shivered as the cold morning began to bite. He hunched in the quilt for more warmth. "I'm very grateful."

She snorted cynically. "I'm sure."

Nevil waited for her to continue. After a few minutes of silence, he said, "I want to talk about the woman in the big house."

"I don't know anything."

Nevil sipped more tea, coming fully awake. "I've read her journal—or at least, some of it. She talks about you—"

"Get dressed," she interrupted. "Leave. She was a mistake, and you're a bigger one."

"What about that story last night. You know something. What is it out there? You've got to tell me."

"Why should I?"

He rose and moved into the main room, taking a seat on a cloth-draped chest, waiting for her to follow him.

Even in daylight, the caravan was lit by two storm lamps, swinging gently. Wisps of dark smoke curled up to the smudged ceiling, the cluttered, claustrophobic atmosphere barely relieved by the thin yellow light that made pockets of darkness at the edges of its beams, hiding more than it revealed.

Draped around the walls and doors of the rickety room were dried flowers and herbs of a confusing variety, books, carved mementos, a basket filled with wooden clothes pegs, some not yet completed, and shelves holding several boxes, two of them lacquered and obviously antiques, plus odd-looking objects Nevil assumed had something to do with the caravan. At one small curtained window there was a table, covered with a gaudy vermilion cloth with yellow swirling patterns and tasseled edges, and stout wooden chairs. The smell of camphor and rosemary lingered.

"Over there," Mother Celina said. She gestured to the table.

Nevil reseated himself, pretending to examine the tablecloth. It looked Arabic, he thought. She sat opposite him and placed her hands together.

Nevil couldn't stop shivering. He did not speak at first because he was sure the quaver in his voice would give him away. He gritted his teeth, waiting for her to make the first move.

After several minutes of oppressive silence, she said, "Why should I get involved. Why should any of us?"

"You said—" Nevil began. "You're responsible. The girl's baby," he finished lamely, looking away. He fiddled with his fingers, catching sight of her through the corner of one eye, feeling like a rebellious schoolboy who'd been found out. She chuckled nastily. "Thought you were an *intelligent* man. It was just a story, is all."

"You said . . ." Nevil spoke more forcefully. "'I helped where I should not have.' You damn well know. You can help me or not, I don't care anymore. It's in your interest as well as mine."

"How's that?"

"If you or anyone here's found to be involved, even if you k-kill th-that *thing* out there, it won't matter. They'll hold you to blame all the same, you know they will. They're just looking for an excuse. . . ."

"Why should you care what happens to us?"

"I don't." He looked up, emboldened, surprising himself at the certainty that filled him. "It's *me* I care about."

She appraised him, pursing her lips, the deep lines making her appear toothless.

"My people believe that man has within him two spirits—an animal spirit and a human. To be whole, we must acknowledge and embrace the beast in us.

"If a man was intemperate and carnal in this life, then his spirit will be earthbound, in the guise of some terrible creature. . . ."

"A werewolf," Nevil whispered.

"Aye."

He shook his head, not exactly disagreeing with her so much as trying to recall where first he had heard the theory. There was something about her, a falseness, that made Nevil consider for the first time that it wasn't as much what she was telling him that was important as what she might be leaving out. "But this isn't a spirit; I've seen it—it attacked me; I *know* it's real."

"What do you know, eh?" She drew back, as though disgusted with his denseness. "How can you even begin to deal with what's out there if you're so adamantly blinded by childish fantasies."

She sniffed in disgust and went to rise. Nevil laid a hand on her arm. "Please."

She grunted, as though calling his sincerity into question, but continued, "A werewolf is an anomaly—sometimes a man, sometimes a woman, sometimes a child. It is a special gift that stretches back, like the Tarot, to our misty beginnings. Just as there are people who can divine water, who can use their minds alone to move things or send messages to another, so we believe in the psychic ability to change into the beast inside us all. Sometimes the change is voluntary, but more often it is because of a curse for some wicked deed."

"But what about *this* one."

Mother Celina seemed suddenly weary, her voice cracking and laden with remorse. "Ten years ago, maybe a little more, a woman came to see me. She and her sister were spinsters, well-to-do, and could not go to others for help because of a dreadful sin one of them had committed that they had to keep secret. Not only was one of the sisters pregnant, she was suffering from a terrible illness that affected her body and her mind. I must help them, they begged me. I was their last hope. Abort the child. If I did, they'd ensure no one would ever bother us around here again.

"Like a fool, I believed them, even though, as now, the people round here curse us and spit as we pass and are always finding reasons to harass us. There were others I had helped like this, though she was too far gone for me to do anything. I promised instead I would help nurse the mother and child through the remainder of the term.

"One evening, our camp was attacked. The police and everybody else came round and tried to drive us away.

When our men resisted, they were arrested and our belongings smashed or confiscated."

She stared at Nevil. "Your mother and her friends were in the forefront, urging everyone on."

Nevil was shocked. "My mother?"

"Aye, I knew her. I know many people around here, though they pretend they don't remember me. They're too good for us, ain't they, 'til they wants something from me. You know. You've heard. But that was when it started."

"You're talking about the Stepan sisters, aren't you," Nevil said. He reassuringly patted the inside pocket of his coat where the journal was safely snug.

"That I am," she replied, appearing pleased with him. "They were here the night the rozzers came and tried to drive us off. The shock of the violence was too much for the pregnant one, and she went into labor on the floor there. The child was terribly deformed and sickly and died within a few days of its birth, which was a kindness, all told. But the woman would not be consoled.

"She called me to her house some time later and insisted she wanted revenge on the man responsible for her baby's death. I, too, was angry at him, at all of them, so like a fool I agreed to help her again.

"I summoned all my skills and put the Evil Eye on him—a terrible curse known only to my people and *never* to be used—though I ignored the warnings of my betters, letting my thirst for vengeance get a hold of me.

"Unless he repented, within five years he would turn into the cruel beast inside him, though he'd be ignorant of his affliction in his human shape."

"He doesn't know?"

"In his dreams, perhaps. In its animal form, as you've seen, the monster's too dangerous to get near. If it were to bite you and you survived, then you too would be cursed with transformation and no one could do anything to help you."

Nevil fingered the scratches on his face, unwilling to believe what she was saying, yet unable totally to discount her story. Too much of it made sense, rang a bell of truth he could not disavow, as much as he wanted to. "Who is it?" he whispered.

Mother Celina drew a deep breath, then let it out slowly. "His name is George Llewellyn."

The name caused a spasm of dread in Nevil. Images of his endless interrogations in the James Street police station, the snarling copper—*"You'll swing for it next time, I promise you!"*—almost overloaded his circuits.

Mother Celina was saying, "The first time I set eyes on him I knew him for what he really was. His eyebrows meet in the middle for one thing. As I predicted, five years ago his wife came to me, desperate to get away from him, needing my help, terrified of him. His evil ways had finally reached their child, and she was powerless to protect her any longer."

Mother Celina added quietly, "Oh, yes, I know George Llewellyn for the monster he really is.

"Jack-the-Lad he was in those days. During the raid on our camp that night he arrested my youngest son—my baby—and stuck him in prison. When he came out he was a changed man, surly, bitter, couldn't get on with no one. Drank like a fish. Llewellyn drove him away from me, from his family. I'll never forgive that black-hearted copper for that."

"What happened to him, your son, I mean?"

"He got hit by a bus after he left a boozer one night. It was all because of that bastard copper. He deserves to die for what he's done to me and mine. . . ." She choked for moment, her voice failing her. "If ever he learns what I did to him I'm finished. But so are you, whatever happens." She paused. "You know him, don't ye. I can see it in your face. You know what I'm saying's the truth."

She seemed suddenly much older, her stoop more pronounced as she rose from the table and crossed to the shelves. Her hands shook as she returned with one of the lacquered boxes, the inlay work obviously hand-carved and -fitted. She placed it before him and motioned with a hand. "Open it."

Nevil gingerly picked it up, at first unable to find any indication of an opening. Turning it upside down, he again failed to find a lock or handle. The box was quite heavy, he thought, as he weighed it in his hands. He ran his fingers over it, seeking cracks, finding none, then pressed a band of marquetry about an inch from the top. When that didn't work he tried sliding the band. On his third attempt, he felt a movement, then a click, and the lid sprang open.

Laying the box on the table, he examined the contents. Nestled in black satin lay a poignard—a thin stiletto of burnished silver with an ivory handle. The knife looked like a white flame and had to be several hundred years old, Nevil guessed. He was awed by it, picking it up and examining the obvious craftsmanship. ". . . only something *silver* . . ." he recalled Camilla Stepan saying.

"It's your only hope of saving yourself," Mother Celina said. Her voice made him jerk up his head. "You must pierce its heart with silver, otherwise it will return as a spirit. Getting rid of it then will be almost impossible, for it will be able to cross from one world to another without the hindrance of flesh it now has.

"That's all the help you'll get from me. Don't *ever* come back again."

181

She removed the knife from his hands and replaced it in its case. Their eyes met. "Not ever," she hissed.

□   □   □

Medford collected George at 6:30 A.M, banging on the front door until he was admitted. "We've got the bastard, George!"

"What you talking about?" At the moment, George begrudged anything but the minimum acknowledgment he was awake. He hadn't even had a wake-up cup of tea yet and was forced to leave Vera Armstrong still snug in his bed. He left Medford waiting downstairs while he whispered to her he had to go. She had mumbled an acknowledgment in her sleep and curled away from him, a terrible ordinariness invading the enchantment of the last few hours.

"Got your end away at last, I see," Medford commented, as the two policemen climbed into a marked police car. "Perhaps you'll be a bit more human now. Christ knows I ain't see hide nor hair of this infamous charm of yours for a while. You're becoming a right surly bugger, George, and no mistake. 'Bout time you got yourself another woman, anyway. You could do a lot worse than her. You did, come to think of it."

"It's not serious," was all George said. He didn't want to let himself consider anything else. "Now, what's this all about. Exactly who have you got?"

"No one yet. Thought I'd leave that little pleasure to you. You got Herbert Williams to thank—he's the one who nailed him."

"What the hell are you talking about, Fred? It's too early in the morning to be playing games."

"The bloke what's doing all them child murders."

Instantly awake, George listened attentively as Medford told him about the attack on DC Williams last night and the discovery of the latest body. "Lucky he's got a head like a block of cement," Medford finished.

"Daft bugger," George said angrily. "I *told* him to go home, not play bloody Bulldog Drummond. Lucky he didn't get himself killed."

"He's gonna be out of it for a while, but he recognized who went for him from the files. You was right."

George's eyes lit up. He *knew* he'd been right—then and now. "Nevil Stimpson," he breathed. He turned to Medford and said quietly, "Anyone been round to see Frank Isley yet?"

"One of the lads is already on his way with him to the hospital. He's going to officially ID the kid there. I thought you and I should have a chat with Mr. Isley later on today. Find out exactly what that kid was doing there in the first place, why he run away from his dad *again*."

"I want everyone in on this, right, Fred?"

"Don't worry, I've already got the rest of the lads out looking. It's a matter of time, George, that's all. He ain't gonna get far."

"Yeah," George breathed in agreement. "That's what it's always been. A matter of time . . ." He fell quiet, daydreaming.

As they drove through the quiet of the early morning, George's nightmare clung to him still, but its content had faded until there remained only strands of uneasiness and remorse, though for what he couldn't recall.

He sat back closing his eyes, the memory of his last meeting with Nevil Stimpson five years ago as fresh as if it were yesterday.

They'd brought him into the station house at four o'clock in the afternoon on a Tuesday. George had first seen him at seven. He'd taken an instant dislike to the man, cringing, red-eyed from weeping, slouched in his chair. They'd gone over the facts of the case: Where had Stimpson been two weeks before, on the afternoon and evening of Thursday the twenty-third, when twelve-year-old Nicholas Davenport had been brutally molested, then murdered.

Stimpson did not have an alibi, had no explanation at all for what he'd done that day. At home, alone, reading, was all he could come up with. His story had so many holes you could drive a lorry through it. What the police didn't have was any hard evidence; what they needed was a confession.

Halfway through the third day of questioning, George had gone out for a cup of tea, then, returning fifteen minutes later, had dismissed the uniform standing stoically by the exit to the interview room. Once George and Stimpson were alone in the bare room, he'd turned toward his suspect, rolling up his shirt sleeves. "One way or the other," he threatened, aiming a finger at Stimpson, "You're gonna tell me how you did it."

"N-nothing happened. Why won't you believe me? You've n-no right to t-treat me like this."

Angrily, George had slammed his hands down on the table before Stimpson, making him flinch and jerk back his chair. "Child-murdering bastards like you ain't got no rights." George snapped away the chair from under Stimpson, dashing it against a wall, almost spilling his suspect onto the floor. Stimpson clumsily regained his balance and backed away. "You keep away from me," he'd shouted.

"Keep away? I'm gonna *have* you. You're *mine*."

"You're crazy. I haven't done anything, I tell you."

"That so? You were his tutor; you saw him twice a week,

Mondays and *Thursdays*. So what happened this particular Thursday, then?"

Stimpson grabbed the chair, holding its back and jabbing the air before George with the legs. "Keep away from me," he yelled.

George tapped the legs; Stimpson jabbed them at George, who smiled coldly. "What's this, then? Assaulting an officer? That what this is?" He slapped at the legs, harder this time, knocking them to one side. Stimpson backed away, managing to bring the chair between them again.

From his cowering stance in a corner of the room, Stimpson yelled, "I haven't done anything. Leave me alone, please, I beg of you. I n-never saw him that day. He didn't turn up for his lesson, ask his p-parents. I called them, I told you."

George advanced menacingly, and Stimpson once more used the chair to keep the policeman at bay. "Help, oh God, please, somebody, help me," he screamed, his voice echoing hollowly in the room.

"You did it," George insisted. "Like little boys, don't yer, Nevil. Like those kids at school—"

"Nothing *happened*," Stimpson shouted. "I never did anything—"

"Yeah? What's this for, then?" George once more swatted at the chair Stimpson had before him. "What you worried about, *Nevil*? You haven't done anything, right?"

"You," he whimpered. "You're going to hurt me. Keep away from me. You're the lunatic, not me. How can you imagine such awful things?" Stimpson jabbed with the chair legs, backing his way around the table in the middle of the room, keeping George from cornering him.

"I don't have to imagine them thanks to scum like you." George grabbed the legs of the chair waving before him and sharply shoved it backward. The curved end of the chair back jabbed into Stimpson's stomach, making him gasp and double over. The chair fell to the floor and George savagely kicked it away. It bounced off the wall with a loud clatter.

At that point, Fred Medford slammed open the interview-room door, bellowing, "What's going on in here, Detective Sergeant Llewellyn?"

Stimpson quickly backed away, warily eyeing both coppers, his arms crossed before him in futile protection at the beating he expected to receive at any moment.

"Nothing, Sergeant Medford," George shouted back. "Kindly leave us alone, I'm conducting an interview."

"No you ain't. Let him go. Orders."

The three men stood eyeing each other, no one willing to give way, the air filled with almost tangible mistrust and violence. "You hear me?" Medford said quietly. "Cut him loose, George."

"You'll *swing* for this, I promise you," George threatened Stimpson, advancing toward him, barging into Medford, who had deliberately stepped in the way.

"That's enough, George, let it go."

"Next time," George threatened Stimpson from behind the obstruction of Fred Medford, "—and there's going to be one, we both know that, don't we—next time, I'll *have* you, you degenerate, murdering piece of shit."

Medford pushed George away. "That's *enough*, George. The inspector wants to see you, right away. Get yourself fixed up. I know how you feel. We all feel the same way, but this ain't gonna do it. This ain't about Wendy, George. We're all sorry about what happened to her, but it ain't about her, you hear me? You're better than this. His brief will kill us in court if we don't do it by the book. I'm asking you nicely, George: Don't do nothing stupid."

So they had let Stimpson go, and the case had remained officially unsolved—*unproven* was George's view. There was no way in hell George was going to let him get away again.

In the car, George smiled to himself. He *knew* the bastard would do it again. *This time,* nothing and nobody was going to get in his way. This time, Stimpson was going to pay for what he'd done.

□   □   □

At 7:30 A.M., George and Fred Medford descended into the subterranean world of Londoners who had become refugees in their own city. They briefly acknowledged the policeman on guard by the sandbagged entrance to the Smiths Common underground station and went inside.

They paused at the top of the stationary escalator that led seventy feet down to the platforms. The cold air outside was replaced, as they descended, by a warm, though rather ripe fog of collective body heat, stale clothes, and tobacco smoke.

"Stuffed up all the ventilators," Medford murmured.

"What?"

"I said, they stuffed up all the ventilators again. WVS comes round, opens them all up, they wait till they've gone, then stuff 'em up again. Jesus H. Christ, you could cut the air down here with a knife." He wafted his hand before his nose as he spoke. "There's some dirty buggers about."

They continued down the steep incline of the stairway, their footsteps echoing off the tiling.

"I've been thinking about your Stimpson feller, George."

"What about him?"

"He's supposed to be into this occult nonsense, ain't he. I mean, he's got the opportunity on at least one of the murders. We got—well, we had—a witness to prove that. Some sort of Devil worship stuff would give us a motive now, wouldn't it? All we got to do is find out how he done it."

"You think these are ritual killings?"

Medford twisted his head, easing a crick in his neck. "No accounting for some, is there. There's all them stories about the Jews and the Gypsies, ain't there. You know what I'm talking about. Stealing babies, blood sacrifices, and all that. Besides, the inspector's getting really antsy with us to get the whole thing over with. He's taking some real stick from Downing Street, apparently."

"I just want to make sure we get him dead to rights this time, Fred, that's all. He's not getting away from me twice."

As they reached the bottom of the stairway they heard a tube train rumble into the station carrying volunteers with tea and simple breakfasts, ready to help the vagrants tackle another day.

Emerging on the platform, George took a mug of tea from one of the volunteers and sipped, gazing around at the waking mass of humanity. "So what are we doing in this depressing hole in the ground?"

"I knows the woman what runs this shelter," Medford said. "They had a lot of trouble here for a while, you know the sort of thing, one kid hits another, the next thing you know someone's got a knife out. So, we puts Mrs. McKray in charge—"

"You mean Bert McKray's old lady's the shelter warden?"

"That's the one."

"I thought he was doing a fifteen stretch in the Scrubs?"

"He is. She's doing her bit for king and country down here." He faced George with a smile. "We ain't had no more trouble since she took over, I can tell yer. Who's gonna play silly buggers with her and her evil brood?"

"So?"

"I put the word out. Seems we found ourselves a cook."

George stopped, ostensibly to light a cigarette and return the mug. Sarcastically, he said, "Just what I need."

"You got no faith, son, that's your trouble. She used to be a cook for the Stepan sisters."

George again surveyed the mass of people getting ready for work and school. Somewhere among them was a woman who could finally shed some light on what was going on. Somehow, Stimpson and the Stepan sisters were connected, George was sure of it.

The tube was to have been extended farther east, and a new section of steel-lined, egg-shaped tunnel had been built beyond the end-of-the-line buffers, though track had not yet been laid. On benches and on each platform, as though sitting or lying on a long streetcar seat, were hundreds of men, women, and children. Rows of still waking forms were clustered together, stretched crosswise, their bodies taking up the whole space. George and Medford stepped carefully across them, trying not to tread on anyone, the sounds of myriad conversations echoing hollowly off the tunnel walls.

Many of the homeless were old and worn, people who had never known much of the good things in life and who were ending their days in desperate discomfort after their homes had been blasted. Those that could took in neighbors who'd lost their belongings and their homes. Those that had nowhere else to go were here, bundled up and patched, the deep lines in their faces betraying the strain of their nightly ordeal. Kids were giggling and laughing together, enjoying the chaos and the adventure. Women not helping others were already sitting together, bulky curlers hidden under scarves, knitting and gossiping. A few smart alecks made cracks about the crowding and the smells, saying how Londoners would turn into a race of tall people with long noses in order to reach the freshest air. Most people, though, just sat after waking from a fitful, nodding sleep, stiff-muscled, backs against the cold tube-station wall. Despite himself, George's feeling of guilt at being better off than these people made him avoid looking at them too pointedly, as though they had become animals in a zoo, curiosities not to be stared at. Bombed buildings were one thing, but the sight of hundreds of poor, opportunityless people lying in weird positions against cold steel and tile, sleeping with all their clothes on, hunched in blankets, lights shining in their eyes from overhead, breathing fetid air night after night—lying deep underground like moles, not fighting back, not even angry, just helpless, scourged, weak, pleased at the release of another dawn—this was life without redemption, George thought. He recognized the feeling, empathized with it. He always had Wendy to remind him, like the Ancient Mariner's albatross, in case he forgot.

Medford by this time had singled out the beefy form of Lorraine McKray, who in turn pointed out the woman the two policemen had come to see. She sat to one side of a group of noisy kids, near the entrance to the new tunnel.

Nellie Lipman was a little old lady in her early sixties with an unruly shock of red hair fading with age, so animated George first thought there was something wrong with her. She reminded him of the fizz in lemonade. She was busy talking twenty to the dozen at her husband, a quiet, thin fellow with sparse, gleaming Brylcreamed hair who would occasionally nod in agreement, muttering, "Yes, dear," whenever she paused for breath, while continuing methodically to tuck in his shirt and tie his necktie.

"Mrs. Lipman?"

She turned from folding blankets to face George. "Yes? Who are you?"

"Detective Sergeant Llewellyn. This is Sergeant Medford. We'd like to talk to you about the Stepan sisters if we may."

Mr. Lipman adjusted the braces on his trousers, then slipped on his bus driver's jacket. "I'm off then, Nell. See you later," he said.

"'Ere, where you going?" she called after him, ignoring the policemen. But he was already making his way over the rousing forms on the platform, heading for the exit.

"You did work for 'em, right?"

"Oh yeah," she said expansively, giving George her full attention. "Right pair they were. Worked for 'em, must have been, what? Two year, I reckon."

"Why'd you leave?"

"Give me my walking papers, didn't she, nasty cow. About three year ago."

"Who?"

"Miss Sofia. Right bloody nutter she was. Always carrying on and creating. I mean, I'm as godly as the next one, anyone'll tell you that, but she used to carry on about 'God is punishing us' this and 'It's God's curse' that, used to give me the willies, it did. I thought at first she'd got the hump with my cooking, but I done for toffs in my time, ain't I, there's nothing wrong with my food. I got right put out for a while though, I can tell yer."

George turned to Medford and with a wink said, "Go get us another cup of char, would you? Like one yourself, love?"

"That'd be loverly. Ta, dear." She beamed a quick smile, her gnarled hands coyly rubbing her face like a squirrel washing itself. Medford made a quiet "Cor blimey" comment, rolled his eyes for George's benefit, then wandered off, grateful to be spared her machine-gun tongue.

"So, tell me about these sisters, then, luv. Sofia and who was it?"

"Miss Camilla. Don't know nothing, do yer. She was a loverly piano player, real serious stuff. Choppin' and Beetovern and all that. Used to do it professional like until about ten year ago or so, but give it up, didn't she, to look after her sister, the loony."

"What makes you say that?"

"Well, she was, weren't she? Not right in the head, poor cow. Nasty mouth wiv it an' all. 'God is punishing us for our terrible sins,' she used to scream. Gawd strewth, what a trial she was! Right particular about their nosh, too, weren't they? All they ever seemed to eat was raw steak and chops, and they'd throw half that away. Nice if you can afford it, I suppose."

"What else did she say?"

"It was Miss Camilla what brought the Devil into their lives, she used to scream. It was Miss Sofia's punishment to have to look after her sister and that 'Devil's spawn.' Mad as a hatter, I told you."

"What was she talking about?"

A strange look came into Nellie Lipman's face. "You know, I never did find out."

Well, if *you* can't, who can? George thought. "Got to have some idea, Nellie. I mean, you was there for two years—"

"Ah, yes," she interrupted, "but I didn't *live* there, did I? Wouldn't let nobody *live* in, like. If I was to guess, not that I'm given to speckerlating about others, especially the dead, Gawd save 'em . . ."

Get on with it! George thought, fighting to keep a friendly look on his face.

". . . I'd say it might have something to do wiv downstairs, like. Used to be some funny noises come from down there sometimes."

Despite himself, George's eagerness got the better of him. He grabbed her arm, waving wildly in front of her, and said, "What noises, Nellie?"

She shrugged off his hand. "Down the wine cellar. Used to keep some really valuable bottles of wine down there, hundred nicker a shot, like, wouldn't let nobody get near them. Frightened me and the char lady was a couple of tea leaves. Used to keep everything locked up, didn't they? All I ever saw was the scullery, the kitchen, *her* bedroom, and the front room—"

"Whose bedroom?"

"Miss Sofia's, of course. When she weren't carryin' on she'd be took poorly and I'd have to bring her food up to her. Them stairs of theirs used to play havoc with my back. Sleeping down here ain't done it much good neither, but you can't complain, can you? I mean, what's the point. Everyone's having it hard these days."

"So it was wine in that cellar, was it?"

"Well, that's what *they* said. I think they must have had a guard dog or something down there. I could hear this whining and growling and that, sometimes. Too frightened to go down there, just in case, you know. Got it to look after them expensive paintings they had, and all that silverware I was forever polishing, I should think. Hated men, both of 'em. So it's gotta be a dog, ain't it? Stands to reason. For protection like."

"So how come this Camilla put up with her sister's bad mouth, then?"

"As I say, she was the one what really run the place, as much as Miss Sofia liked to *think* she was in charge."

George said, "You, er, busy this morning?"

"Course I am. I'm a very busy person."

"I was wondering, like, if you'd help us out. See, we found one of the sisters still alive, I reckon. Only we don't know which one. She's round the hospital. I'd really appreciate it if you'd take a quick gander at her, identify her for us. Could you do that?"

Medford arrived with the teas and took the opportunity of the pause in the conversation to hand one to Nellie. She sucked at it noisily, wrinkled her nose, and said eventually, "Why not. All got to do our bit, ain't we?" She sipped more tea.

"Thanks, missus. You're a real brick. Sergeant Medford here'll take care of you."

They were interrupted by the breathless arrival of a uniformed PC who scanned the tube station until he spotted the sergeants and quickly made his way over to them.

"We got real aggravation down the station. Inspector says he needs you both, sharpish."

"Don't you even say good mornin' first, Derek?" Medford complained. "Take this lady round the hospital soon as she's fit, get her to ID the woman we pulled out the wreckage the other day. You know the one, right?"

"Sure thing, Sarge."

He accompanied the sergeants back to the street, explaining that a deputation of locals was crowding the lobby of the police station demanding that something be done about the Gypsies and refusing to leave until someone gave them an answer they liked.

"It's that bloody Sybil Tunbridge," George muttered.

"Lock her up for a bit. That should take the wind out of her sails."

"Don't tempt me, Fred."

□   □   □

The day was cloudy and threatened rain, or maybe sleet. Nevil crouched in the ruins of the semidetached houses across from the James Street police station. He had retrieved his blanket, the material at first stiff after a night out in the bitter cold, and refilled his thermos with hot tea bought from a nearby café. He settled in the shell of a small house behind a glassless window and waited, blanket around his shoulders, passing the long hours alternately watching and trying to decipher the crabbed handwriting in Camilla Stepan's journal. Featured prominently in it, though without being named, as Mother Celina had predicted, was then Detective Constable George Llewellyn and his brutal police raid on the Gypsy encampment ten years before.

Nevil fingered the silver dagger hidden inside his overcoat; his determination was evaporating, and the knife, instead of reassuring him, became a reminder of his awful predicament. He shivered and pulled the blanket closer.

The police station was an imposing Victorian edifice sited at the right-angle junction of two roads. It had a parking space at the back, partially obscured by mesh fencing, and several steep steps that led up to the double front doors. A regular stream of police officers and civilians came and went through the entrance most of the morning. The manhunt for him had begun in earnest, it seemed.

Despite himself, Nevil dozed in the cold, jerking awake several times, then gradually nodding off again. Awake or asleep, he was harried by demons.

In his dreams he once again endured the terror of that night in the trenches in France. . . .

It was a long time before the shelling finally stopped, the machine guns at last silent. Lance Corporal Atkins was still moaning, suspended puppetlike on the barbed wire in no-man's-land. The sound tormented Nevil—he was the only one left alive now to hear it. Each groan was a claw, shredding his tattered nerves still further. Time lost its meaning, the night interminable and vicious. Gradually it dawned on Nevil that the silence meant he could try to reach Atkins—anything to stop that awful gurgling moan.

In his dream Nevil again found himself sinking in the muddy, churned earth as he crawled, inch by inch, toward the wire. He was ten feet away, near a shell hole, when a flare once more blazed in the night sky like a sun. Nevil froze, a panic gripping him so completely his mind went white with fear.

He didn't know how long he remained that way, but it was the guttural stutter of machine guns that brought him to himself again. He found he was whimpering, immobile, his fingers locked in fists that clenched the earth, as if to heave himself bodily into the ground out of harm's way. A shellburst killed the eight Tommies huddled nearby.

He heard Atkins cough, gurgle, then fall quiet.

Nevil remained where he was for the rest of the night. Those hours lying exposed, a shell hole only yards away, went on forever. Tracers sliced above him, the shelling recommenced, his every muscle twitch attracting gunfire.

By the time a British patrol found him, he was incapable of speech, both from the cold and the terror of that long vigil. Not knowing any better, they had called him a hero—but Nevil knew the truth. Atkins had died because of Nevil, because he had been too cowardly, too frightened to make the attempt until it was too late, and then he froze at the critical moment, once more a failure, paying for it with someone else's life this time, marking him as surely as God had marked Cain.

In the manner of dreams, his dead comrades-in-arms,

George Llewellyn, and Mother Celina stood at the head of a noisy mob of angry soldiers, policemen, and Gypsies, all staring threateningly at him, slapping truncheons and fists into open palms. . . .

Nevil jerked awake, the noise of a boisterous crowd across the street filtering over to his hiding place.

He eased himself to the side of the empty window frame and watched as Sybil Tunbridge and Edith Bullfinch headed up a deputation with a local councilor Nevil recognized. It disappeared inside the police station, while at least twenty other people formed a ragged picket line outside in the road. Despite the angry voices, they looked for all the world as though they were waiting for royalty to emerge. After a while, they slouched into their coats, turning sideways to occasional gusts of wind, hands thrust deeply in pockets against the cold.

Nevil was too far away to hear what was said, but as the morning wore on the police ineffectively tried to disperse the crowd though it was clear none of the locals were in a mood to back down.

Nevil waited patiently. It was nearly lunchtime when a uniformed sergeant escorted the deputation outside again, followed by a small phalanx of policemen who firmly but gently shooed the rest of the protesters down the street, though many shouted angry comments toward the police station as they wandered off. "It ain't finished yet, Medford," Nevil heard a man shout.

□   □   □

When the streets were once again clear, George Llewellyn descended the front steps of the James Street police station, pulling up the collar on his overcoat, pausing to light a cigarette before continuing down Waterloo Road, heading toward the hospital.

George found Dr. Phelps drunk and snoring. The pathologist sat behind a large wooden desk in his office, head slumped over a green ink blotter. A three-quarters empty bottle of gin open beside him, an overturned glass near a hand, an arm sprawled out as a pillow under his cheek.

"Jesus," George muttered in disgust. He pushed back his fedora, and hands on hips, surveyed the room. Books and papers were scattered randomly on available flat surfaces, while many more were piled untidily along the walls, wobbly stacks waist-high.

George cleared off a chair and pulled it up to the front of the desk. With a handkerchief he wiped clean a shot glass he retrieved from a nearby shelf, then pulled over the bottle, sat in the chair with his feet cocked on the desk, and poured himself a stiff drink.

He stared at the crumpled, snoring form before him. A wave of disgust went through George, and with it a realization that he could be looking at himself in a few years. Alone, self-loathing, drunk, a shell of his former self.

Phelps raised his head unsteadily and peered at George with red eyes. He belched and dropped his head back on his arm.

George leaned forward and poured another shot. *If you can't beat 'em, join 'em,* he thought. He raised the glass in an ironic salute to the near-insensible Phelps, drained it, and poured himself another. The bottle looked dangerously low. *Here's to the hero,* he thought, saluting Phelps once more. *Home safe and in the bosom of his family.*

It was another half-hour before Phelps looked up, groped for his bottle, and came more awake as he realized it was empty. George took out his brass hip flask and handed it to Phelps.

"It's whisky, I'm afraid."

Phelps drained the flask, tipping his head back and wincing as the liquor burned its way down. "Not much left, was there?" he said accusingly, his voice a tobacco-scarred rumble.

"I got bored waiting."

"Leave me alone." Phelps patted his waistcoat pockets and pulled out a cigar stump. He spent several minutes trying to strike a match but his hands shook too much. Eventually, George leaned forward and flicked his lighter, cupping his hands around the end of the stump until they were lost in a thick fog of noxious smoke.

"What the hell happened to you?" George said. It was a rhetorical question and had been more a thought than something he had meant to say out loud, but his disappointment and repugnance had got the better of him. Or maybe it was the alcohol?

"Who the hell are you to judge me?" The anger in Phelp's voice seemed to return him fully to the present. "What do you know," he sneered. "Didn't say that five years ago, did you, *Sergeant*? Oh no. Then it was a phone call at one in the morning, 'Help me doctor—'"

"That's enough."

"These things are never over with, though, are they, *George*. They stay with you." He slumped back in his chair, falling silent, aware that he had said too much.

George leaned forward, jabbing a finger at Phelps. "What do you know?" he insisted, thinking both about Stimpson and the investigation.

Phelps started to chuckle. There was no humor in it, however, and it reminded George of a hyena he'd seen in a zoo, braying with possessive victory over a carcass. "It's a werewolf." The braying grew louder but was cut short by a racking fit of coughing that left Phelps winded and red-faced.

George reached across the desk, grabbing the pathologist by his shirt. "Don't mess me about," he hissed. "I'm not in the mood."

Phelps's breath was sour and reeked of booze as he said, "I'm not," into George's face. "I've seen one."

George threw him back into the seat and lit up a cigarette. His own hands had started to shake. "Seen one *what*?" he asked, clenching his fists.

"'What happened to me?' you asked. Remember? I *saw* one, what it can do, twenty years ago. A native; an Eskimo."

"Don't be bloody ridiculous, you drunken old fool," George said.

Phelps ignored him, rummaging around in his desk. A few moments later he reemerged with another half-filled bottle of gin that he plumped victoriously on the table.

"You think werewolves don't exist?"

"Course they don't bloody exist! I know *who*'s responsible; what I need to know is *how* he's doing it."

Phelps hunkered down in his chair. "Then we have nothing more to talk about."

An ominous quiet clouded the room, each man sunk into a petulant silence.

"Kids are being *butchered* out there. Damn it, tell me what you know."

"I already have," Phelps whispered.

George launched himself from his seat, slapping Phelps's desk in frustrated rage, pacing the room until he had control of himself once more. "Don't play silly buggers with *me*. I won't stand for it."

"You don't want to hear the truth. That's always been

your problem, Llewellyn. You try and make everybody live in your own little carefully ordered universe, even if they don't fit. It's why your wife left you. Why you're always losing your temper. Just find someone to arrest . . ." His gravely voice broke. Then more quietly, he added, "Maybe it's come for you, at last." He looked up at George, his red eyes gleaming with malice. "To punish you for what happened to Wendy. Maybe it's come back for me. We've all got our dark secrets rotting away our souls, haven't we?"

George leaned over the desk intimidatingly, grabbing Phelps by the shirt once more. "God damn you, tell me!" There was no reply, and in disgust George let him go and sprawled into his own chair again.

After a long while, Phelps went on, "Where do you think all the stories come from? Someone just made 'em up?"

"I'm not interested in stories. How is he doing it? Some sort of instrument, is it? Steel false teeth? What?"

"It's come for us both." Phelps tossed back his drink and poured another, the bottle clinking noisily against the tumbler. "I used to be like you. A *rational* man, *rational* ideas. But how can anyone be *rational* in a world gone mad? Look around you.

"I read about them afterward, when I got back. I had to find out, you see. We're in Hell now. Condemned for the 'sins of the wolf.' This war, it's spawned evil things. It's our punishment for being seducers and hypocrites, thieves and liars, magicians—"

"You daft bastard. This is a waste of time." George stood and shrugged into his overcoat. "Are you telling me some escaped *wolf* is out there doing this? Not a man? Is that what all this gobbledygook is in aid of?"

"Not a wolf, no." Phelps began chuckling again.

"Right," George murmured, almost relieved.

"It's come for us, George. You want to know what you're

hunting? A creature of perpetual gloom, the beast in all of us, the end of civilization. *Um elfe kommen die wolfe, um zwolfe bricht das geweölbe.* At eleven comes the wolf, at twelve the dead rise—"

"You're insane. They ought to lock you up, you daft sod."

"You think you know it all, don't you?" Spittle bubbled from the corner of Phelps's mouth, clinging to his beard. "Well, let me tell you, you don't know anything. There's a skin disorder called *lupus vulgaris*—the common wolf, where the victim is covered from head to foot with ulcerated lesions and tubercles; then there's *lupus erythematosus uniquium mutilans*, the 'red talons of the wolf,' where the victim's hands and feet are so disfigured the skin and nails look like paws. Eight out of ten victims are women, mostly of child-bearing age. Then there's pyphoria, common in South Africa, certain types of severe schizophrenia, congenital syphilis . . . the victims don't look like people. They look like *wolves*, Llewellyn. They act like them, *eat* like them. And they're all incurable."

"I don't understand. What are you saying?" George whispered. As much as he wanted to be far away from this drunken, crazy man, something held him back. What was Phelps telling him?

As if reciting a familiar litany, the pathologist went on, "Giles Garnier, who lived with his family in a cave outside Lyons, found one day scavenging a dead body in the woods for food, burned alive and his ashes scattered on the wind; Michel Verdun and Pierre Burgot convicted of having sexual relations with wolves and executed. Or maybe Jean Grenier, who confessed he was a werewolf, indicting his father. Because he was only fourteen his death sentence was commuted. He spent the next eight years running around on all fours in a Franciscan friary in

Bordeaux, physically deformed, demented, pathologically attached to wolf lore. He was lean and gaunt, his hands deformed, his nails like claws, he could run with great agility on all fours, and ate rotten meat, only came out at night, and howled at the moon. Or there's Victor, the wolf boy of Aveyron, who ate raw meat and built dens in a corner of the house of the doctor, Jean Itard, who found him in the wilds. Lots of stories of children like that. All over the world. Creatures of the Devil, abominations, the beast in us running amok, *werewolves* . . ."

George left quietly, Phelps still rambling behind him, unable to make sense of the disturbing meaning buried somewhere in all the pathologist's nonsense.

□　　□　　□

Feeling the dagger again for reassurance, Nevil watched Detective Sergeant Llewellyn walk down Waterloo Road toward the hospital until he disappeared from sight. Nevil lay back, safe for a few hours, certain his hideout so near the police station was the last place they'd look for him.

Settling back, he opened Camilla Stepan's journal and began reading, skimming the cramped handwriting, then returning and rereading the weekly entries more carefully. As he read, Nevil was reminded of his own abused childhood, until the tears streamed down his cheeks:

July 8, 1929.
　　Etan has returned from South Africa. Sofia and I had a wonderful gathering of old friends to welcome him home. Robert and Cecily and the children are doing splendidly, Etan says. I'm so pleased for them. Etan insisted I play the

pianoforte for him, and I tried out the Ravel, which was wonderfully received. I shall use it next month at Lady Astor's.

Etan has become such a debonair man-of-the-world. The attention he pays to me is quite intoxicating, I must confess. I can scarce catch my breath at times. He is handsome, bronzed, rich from plantations he and his brother own. He has come back, he says, to raise capital for a cattle ranch out there. Everyone at the party was envious of his new life, and several of the men spoke earnestly of investing. He has such a winning way about him. What an entertaining, eligible young man he has become. I'm so proud. Etan regaled us with the most marvelous stories of how beautiful South Africa is; the purple veldt, arrogant prides of lions, herds of water buffalo, safaris for ivory. He claims to have been carousing and hunting with Hemingway, and to be close friends with the grandson of Cecil Rhodes, though I fear he may have been a little carried away by the wine and the gaiety of the evening, to be honest.

We all went to bed, drunk with possibilities and hope.

January 22, 1931.

Etan has gone. Sofia has reacted to his departure worse than I. She has taken to her bed in a deep depression, crying endlessly into the night, every night. How could we have been so foolish, so easily deceived?

Men are such inconstant creatures, such betrayers. Even here, I can not give utterance to the depths of my bitterness. I am sure now, it was not Eve who tempted Adam, but the other way about. Sofia refuses to see a doctor. I don't know what to do for the best. I'm sure she is suffering, like me, from a broken heart. Oh Etan, how could you have been so faithless?

February 24, 1931.

What a despicable character James is. He had the audacity to turn up here looking for Etan this afternoon. I find it hard to believe, even now as I write, that he could have had the indelicacy, the crass, insulting vilgarity to ask me, point blank, if I had ever been intimate with Etan!

We walked in the grounds after he insisted he had to talk with me, and would not leave, indeed, he threatened to make a scene, unless I agreed to accompany him. I did so with abhorrent reluctance. Though I clearly explained I did not wish to hear from such a cad and a rotter, a man so depraved he could court two women without either of them knowing about the other's involvement with him until he left, promising the world, dallying with us merely for sport, as if we were no more than the creatures he hunts in his wretched safaris. If there is a name for the black, evil side of Man's nature it is not Mr. Hyde—but Etan Henderson!

James told me, while we walked about the rose garden, that Etan has a disease! James actually seemed relieved, when, from my outraged reaction, it was clear to him, as I had not meant it to be, that I had never been intimate with Etan, despite our engagement. I must confess now, in the privacy of this journal, I am relieved beyond measure that he ran away when he did, without my resolve weakening. We came so close. . . .

February 26, 1931.

Finally, I have had the courage to face Sofia with the news James brought of Etan. His creditors have now reached across the ocean to find him and claim their due. If only I too could join with them and exact my revenge. I lie awake at night, plotting the most horrible demises for him. His intentions towards us were never honourable. We were playthings, foolish spinsters caught in a devilishly magical web he wove for us. How he must be laughing at us, entertaining his brutish friends at our expense.

But the worst of all this wretched mess was yet to come. When I told Sofia what James had implied about Etan's state of health, her face drained of color. She knew!

What choices did she have left, finally, than to reveal to me the depths of her depravity and the awful price she has paid for her sins: of the flesh and of envy. My hand shakes so from anger, even now. I have fired all the servants, for they must not know. No one must know. My penance for my trusting stupidity, I see now, is to care for Sofia. I can no longer play the piano in public, or even be a member of society. We have foresworn civilisation by what has happened. My foolishness is not only boundless—it has made us morally bankrupt. I thought I had a fiancé, and find instead he has befouled my sister's body—and my life, with not even a backward glance. There is no one I can turn to—no one.

Sofia knew already what James had tried to tell me! It was she he had come to see, unwittingly perhaps, not knowing the full depravity to which that man—whose name I will never utter more—could sink. Not only is she sick from his foul infection, she is with child by him. No one must know, she insists, and I agree.

He is a wolf—the embodiment of all Evil things; like that story by Wilde, "Dorian Gray," pleasing on the outside and rotten on the inside, morally and physically. He has managed to infect us both in a way, and I fear for Sofia and the child, despite her betrayal of me. She, surely, is paying the price for her wickedness. My hatred for her is but slight in the face of my hatred for him. It possesses me totally. But she is my sister; what else can I do to redeem myself from this nightmare but suffer with her the purgatory we have fashioned for each other? I must constantly remind myself it was him, not her who is to blame for all this. Truly, we were Little Red Riding Hoods who met the wolf in the woods.

May 12, 1931.

The Gypsy woman will not help. Sofia is too far gone with the child to abort it. It is too late for us, even by this murderous route. I am pleased that <u>he</u> has not also turned me into a murderess, despite Sofia's agony. God has turned away His face. What will become of us?

December 23, 1940.

It has taken me many years to understand, but we have betrayed ourselves in allowing <u>his</u> betrayal to consume us so. There are many things for which I will spend my next few lives atoning, I am certain. Even Stimpson, that funny little man who has unknowingly become my contact with the outside world, has become infected with my wretchedness, which spreads—like a moral cancer. I know of his trouble with the police, more than he believes I know. But who am I to judge another? What pitiful creatures we humans are. That my sister's youthful gentleness should have been so viciously destroyed by her immature inadequacy, her jealousy at my music, my intended marriage. Why should I have had both when she had nothing, and would have been left alone in this cruel world? She determined to have the man, thinking it fair trade. I have forgiven her, and I pray that some day, when her sanity returns, if but for a short while, she will forgive me also.

But nothing that happened comes close to the heinous betrayal we have perpetrated on the child of that ungodly union, to save the vestiges of our own corrupted natures. God knows, I am utterly ashamed and repentant, yet powerless in my paralysis of guilt and obligations, which weigh like Marley's shackles on me.

Sofia's illness is much worse, and she is bedridden much of the time. Her rages and her wicked tongue, her desperate pleas to God, unanswered as are mine, our hopelessness—it is consuming us. The only silent ear I have left is this Journal. I force myself to confess to it, for a priest would be aghast if he knew what we had done. But this diary has become more than that. Increasingly, it is as though the years have neutered me; our alienation from the world, our imprisonment, self-imposed though it is, has become our atonement for our grievous sins. But it is too late for the child. God help us all! While it exists, while I have the strength to write, though it ebbs from me like an endless hemorrhage, I have come to see that this Journal is what is left of <u>me,</u> my essence. While I can find the strength to ask God for forgiveness by naming what should be unnamable, a part of the <u>real</u> me will continue to exist too.

If ever, after my death, this should be found and read, forgive us our trespasses—forgive us.

The bombing is terrifying, more so because of what it could unleash; if only they knew. Hiding in the cellar is out, for obvious reasons, and I can hardly take Sofia to a shelter the way she is these days. She lies in bed, or under it when in her more lucid moments, but is hardly able to walk. During the raids, I have taken to hiding under the piano, the only thing I can honestly say I still love, though that, too, has been corrupted, and decays. It is not so much for the protection as the comfort, I think, little as that may be, that I draw from even this glib nearness to music. In a way, this war has made me realise that we have nurtured in our bosom a monster bred of his times—a perfect reflection of the horrors here and in Europe.

The child has lost all vestiges of humanity. I think on what he has become, what I see now we have helped to make, in our gutless, wicked, misguided attempts to save ourselves, and I know there is no more goodness left in this world. For the longest time I could not bring myself to murder in the flesh what I could not condone extinguishing in the womb. Nor would I allow Sofia to do so. It is as if the hand of God—or more likely the Devil—is protecting him. Too late, we tried to poison it, but failed, and we cannot get close enough now to destroy it any other way than to starve it. It has become its father's son tenfold! We have bricked it in, hoping he—it— will die. It's the only sure way left. But it has found some source of food. I suspect wild animals. Still it lives and rages, like its mother. Such an atmosphere of anger and hatred. It is crushing the last of my spirit from me. It cannot last much longer—it must not.

The irony is bitter to me: I, who was so set against Sofia's abortion, who screamed murderess at her all the way to Mother Celina's dreadful hovel-on-wheels; who later so rejoiced when Sofia screamed and the child's head popped out on the caravan floor into this unforgiving, brutal world; I am responsible now for its living death. This child has proven to me that God is indolent, and the Devil rampant, for what has happened to us is surely the Devil's work, not God's.

At night, as I wrestle with nightmares sleeplessly in my bed, I curse my trusting foolishness at being so easily taken in by that unspeakable soulless wretch whose fault this is. But he is not alone. He is like all other men–depraved, brutish, corrupted in body and soul, cursed. In the still of the night I can sometimes hear, or imagine I can anyway, the raging anger of that Werewolf's offspring we have caged but cannot kill. It has survived where none else would. I keep asking that Troll-like little man to read the cards for me, in the hopes that there I will find an answer or at least a sign before it is too late. So far, he has proven useless.

If ever there was doubt of a creature of the night, a twisted snarling, prowling, flesh-eating thing, it exists now. It is the dark part of our souls released, and will not die a normal death, even in the barren hell to which we have confined it all these years. It has surpassed its father, fulfilled his malignant, diseased legacy to this world, its spirit, if it still has one, trapped forever within a wretched shell.

There are many strange and unexplained things in this world, I have discovered. First that man, whose name I refuse to utter, who caused us so much suffering; then that bully of a policeman, bursting into the caravan, attacking the young man who came to our aid, causing Sofia to go into premature labor—he too is responsible. While the child lives, an accuser stands before him, even in his willful ignorance. He, too, must be made to pay for his penance one day.

When that gnarled hag Celina came to us to ask for money, she said it was God's way of exacting revenge, so that the policeman's wife could run away from him. I gave it to her willingly, as she knew I would.

We are the caged keepers of a caged monster, and it's not fair nor just that we alone should have to atone for our wickedness; others must—men must, as well. They made us open Pandora's box, and now we cannot properly close the lid. One day soon the fascists will bomb this house and release this festering male wickedness into the world. That, I begin to see, may be the price Sofia and I must pay for peace.

If there is truly a God He will show His mercy and release us all soon from this torment.

Several hours later, Ethel Tanner wheezed as she descended the narrow staircase to her kitchen. She was fussing clumsily with a teapot and kettle when the front doorbell rang. Cursing softly under her breath, she heaved herself and her throbbing legs to greet her visitor and was surprised by a somber-looking George Llewellyn.

"Thought I'd come round for that chat I promised you," he said.

"I just put the kettle on. I suppose you want one, don't yer."

"That'd be nice." George grinned at her.

"Don't you try that smarmy rubbish on me, George Llewellyn." Her gruff tone belied the obvious pleasure she had in seeing him once more. "You're after something; I know you of old."

"No, not me, Ethel. Just popped round for a visit, that's all, like you said."

"My arse you have."

The tea brewed and poured into large mugs, George and Ethel retired to her front room.

"So," she said. "We won the war yet?"

"It's a villain's paradise out there, these days. We're all too busy running on the spot to do much more than file a report."

"Things ain't changed much, then," she chuckled.

"They've got worse, Ethel."

"Signs of the times, I suppose."

"Well, funny you should say that. Old times was what I come round to talk about."

"Don't know as there's much I can help you with there, George."

He reached into an inner coat pocket and produced a sheet of paper which he handed to Mrs. Tanner. "What do you make of that, then, Ethel?"

She examined the paper, squinting to see better. "Do us a favor, George, hand me my magnifying glass, would yer? My eyes is gone these days." As George rose she said, "On the mantelpiece over there."

With the magnifying glass held over the paper in her stiff fingers, Ethel Tanner saw clearly that it was a death certificate for a child, dated September 6, 1931. "Where'd you get this then, George?"

"One of Fred Medford's lads turned it up for me. That's just about the end of your time with us, weren't it."

"About then. This supposed to mean something to me?"

"We live in hope, Ethel," George said, a little too glibly. "Problem is, the war's screwed up all the records for round here since they hit the town hall. I was hoping your memory might serve. Got that from one of the lads who did a search for me in the records at Somerset House. It's a bit of a long shot, I admit, but the funny thing is, like, we got a *death* certificate, signed by a local doctor no one can remember ever having been around here, and nothing in any of the parish records to show it was actually buried or cremated, no grave we can find, and oddest of all, no matching birth certificate."

"You *are* joking, George, right? How am I supposed to help yer."

"Can't die without being born, Ethel. Stands to reason, don't it? Why would anyone file a death certificate, but nothing else? Look at the name of who signed it. On the bottom. Supposed to be a doctor, right, but I don't remember anyone round here with a name like that who could have been involved. Thought you might. Hoped, anyway."

Ethel reexamined the certificate, staring through the magnifying glass at the near-illegible signature. "What's this say, then?" she asked irritably. "Looks like Cameron, is it?"

"That's what I reckon. C. Cameron. You ever heard of him?"

"Cameron, Cameron," Mrs. Tanner murmured, searching her memories. "Should be familiar, shouldn't it?"

"That's what I thought. But it ain't, least to me. Another thing, see the mother's name?"

Ethel Tanner peered at the paper once more. "Henderson?"

"That's right. Except the only Henderson round here we can't account for is the bloke you was telling me about. That young copper's a sharp lad. It was the names, and the fact that it's local, that caught his eye."

"No, no, it couldn't be anything to do with him. I told you, him and his family went orf to South Africa, must have been, what? Nineteen twenty-three, somewhere around there anyway. Ain't never come back. 'Sides, no one in his family called Sofia that I knew about what could have been the mother."

"But there *is* a Sofia Stepan in hospital, though, who looked after Robert Henderson's house after he went abroad. Bit of a puzzler, isn't it?"

"Not only that, George, but why choose Henderson as a last name. Why not something different?"

"Maybe because if it all ever came out, she wanted to make sure he shared in the blame in some way. Make sure everyone knew at that point he was the father—I don't know."

"Oh my Gawd," Ethel whispered at last.

"What?"

She sighed deeply. "Trust you to open a can of worms like this, eh, George."

"It's a cover-up, isn't it. What for, that's the question, Ethel?"

"Henderson—Robert, that is—had a brother who did come back for a while about this time. Right wide-boy he was." She waved the certificate. "This is probably a mistake. Must be a chance in a million you'd ever come across it, let alone think to question it if you did."

"Come on, Ethel, out with it. This is important."

"Celina Cameron. She weren't no doctor. She was a midwife. You think about it a minute, you'll remember her too. Ten year ago. Lots of stories about what she used to do round here, besides her regular duties."

From the recesses of his memory an image started slowly to surface in George's mind. He sat up straight. *"Christ. The abortionist."*

"It's one of the reasons my Sid and you lot tried to clear them buggers orf the common, ain't it, if memory serves."

George became lost in thought for a moment longer. "But this couldn't have anything to do with that."

"You're probably right. But what if there weren't no *birth* certificate, because they wanted to *hide* the birth for some reason—"

"But there *is* a death certificate, 'cause they were trying to hide the fact the little bugger's still alive." George added, in a rush, "So what happened to the baby, Ethel?"

"Don't ask me, George. Why don't you ask *her*." Ethel Tanner nodded in the direction of the common. "She's only down the street, ain't she."

Then, muttering to himself, George added, "But how does this bastard Stimpson fit into it, that's the question."

Dusk fell shortly after George left Ethel Tanner's, the winter evening forcing him to muffle against the pinch of the cold air. Within minutes his nose and fingers had become numb, though he was sure that the gin he'd drunk earlier contributed to his fuzzy condition, despite Ethel's tea.

He passed the back door to the morgue, where ambulances and hearses pulled up late at night, the hospital grounds deserted and desolate. It was a miracle the buildings had not been hit in the raids, their square, ivy-covered Gothic severity, amid the fractured ruins of

Smiths Common, somehow silently chastising, like an irate old gentleman facing savages with indignation alone. George's disconcerting interview with Phelps still played on his mind as he combined it with the evidence of the death certificate—but Stimpson wouldn't fit; and as much as George tried to ignore it, snatches of his nightmare, where he had found himself shackled to the wall in that cellar, stubbornly refused to evaporate into the ethereal stuff it had come from. He had a clearer notion than he wanted to admit of what was going on.

His growing depression was fueled by the knowledge that the thing would strike again. The pattern was becoming clear. It killed to eat, and it needed to eat at least once a day. That meant it would probably be out again tonight, and there was no way he could think to find it, trap it, or stop it.

He *knew* what he was chasing was connected to the sisters and that appalling cellar. What could they have kept down there? And why? *I wouldn't have kept a mad dog in that abominable place,* he thought.

The answer stayed tantalizingly just out of his grasp.

Phelps, along with that daft pratt Williams, insisted what he was after was a *werewolf*. Utter balderdash! Who did they think he was, some sort of cretin? What were they all hiding? Werewolves were fairy stories, scientific impossibilities.

Reluctant as George was to accept the idea, though, the werewolf theory did explain *what* those weird women had been so secretive about, and why it had been kept in that cellar all these years.

He hawked and spat in disgust. He reached the main road, the desolation making him feel he was the only human left in the world, then ducked into an alleyway, taking a short cut to the station house. The alley was about four feet wide with high, rough black slatted wooden fencing, and it wound through several gentle *S* bends that obscured a view of the exit. With no street lights it was buried in shadows.

As he carefully made his way along the narrow pathway, running a gloved hand along the fencing to orient himself, George decided that Phelps might have been talking about a werewolf, but not the mythological kind. He could not get rid of the idea the pathologist had planted that *werewolves might exist.*

No, there was no way George was going to accept that what he was chasing was anything other than some real—if demented—creature. Fred Medford's idea that Nevil Stimpson was into Satanism and therefore had a motive, means, and opportunity was becoming more appealing by the hour. It would explain the werewolf ideas, for example. Who better would know how to fake it? And then, if you took that absurd idea to its logical conclusion, maybe *he* was the creature. Find Stimpson, George was certain, and he would find the answers to most of his nagging questions. It was grabbing for straws, though. . . .

He rounded the last curve of the alleyway and was near the exit when the shadows coalesced into a shape, and before George realized what was happening, the shape was howling and charging toward him. He felt something sharp pierce his chest and fell back from the weight of the man—he was sure of that much as his addled brain fought to react.

George fell heavily against the fencing, making it rattle, smacking his head on a sharp edge, and collapsing to the ground, one arm trapped painfully beneath him. The man on top of him, face smothered with a scarf obscured further by darkness, whimpered and growled, struggling to free a hand that was trapped in the folds of George's overcoat.

George tried to free an arm and found he couldn't push himself away from the fence. His attacker finally freed the entangled hand, and George saw a flash of metal. In raising the hand to stab again, the attacker also freed George's trapped arm. George immediately swung a punch that glanced off a shoulder, managing to hold off the knife blade just short of his throat. It dawned on George, rather belatedly and with avalanching shock, that this bastard was trying to kill him!

He struggled fiercely, grabbing a coat sleeve as the knife swung in again, but he slipped further down the wall toward the floor and cried out as he felt ripping and then a hot needle slide across his chest, followed by the slow seeping of blood.

A sudden panic at the seriousness of his situation caused George to lash out with his feet, fending off the other man. He thought for a moment he had freed himself, then the knife came slashing down once more. Rolling to one side, George felt the blade skid along the cobbled street next to him. He slammed upward with the palm of his hand, catching the assassin in the chin and driving head and body backward.

George turned, intending to get to his feet, but somehow he slipped on the icy cobbling, cracking his knee on the stone, realizing, as the blinding pain subsided, that the wetness in his sleeve and dripping down his hand was more blood. He sensed his attacker closing for the kill behind him and, still on all fours, kicked backward, felt his leg judder as his foot connected solidly with something hard, and heard a bellow of pain. He lashed out again, felt his foot connect solidly once more, and heard a crunch.

Obstinately, George ignored the insistent dizziness that

was hovering and managed to turn himself so that he was sitting with his back to the fence, legs splayed before him. He scanned the alleyway, but the assassin had gone, echoing irregular footfalls fading into the night.

After what seemed a long while, George started to shiver from the cold and shock. He was bleeding badly and knew he couldn't stay where he was much longer or he'd freeze to death. Yet making the decision to move, and actually doing it, forcing his leaden, stiff limbs to obey, took forever.

Stooped but standing, and leaning heavily against the fence, George forced himself to stagger toward the end of the alley. Pain flared in one knee when he put weight on it. His only concerns were staying alive and finding the bastard who'd just attacked him; and the only way to do that was to keep moving. He bounced off the fencing, finally reaching Waterloo Road, only to realize it was deserted. George made it five feet into the roadway and lost his sense of geography. When it returned a few minutes later, he was lying in the street, his shirt soaking wet now, and feeling ever colder as it stiffened. *I'm dying,* he thought, and closed his eyes.

□　　　□　　　□

Nevil could not guess at why cosmic forces—he could express the recent confluence of events no other way—had chosen *him* as this poor creature's executioner, the one man who had even an inkling as to the depth of suffering Sofia Stepan's son must have been through; to whom she sister had entrusted her journal; who could emphathize with the injustice of it all enough to forgive the child—or at least, what it had become—for the dreadful butchery it had unleashed on the world now it was free.

Nevil was still in the ruins opposite the police station, and he guessed it must be time to move on: didn't pay to stay in one spot too long. Then it occurred to him that perhaps the one person best suited to ease the creature's suffering was indeed himself *because* he understood. *A mercy killing,* Nevil decided. *That's what all this has been leading me to.*

Under cover of darkness, he gathered his meager belongings and started down Waterloo Road. He hadn't gone far before he was forced to duck into the shadows of a doorway as a drunk staggered toward him. It was only as the figure drew closer that Nevil realized it wasn't hunched from drink, but from pain. He was about to step forward and ask if he could do something to help when he stopped himself. That was a plain foolish idea. Then he recognized the man as the tall Gypsy he had seen leaving Mother Celina's caravan. What had she called him? Gus, that was it.

The Gypsy stumbled, groaning, colliding with a lamppost and dropping to his knees. Something slipped from within his coat onto the roadway. The man heaved into the gutter, then stood up again and lurched past Nevil, oblivious to his surroundings and to Nevil cowering in the doorway. Nevil waited until he had passed, then crept into the street and picked up what Gus had dropped. It was a knife, a poignard to be exact. Trembling with blossoming outrage, Nevil withdrew the knife Mother Celina had given him and compared it to the one he had just found. They were a matched pair. What did it mean? "Fix him good for me, Gus," Nevil recalled Mother Celina calling out to the man.

Remembering her hatred and bitterness, thinking about his own perilous position after his attack on the policeman, suddenly fearing the worst, Nevil hurried down the street.

As he had dreaded, a body was lying in the middle of the road, no doubt stabbed to death.

It was when Nevil gingerly rolled it on its back that he recognized Detective Sergeant George Llewellyn. Nevil should have felt triumphant and yet he did not. A moment of relief was quickly replaced by the thought that *he* hadn't done it, but *they* would now believe he had attacked *two* policemen and killed both of them. It was all that bloody Gypsy woman's doing! She'd set him up. He heard his mother's voice screech down the years, *"I told you it would be the gallows for you, my lad!"*

Nevil was torn from his self-loathing by a groan from the man he knelt over. That evil copper wasn't dead, after all! Perhaps Nevil still had a chance to save himself, somehow.

How badly hurt was the man? There was an awful lot of blood on his clothes. Nevil backed away, feeling the two knives inside his coat pocket. *If they catch me now . . .!* The thought made him nauseous.

But the policeman was only semiconscious. He would die soon if Nevil did nothing, that was sure. Once again, the irony of his life did not escape him. Either way he was doomed, Nevil could see that clearly. He sighed resignedly. He could not find it within him just to walk away and let the man bleed to death. That Nevil should find himself in this situation *again*, after he had failed both Atkins and then the boy—it was too much.

But where to take him? Nevil looked around the street, then back at the policeman. He was too heavy for Nevil to carry very far. Nevil's gaze lit upon the massive form of a church, tucked in from the roadway, perhaps a quarter mile away. That would have to do.

He struggled to heave the policeman to his feet, not knowing quite where he found the strength, slapping the man's face to bring him around enough to stagger down the street with Nevil's arm supporting, knees almost buckling from the weight, blood dripping into the road behind them.

At the church, he leaned George against the stone wall and battered at the heavy wooden door until a light came on inside. Pounding more urgently, Nevil waited until he heard someone coming, then ducked into the shadows.

"Oh my Gawd," he heard the caretaker exclaim. Then Nevil heard him shout, "It's George Llewellyn, Father. He's been hurt!"

Nevil slipped out of the shadows and stood a safe distance from the doorway, confident he was in shadow, at least partially. "I didn't do it," he said to the caretaker, who was still leaning over George. The old man looked up, squinting into the night.

"Who's out there?"

"I didn't do it," Nevil repeated. "I tried to help." He could find no more words to give shape to the damned emotion within him. He and the church caretaker stared at each other until Nevil heard the bustling approach of the priest. "You tell him," he called out to the caretaker. "I didn't have to—" His voice choked and he turned away, hurrying into the darkness before the priest arrived. "You tell him," he called over his shoulder with a sob.

□　　□　　□

George was only vaguely aware of being carried into a room and laid on a bed. He felt cold, and despite a resolve to remain conscious, another world tugged powerfully at the cords anchoring him to reality. He found himself slipping away from the echoing, urgent, sibilant sounds that washed over him, from the hands tugging annoyingly at his clothing. . . .

Instead, he found himself floating in a suffocatingly dark place that smelled of coal dust. Yet he did not question the oddness of the situation or how he had arrived there.

As he became accustomed to the darkness he gradually made out a phosphorescent shape; and it wasn't until he drew nearer that he could see it was a figure sitting in a chair, its back to him.

George hesitated, a fear descending darkly on him that he could not explain and could not shake. The figure in the chair slowly turned, and George saw, a leap of joy mingling with the fear still stalking his veins, that it was his daughter. He had found her at last! She was smiling, he thought, though her luminous quality made it hard to be sure.

"Daddy," she called out. Her voice sounded odd, hollow and far away. At least, while George wasn't sure the figure had spoken, he had no doubt it was his daughter's voice he heard. He moved toward her, wanting desperately to embrace her, but somehow, she managed to keep the distance between them. George couldn't understand how this could be, but it made a sort of sense to him. He smiled at her.

"Hello, *caraed*."

"Where am I, Daddy?"

"I don't know. Come here to me. I'll make it all better. I promise . . ."

The figure retreated, her glow dimming, before she cautiously approached him again, keeping a little beyond arm's length.

"Where have you been?"

"I'm so sorry . . ."

"That's what you always say afterwards."

George had no answer and was overwhelmed with feelings of guilt and remorse.

"I want to go home."

"I know." He felt tears burn his eyes.

"You hurt me, Daddy."

"I didn't mean to. It was an accident. I couldn't help—"

"You *hurt* me. Why, Daddy? Where am I?"

In despair, George said, "I don't know," and turned away. Shielded from her brightness, he was once more engulfed in the suffocating darkness.

When he turned back, she had receded until all he could make out was her glow. He moved toward her again, hearing her voice echoing as she called his name, unable to reach her, to hold her and make it all right again. He felt her loss as though he had been poisoned, a numbing ache spreading through his body.

The ground bulged between them, and around it spun a whirling blue light spitting sparks, keeping George at bay, until he became giddy with the sight. He blinked, and in the instant he reopened his eyes, he saw a bent, though human-looking creature grinning at him, its wolflike jaws gaping and drooling, its slitted yellow eyes flashing with mockery. His father! As the creature turned away from him, George was overcome with revulsion, frozen by infantile panic.

A wail of despair began deep within him, and he leapt at the creature hunched over his daughter's body, finding himself in an iron embrace with it, as much struggling to avoid its slashing claws and snapping teeth as to throw it to the ground and break its back. Hot breath scorched his face, and through the haze of rage that possessed him, burned in his chest, braced him in his struggle, he heard

223

his daughter's plaintive voice call out, as he could not, "Daddy, help me . . ."

George opened his eyes and stared into a pocked, ruddy face.

"He's back among the living, at last," Fred Medford said to someone in the room. His face loomed into view again. "You gave me the right wind-up there for a while, George. How you feeling?"

George tried to speak but his mouth was dry, and besides, he felt too weak. His nightmare receded quickly, though not totally, from his conscious mind. Someone propped up his head and gave him a sip of water. He smelled a vague, familiar scent. Closing his eyes, he lay back in the bed. He didn't seem to have much control over his shivering body, though he was too weary to care. After a moment he opened his eyes again and saw Vera Armstrong standing beside Medford, staring down at him, holding the glass of water as though it were an offering.

"What happened?" he croaked.

"Father Perbrick couldn't get no-one out here in a hurry; and needed help getting you to a hospital; so he called me. We all thought you'd had it, George. Anyway, I got Vera Armstrong to make a house call. Lucky for you she was off duty."

"You've lost a little blood," she said in a calming understatement. George shifted his gaze, having difficulty concentrating. His eyelids felt as though they had lead weights on them. "I really want to get you into hospital, but Sergeant Medford knew you'd kick up a fuss and insisted I stitch you up here. It looked a lot worse than it was. You're very lucky. Chest wounds bleed a lot, but this one's not too serious. A few days bed rest should take care of it."

"We don't have a few days," George whispered, then surrendered to the overwhelming urge to sleep.

□   □   □

Nevil made painfully slow time as he headed toward the Gypsy camp, scouring the night, pausing every few minutes to catch his breath and stare into the darkness behind him for any pursuers. He wasn't really certain what he would do when he got there, but he had to get Mother Celina alone.

The darkness was both a curse and a blessing, the streets deserted, the evening growing old as he paused once more, a wary eye out for the predators hunting him. He knew helping the policeman had been a thankless act, even if the caretaker recognized him, which Nevil doubted. But somehow, he was determined that in the face of such adversity he would try to do something right—for his own sake if nothing else. That old Gypsy woman had deliberately played him for a fool—and he'd taken the knife and fallen for it hook, line, and sinker. *I'm so stupid. It's no more than I deserve* . . . he started to think, then stopped himself. The fact was, it *was* more than he deserved. A lot more. He had done nothing to hurt anybody else, ever; nothing to warrant the kind of injustice he'd endured in his life; nothing to any of the children—Christ, he *liked* children.

Clambering over several mounds of rubble, he pulled up short when he heard the sounds of voices nearby. He peered through a tangle of wood and bricks. It took him a moment to spot three men bending over something on the ground. One straightened triumphantly, holding up Nevil's binoculars. They'd found one of his hiding places! Shifting position, Nevil was able to take in more of the scene.

The men milled around, scanning the area for more

signs. Nevil could see clearly now that two of them held clubs of some sort. They gathered and spoke in low voices, comparing other things they had found: empty tin cans, a cup he had forgotten to re-cover the thermos flask with, a newspaper—clear signs someone had been there recently.

The men turned their attention back to a bundle of clothing on the ground. One of them launched a kick at it.

After a few minutes the three men wandered away, pursuing other prey. Nevil watched them, saw one come back and growl with anger as he kicked the bundle several more times. One of his friends restrained him, and Nevil heard someone say, "That's enough, Frank. You're gonna kill him. 'Sides, he don't know what you're doing to him. He ain't the one we're after, anyway, is he?"

"It was my son got killed, not yours, Hardesty! You hear me? He's one of them murderin' bastards, ain't he . . ." Frank Isley's voice crackled with a grief and anger Nevil could feel twenty yards away.

"Look at him, Frank. He ain't going nowhere. We'll get the others and come back. Do 'em proper."

The second man returned to see what the fuss was about, and the three of them milled around the body on the ground until Frank's friends dragged him away.

Nevil collapsed in a heap, his back to the rubble, his heart pounding. He could almost taste his fear. That was what they would do to him if they caught him: beat him to death, kick him into oblivion. Who would save him? The police? An exhaustion overwhelmed Nevil. How much longer could he go on living like this, homeless, unemployed, worse—like an animal, scurrying from hiding place to hiding place, scavaging what he could to eat? Constant prey to predators, bigger and stronger? Which reminded Nevil, he hadn't eaten since yesterday—almost twenty-four hours. As if possessed of its own awareness, his stomach gurgled its emptiness.

Nevil placed his head between his knees and wept, a familiar though long-forgotten pins-and-needles feeling reminding him of all the times he had sat in that dark understairs closet, waiting for his mother to release him and end his punishment. Only this time there was no one to set him free. All he could do was wait until they caught him. End it, once and for all.

After a long time he raised his head again and scanned the area. The Gypsy lay motionless. Then an idea came to Nevil, so outrageous he cried aloud in surprise.

Quickly, he glanced around, a rodent wary of hawks, and scurried over to the Gypsy.

The man lay on his back, unconscious, breathing stertorously, his arms and legs splayed, his face and hands bloodied. Nevil recognized him once he crouched down. It was Gus. Another two hundred yards beyond the rubble and he would have been home, Nevil thought, glancing towards the Gypsy camp.

Fumbling in his greatcoat, Nevil removed the silver knives, wiped them with his scarf, then carefully hid them in the inside pocket of the Gypsy's coat. That, at least, might take some of the heat off Nevil. He experienced an exhilaration, a heady, gleeful sense of justification at the prospect of turning the tables so neatly, that was abruptly cut short.

Sensing danger he spun around, not sure why his senses were suddenly so acute, but not prepared to ignore the instinct. He could smell danger these days. Still crouching, he crabbed backward into the shadows and waited, scarcely breathing lest he make too much noise.

As he waited, he was unable to prevent the loud chattering of his teeth; then he saw a shape materialize from the curtain of nighttime gloom and approach the body on all fours.

Nevil cowered deeper in the shadows, horrified at what drew near.

He had finally found the werewolf—and left himself defenseless. The realization left Nevil breathless and rooted to the spot. His skin felt covered in insects and he had to force himself not to rub away the feeling.

The creature sniffed the air and sidled nearer to the Gypsy. It prodded the still form, then pushed it. The Gypsy didn't move. The creature's hair reached its waist and flailed in the chill night breeze, obscuring much of its naked form, but Nevil saw enough to know what he was staring at, to connect it to the child in Camilla Stepan's journal. It bowed its head until the shadow of it merged with the still form of the Gypsy. It was a moment before the slurping sounds told Nevil it was licking the blood off the man's face.

The Gypsy jerked spasmodically and made a sound unlike any Nevil had ever heard, then a spray of arterial blood spouted into the air. The creature writhed in ecstasy and began noisily feeding while the man jerked and twitched as though electrocuted.

Nevil felt bile rise hot in his throat and ducked away. He cried aloud—the end of the world had come; Armageddon was upon them. Terrified he'd given himself away, Nevil nevertheless forced himself to look once more, to face the worst.

The creature had not heard him! It continued to gorge itself. The wet sounds of snarling and tearing, the brittle crunch of gnawing on bones, made Nevil feel faint, his knees weak. He could not watch any more of the appalling primeval spectacle. He squeezed his eyes tight shut and covered his ears with his hands.

How long he hid Nevil did not know, but eventually he found enough self-control to look up again. The noises had stopped. The creature was sniffing the air, as though sensing interlopers—danger. It swung its head from side to side, lifting its face to the starry sky, howling victorious rage, then it left the Gypsy and retreated into the darkness from whence it had come.

Nevil could wait no longer. He quickly closed the distance between himself and the corpse, skirting the blood-soaked earth, following the creature, not knowing what he would do if the thing turned and attacked him, but knowing he had to track it to its lair if he was to have any hope of redemption.

TUESDAY

January 7, 1941

George awoke on a camp bed in the church vestry at about four in the morning to find Vera Armstrong, fully clothed, cradling him, dozing with her back against the wall. As he moved she too awoke, and he lifted himself stiffly from her lap, feeling embarrassed.

"How are you feeling now?" she whispered.

George looked at her quizzically. "You were having a nightmare. Talking in your sleep. I didn't want you to pull out your stitches," she explained, to indicate why they had slept together this way. As they both came more fully awake, the chill of the room seemed to infect their relationship.

"Thanks," George finally whispered. He could not forget the image of being locked in that monster's embrace—but what was it—his father or his own dark nature that he had been finally forced to confront. It seemed they had become the same thing.

"Do you want to talk about it?" she asked.

"What did I say?"

"I didn't listen too closely."

George closed his eyes, basking in the warmth of respite, feeling the tightness of his bandaged chest, knowing she was lying. From her embarrassed tone, she must have clearly heard every word he'd muttered. It probably hadn't been very nice if his recent dreams were anything to go by. The idea of revealing so much of himself haunted him: What did she really think of him, want of him?

Vera Armstrong saw the shadow that passed over George's face and went on, "You talked about your father mostly—and Wendy."

She'd confirmed George's worst fears. He struggled to sit up, but the effort was too hard. *Christ, I can't get sick now!* he thought.

"I take it you don't get on very well with him."

"No," George admitted. She helped him prop himself up in bed.

"Why is that?"

"We've never got on, even when I was a kid."

"You sound angry."

"I'm not sure anymore." He paused, then, catching her eyes for a moment, said softly, "I feel like I'm in sight of a shore finally. Is something happening between us?"

She primly smoothed her clothes and occupied a chair pulled up to the side of the bed, emphasizing the distance between them. "Perhaps. I don't know. I like you well enough"—she smiled briefly—"you're a nice lover, I enjoy your company; but there's something about you that really disturbs me."

"I know the feeling."

"You frighten me."

George chuckled, breaking into a fit of painful coughing for a moment. "Sounds like passion to me."

After a long pause, he went on, "Maybe it's me. I thought we had something, maybe. It's hard competing with a ghost, you know. They don't make mistakes. I sometimes get the feeling your husband's memory's more important to you than he was."

"You think there's a competition? You take too much for granted." The cold ambivalence of her comment was followed by a long silence. Eventually she added, "Your Sergeant Medford's outside. I should tell him you're awake. He's been quite worried about you, you know. He seems a good friend."

"Yeah, I suppose he is." Again there was a long silence. The aches and pains in George's body settled into a dull throbbing. With another effort he managed to sit up and swing his legs to the floor. A wave of dizziness swept over him but he held his ground and it dissipated. He felt weak, but back in control again. Nurse Armstrong watched him with obvious disapproval. "You're going to pull those stitches out."

"I'll be careful."

"Get some more rest."

"What about you?"

"I'll be all right."

"I take it our one night together was just that, then." He could not keep the hurt from creeping into his voice.

"I don't know. It was— Don't rush things, okay?" George sensed an element of pleading. Perhaps she wasn't shutting the door on him completely, after all. "I was going to say it was a mistake—but that's not true. You're the first man I've been with since Robert, you see. Perhaps . . ." She hesitated, then went on, "Perhaps we both just need some time."

George held his tongue on the retort that sprang to

mind. It occurred to him she was really talking more about herself. "Believe it or not, patience is one of my few virtues." Thinking of Stimpson, he went on, "I can wait a long time to get what I'm after if I have to. If it's worth it."

Vera sighed and sat on the edge of the bed. George lay back, holding her hand. The last thing he was aware of before falling asleep was her arm around him and the thought that perhaps things would turn out all right after all.

□   □   □

Nevil watched the creature go to ground near a squat, ruined building abutting the common, hidden by hilly terrain and overgrown shrubs until he was almost on top of it. About fifty yards to his left, and beyond a screen of blackberry bushes, waist-high thistles, and stinging nettles skirting the north edge of the common, was the Gypsy camp. From somewhere, birds started to chirrup to each other. Dawn began to spread bloody streaks in the sky.

Nevil carefully made his way to the Gypsy camp, following the shrub line until he was able to creep undetected through the low-lying ground mist. He crouched under Mother Celina's caravan peering around. There was a pristine hush that combined with the gauze-like mist to create a mystical effect.

A low, throaty growl close by interrupted his reverie. Turning slowly and with difficulty in the narrow space beneath the caravan, Nevil was confronted with a mongrel dog, its coat muddy and matted, its lips pulled tight to expose jagged white teeth, its notched German Shepherd ears laid flat as it bellied to the ground and wriggled its way under the caravan, a long leash trailing behind.

Nevil looked around desperately for a weapon, even as he backed out into the open, cursing himself for not keeping one of the silver knives. The dog inched nearer, obviously waiting for Nevil to break and run for it. With the utmost difficulty, Nevil stood his ground, keeping one of the wagon wheels between himself and the advancing animal. The dog crawled closer still, growling loudly, its hackles bristling, its eyes gleaming.

A moment later, Mother Celina jumped to the ground and, looking around, spotted Nevil. "I told you not to come back here."

Glancing at the dog, Nevil shouted, "Call it off!"

"Git him!" she screamed at the animal.

The dog hesitated, its paws kneading the ground as it prepared to leap free of the caravan and rip him with its teeth. Scanning the common, Nevil sought a haven but found only the shreds of mist swirling around the camp, partially obscuring the stark shapes of the wagons.

Desperately, he yelled, "I know where Gus is. He's hurt. Call it off and I'll take you there. You'll never find him otherwise!" He glanced at the dog again. Any moment now . . . "Call it off, for God's sake!"

"Stay!" she ordered the animal. "What do you know about Gus?" Mother Celina menacingly closed the gap between them.

Nevil's answer came out in a rush. "I know he tried to kill that copper and get me blamed for it."

"Is that right?" she said nastily and moved toward him.

"You k-keep your distance," Nevil called out. He took a couple of steps backward, bumping into the wagon. He'd thought his revelation would rattle her enough to give him the upper hand. Instead, she had managed to unnerve him. His plan was already going wrong. "Why me?" he asked her.

"You was perfect for it, you daft sod. You was there." She advanced on him again. "Now then, what's all this about Gus?"

"Y-you know, don't you? What's really going on, I mean. What's really out there."

"You said Gus was hurt. Where is he? What's up with him? You better not have done nothing to him . . ."

"I think he's dead."

This time the news did have an affect. Quietly, she asked, "How?"

"Same way as the children." Gaining more strength in his voice, Nevil went on, "The coppers think *I* did it. But you and me know otherwise. You've got to tell them the truth."

Her sharp-edged laughter sent a wave of anger through him. "I'll m-make you," he threatened, taking a step toward her. Her laughter grew louder.

"I can prove it," he hissed, tapping his overcoat where the journal was still safely snug. "She wrote it all down."

"Don't need me then, do ye? I didn't do anything, and you can't prove any different. Who cares what you say or what she wrote down. It weren't nothing to do with me."

"But you want to know where it is, don't you? You want to get it before it kills more of your people. What would they do to you if they found out you're one of the people responsible for all this. 'I helped where I should not have,' remember? The baby, Gus—who's next? I'm the only one who can help you. But you've got to help me first."

"What can you do? Look at ye."

237

"One w-way or the other . . ." Nevil stuttered, stepping closer.

"Billy!" Mother Celina called. Nevil paused, and she yelled the name again. A moment later a beer-gutted man in his thirties stumbled through the door of her caravan, rubbing sleep from his eyes with tattooed hands, blinking and squinting.

"What's up?"

"Him."

Billy blinked several more times as he examined Nevil. "What's he want?"

"Go with him. Fetch home your sister's husband."

"What's that daft git been and done now?"

"Just do as you're bid," Mother Celina snapped. "You hear me?"

"Yeah, I hear yer. Don't get your bloody knickers in a twist. Middle of the bleeding night . . ." He continued mumbling as he jumped to the ground. He buttoned his leather jacket as he joined her, staring down at Nevil, who was a good head and shoulders shorter.

"I'm not s-saying anything else," Nevil said petulantly, looking from one to the other. This was not at all what he had imagined would happen.

Billy's haggard, hawk-nosed face loomed close to Nevil as he was corraled against the wagon. The Gypsy's foul breath caused him to turn away. A finger poked into his chest made Nevil more uncomfortable.

"I don't want to hear this shit, cocker. Now, my ma says you know what's happened to one of ours. That's enough for me. It's too early to play silly buggers and I've got a splitting 'eadache, so don't mess me about. You're gonna take me to where Gus's at or I'm gonna have to get nasty with you. You understand what I'm saying?" The finger jabbed several more times to emphasize the point. Nevil pouted, refusing to show his intimidation.

Realizing he'd walked into the middle of something he didn't understand, Billy turned back to Mother Celina and asked, "What's going on, Ma?"

"*He* says Gus's hurt bad. Maybe dead."

"Dead? How?" Billy turned to face Nevil again, menace clearly in his bearing. "What's he doing here?"

Mother Celina remained stoically silent.

"Go on then, tell him," Nevil taunted her, surprised at his audacity.

"Watch it." The finger stabbed Nevil once more.

"Gus got killed by the same creature that's killing the babies. And it's *her* fault."

"Shut up, you!" Billy shoved Nevil hard, and he stumbled heavily against the wagon, losing his footing and ending up on his arse feeling foolish and angrily frustrated that no one would take him seriously. "It's all *her* fault," he said, waving a finger at Mother Celina. "She brought it into the world, helped keep it alive—"

"That's a bloody lie!"

"*She's* responsible, not me. Ask her what's going on."

"If he ain't gonna tell us, Ma . . ."

"Make him."

By this time they could hear the sounds of rousing in the camp. Their loud voices had awakened others. A couple of men jumped down from their caravans, glowing lamps in hand, to see what was going on. Horses stirred, stretching and snorting, and several dogs began barking.

Through the mist, Nevil spotted a rapidly approaching group of people. The flimsy clouds swirled and rose around them, the breeze carrying snatches of raised voices. As Billy and Mother Celina turned to see what was happening behind them, Nevil noticed several interlopers break away from the main group and throw their shoulders against a caravan, rocking it violently from side to side. Raucous voices shouted at the people inside to come out. With a tearing sound the wagon overbalanced. It crashed to the ground, cracking like an egg, wheels spinning aimlessly. Several panicking Gypsy woman and screaming children tumbled to the frozen earth. Another group attacked a second wagon, trying to demolish it with hammers and axes. Dogs howled, and irate voices continued to rip the early morning air. Within minutes the place was in pandemonium.

The dogs were unleashed and bounded with snarls toward the Englishmen while the Romany men, some half-dressed and still groggy with sleep, found themselves grappling with vengeful locals, many crumpling immediately under a murderous clubbing onslaught as soon as they emerged into the cold morning air.

Nevil heard thwacks and thuds as ax handles bounced off wood and impacted on flesh, the screams of the injured and the terrified, saw several men wrestling on the ground, fists and legs flailing, while Gypsy dogs leaped and snapped at the assailants, several biting exposed forearms, other laid flat with a cringing whine by judicious blows.

Nevil fought an overwhelming panic as the tidal wave of violence crashed around him. He cowered by the wagon wheel, peering around it at the melee of figures running to and fro, screams of "murderers" and "baby butchers" and cries of rage and pain adding further to the bedlam, Mother Celina and Billy forgotten for the moment.

Men reeled and swung their arms, heads were slammed against wagons and the frozen earth. Several of the mob renewed their ax attacks on the caravans. Bodies littered the ground, a few of the injured who were able crawling off into the misty common in hopes of escape.

A chilling chorus of victorious yells went up, and as Nevil watched, flames licked through the windows of several overturned wagons. Palls of smoke billowed into the slowly brightening morning as the first rays of the sun burned away the ground mist.

Police whistles cut through the din, and then Nevil heard the clanging of emergency bells as two Black Marias arrived, followed closely by the first of several ambulances, tires screeching as the vehicles braked to a halt by the common. As Nevil continued to stare, a contingent of burly coppers ran into the camp, truncheons swinging, several helmets flying, as they roughly separated and began arresting the warring factions.

"Oi, you two!" a voice bellowed. Nevil spotted a burly, uniformed police sergeant, with several constables just behind him, running toward where he stood. "You stay where you are. You're both nicked."

Not knowing who was being addressed, as if scalded Nevil took off toward the shelter of the shrubbery and the ruins beyond, imagining the pounding feet of vengeful policemen just behind him, expecting the iron grip of the law at any second.

When it came, he had almost gained the cover of the shrubbery. Someone heavy crashed into his legs in a rugby tackle, and his head slammed into the iron-hard ground, dazing him. He gasped for breath that would not come.

With the wind knocked out of him, Nevil could only flounder face down as his arms were roughly snatched backward and he felt the cutting pinch of ratcheted handcuffs secure his wrists behind his back.

"Got you, you bastard!" the policeman said. He jerked Nevil upright and added breathlessly, "Nevil Stimpson—I arrest you for the attempted murder of a police officer . . ."

□   □   □

George stood with Sergeant Medford surveying the wreckage on the common. His chest ached, and his knees were rubbery, but his determination to see this thing through had become an engine driving on reserves George had not known he had.

More ambulances were arriving, crossing paths with Black Marias carting away the less injured rioters. "What a bloody mess," George complained. Medford didn't reply. Many of the Gypsies' homes were burned, smoking wreckages, overturned and splintered, though some still stood, barely scratched. People wandered around, dazed and weeping, trying to comfort each other and the blood-spattered injured. Near the two policemen one woman sat on her haunches beside a crumpled young man, her clenched fists threatening the sky, wailing with enraged anguish, one voice in a chorus of such suffering. They were a counterpoint to moans and the loud, pragmatic voices of police and ambulance crews.

Beyond the two policemen, four civil defense volunteers were carrying a stretcher with difficulty onto the common. A long arm dangled from beneath a blanket and the hand dragged on the sickly yellow grass as the stretcher bearers negotiated the treacherous terrain.

Turning to Medford, George asked, "How many arrests?" He winced at the burning ache in his chest like a heartburn he couldn't dispel, looking around disgustedly at the scene.

"Thirty-odd, I think. Not sure, Taff, to be honest, till I get back to the station."

"I'm gonna swing Frank Isley by his balls for this. Bloody brownshirts!"

"It was bound to happen—"

"No it wasn't. English bloody Nazis, that's all they are." He turned to face Medford. "Shoot the lot of 'em if I had my way." He spat. "It's bloody nice, isn't it? What the hell are we fighting this war for?"

They began walking back to the road, passing several locals who were helping the remaining Gypsies patch up bruises and minor cuts, comforting the groaning and the stupefied, stunned at the sudden violence of their neighbors, trying without much success to make amends. Despite the early hour, the riot had attracted sightseers, some still in their nightclothes under overcoats, now lining the edge of the common near the road, subdued witnesses gathering in numbers.

"Get them out of here," Medford shouted at several uniformed coppers, motioning toward the crowd.

"It's too easy."

"What's that, George?"

"I don't like these buggers being here any more'n anyone else, look you. But that ain't no excuse for all this, is it? Like a bunch of animals."

There was a long silence as the two men stared around the battlefield. Nearby, the stretcher bearers had reached an ambulance and George heard someone say, "Found this one in the ruins over there. Watch yourself, there's blood all over the place. . . ." The voice faded away, masked by others.

Eventually, Medford said, "We'll have to let her go."

"Who's that?"

"That old cow—the Gypsy woman."

"Not on your life! I want her charged with conspiracy to cause an affray, along with everyone else."

"Can't do it, George. We've had the word from Downing Street. Only the men."

"God damn it! And where's that toe-rag Stimpson got to?"

"Ah, well, you're in luck there."

"What?"

"Derek Cooper nicked him. He was trying to bugger orf out of it before anyone saw him. Thought you'd be pleased."

"Thank Christ for small mercies."

"Nearly lost him again, an' all. Some wanker smacked Derek round the head with a piece of two-by-four. Thank Gawd he was still wearing his regulation titfer. Near enough split his head open. Poor bastard's still seeing double. He ain't the only one, neither. At least three more of our lads got knocked about."

"Where is he?"

"Took him to hospital."

"Stimpson."

"Oh, he's in a car over there. He's all right. Station's a right bloody nuthouse. I thought it best to keep him handy."

"You spoken to him?"

"Not really. He's been asking about you, though."

"You're joking!"

"Don't ask me what's going on, George. I ain't got the faintest."

They were nearing the edge of the common by this time, and George saw several police cars, headlights blazing, emergency lights still flashing, parked at an angle blocking the roadway.

A policeman yelled out, "Sarge, you better come take a look at this."

George crossed to the ambulance the constable stood beside and was ushered into the back by one of the ambulance women. He pulled down the blanket and briefly examined the injuries on the Gypsy. "Jesus Christ," he muttered.

"Where'd you find him?" he asked the policeman standing by the open rear doors. This made victim number six.

"It was in the ruins over there. We found these on him." He handed George the silver knives. George examined them, missing pieces of a puzzle beginning to fall into place. He stuck the knives in a coat pocket and nodded to the constable to carry on.

George took his time, climbing out the ambulance with difficulty, then said to Sergeant Medford, "Right. I want to see Stimpson. Even if he didn't do it, he bloody well knows what's going on. I'd stake my mother's life on it."

Medford gave George a strange look, but said only, "Over here," and led the way.

□   □   □

George made himself comfortable in the passenger seat facing Nevil Stimpson seated in the rear. He smelled ripe from days of living rough, and his clothes were ripped and muddied, his hair awry. George wrinkled his nose but said nothing, studying Stimpson's stubbled gray face. Stimpson sat, head bowed, his hands still handcuffed awkwardly behind him. George leaned out the door and motioned to a constable to release him.

"You sure, Sarge?"

"He'll behave himself. Won't yer," he said to Stimpson. The policeman uncuffed Nevil, who looked up for the first time, staring in surprise at George, rubbing his wrists to get the circulation flowing again. "Th-thank you," he murmured.

George faced Nevil once more. "You're in serious trouble, Mr. Stimpson. Very serious. Do you understand that?"

Nevil nodded.

"Right. Your only chance is to help me sort all this out." George paused, remembering splinters of a dream in which he was half carried, half staggered down a road, feeling his life leaking from him. Ignoring the disturbing mental images, he went on calmly, "Make no mistake: I've got you dead to rights for attempted murder. I told you last time, didn't I? I *know* you."

Stimpson's bottom lip quivered, as though he was about to burst into tears. He continued to hang his head in silence.

"So," George continued brusquely, "what's your connection with these gypos?"

"Nothing," Nevil whispered.

"Now don't start that." George felt his temper rise. "I'm trying to be reasonable, much against my better judgment. Your days are numbered, my lad. I'm trying to give you a chance here. Your last chance, and what do you do? Spit in my face."

Nevil shook his head. "N-no. I'm f-frightened."

"You will be, boyo, if you don't cooperate, I promise you that. Now, tell me about these gypos. What are they doing back here? What are you doing with 'em?"

"I went to see the old lady. Years ago she helped those two women. I thought. . . ." He broke off.

"Spit it out, lad."

Nevil looked George in the eye and this time held the gaze. "It's *your* fault, all this, not m-mine. She blames you for the death of her son; one of them anyway. Ten years

246

ago. The last time something like this happened. That's why that Gypsy Gus tried to kill you. He was her son-in-law. It was his kid who got killed. I suppose she convinced him killing you would somehow even it all up. Ask her."

"I intend to, don't you worry. That don't explain nothing." George leveled his finger at Nevil, who cringed despite himself. "I don't like you. I didn't like you the first time I clapped eyes on yer. You're dangerous. Little kids aren't safe with weird bastards like you about. I couldn't make you tell me what you knew last time, but by God. . . ." He stopped himself, the burning sensation in his chest intensifying. He waited, wincing, until it had passed. "So why have you been living rough since Thursday, then? You've got a nice house to stay in. I know, I've seen it. That's more than most have got around here these days."

"I k-knew this would happen, that you wouldn't b-believe me. I ran away because I'm f-frightened."

"You're full of it, ain't yer?"

"If I help, you've g-got to drop the m-murder charge. I didn't . . . I n-never meant to hurt that c-copper, you know that. He attacked me in the dark, I was j-just defending myself. I'm a victim of circumstances."

"Tell that to the magistrate. I don't want to hear it," George said, disgust evident in his voice. "You nigh on topped a policeman, during wartime yet. Split his skull open. You think you can get away with something like that? You think I'd let yer? You've gotta be off your rocker. I've got six mangled bodies out there, and *you* know all about them. You deserve locking up as far as I'm concerned. You ain't getting away from me again, you bastard, you hear me?"

"I've d-done n-nothing wrong, I told you. I n-never did what you said. I don't know who hurt those kids—your kid. I don't *know*." He hunched himself tighter and seeing George's angry scowl added, "P-please don't hurt me."

"Don't tempt me, you miserable excuse for a human being."

"You're j-just like me, I know *y-you*. Only you try and hide it with bluster and by tormenting people before they do it to you. Oh, I know y-you all right. Makes you f-feel good, does it? P-powerful? Get your own back? I'm not saying another w-word 'til I see a solicitor." He stared out the misted window, ignoring George, wrapping his arms about his body, his nervous tic making him appear to wink knowingly.

His attitude incensed George. He felt like smashing Stimpson in the face. Abruptly, George faced the front instead, feeling his anger burn within him and the pain in his chest grow almost in proportion. If he wasn't careful he'd rip out his stitches. He breathed deeply and without looking around said, "Plead guilty to grievous bodily harm, and I'll see what I can do."

"No. I n-never meant . . ."

"I'll get that thing out there with or without you. You hear me? The choice is yours. Take it or leave it."

There was a long silence. Eventually, George waved Camilla Stepan's journal. "Where'd you get this?"

"She g-gave it me."

"Who?"

"The older sister—Camilla."

"And why would she do something like that?"

"She was frightened."

"What about?"

"Everything." Nevil looked up, his eyes bloodshot pale-gray pearls. "These are f-frightening t-times." He ducked his head once more."

"What did they keep in that cellar?"

Clearly frightened, Nevil mumbled, "I don't know."

"Don't lie to me."

Nevil stared at the floor. Eventually he muttered, "Her son."

"Her what?"

"Sofia Stepan's illegitimate child." He pointed to the journal George held. "It's all in there. She wrote it all down. You're in there."

There was no more dodging around what George had suspected since visiting Ethel Tanner. It was all making appalling sense at last. It was what Phelps had been trying to tell him. But it also meant admitting Stimpson was more innocent than George had believed, something George wasn't yet ready to do. "Where is it now?"

"Are you going to kill him?"

"Just answer the bloody question. You've been protecting it, ain't yer. That's what you've been doing all this time out here."

"No. I-I never did. I've been looking for it, like you."

"You expect me to believe that?"

With a sign of defeat, Nevil whispered, "He's hiding in the ruins somewhere. I'll have to take you there."

"You're right about that," George threatened. "You aren't going anywhere without me from now on, boyo." He opened the car door and strode over to a group of Home Guardsmen, chatting with some coppers while eyeing the crowd several yards away behind a makeshift rope barrier. "Who's in charge here?"

A bearded, fair-haired man, looking like a consumptive Viking, stepped forward. "Um, the name's Googe," he said rather self-deprecatingly. "I'm the, er, captain of this squad."

George pointed at the rifles the Home Guardsman were carrying and said, "Are those loaded?"

"Yes. Of course, we don't have much—"

"Who's your best shot?"

There was a general murmur of brief discussion before one of the men said, "Ben, I'd say." Others nodded agreement. A teenager, angry pimples dotting his cheeks and forehead, was pushed to the front, awkwardly holding his rifle.

"How good is he?" George asked Captain Googe, with obvious skepticism.

"Well, at targets . . ."

"You ever killed anything, son?" George asked.

"Some squirrels, couple of crows."

"You'll have to do. Come with me. The rest of you, keep that crowd out the way."

Without waiting to see if the sharpshooter was behind him, George motioned for one of the constables to bring along Stimpson. They were on the verge of the common when a series of bloodcurdling screams went up. The Home Guardsman visibly started, but George was already stumbling toward a dip in the common where other policemen were rapidly heading. Overrunning the Home Guardsmen, the onlookers too surged onto the common, heading for the same spot.

George breathlessly reached the brow of the hill, his chest burning with every gasp, feeling light-headed from the effort. He looked down: The hillside overlooked a grassy crater some twenty feet deep, ringed by policemen and onlookers, gawking downward.

"My God," Medford murmured from beside George.

Below them, one of the injured Romany men who had crawled off from the fighting, obviously trying to hide, had heaved himself partway up one of the grassy slopes. His leg looked broken. Several yards before him, crouched by a large broken pipe at least four feet in diameter jutting out the opposite bank, was the creature. The chill breeze wafted its hair, and it stared about, scanning the circle of people stark against the white sky above it, obviously unsettled, hissing and growling.

The young Home Guardsman took a prone position, sighting down his rifle.

George stared at the tableau. "Hold it!" he said. He whispered to a constable standing nearby, and the policeman raced off toward some distant garden allotments.

"What the hell is *that*?" Medford said.

"A werewolf," George said, more to himself.

"A what?"

George gazed at Medford. "You heard."

"Oi, you stay where you are. . . ." a voice shouted. Distracted, George looked around. He glanced down into the grassy crater and saw Stimpson cautiously making his way toward the injured man, who, in obvious difficulty, had slid back down once more.

"How'd he get down there? You got it?" George snapped at the sharpshooter.

"Yeah." The reply was querulous. "What the hell *is* that?"

"Just don't you shoot until I tell you," George turned to Medford and said, "I'm going down there. You make sure no one follows me."

"This is stupid, George. Just shoot it."

"I *can't*, not like this. Besides, what happens if he misses?"

"You're a lunatic, Llewellyn! If I had my way . . ."

"But you don't, do you."

Stimpson had reached the injured man by now and was trying to help him. The creature roared at the assembled crowd, took several paces toward the two men, then backed away to the pipe until it was crouched just inside the protection of the duct.

"Damn it," young Ben muttered.

"Here," a winded copper said to George and thrust some netting from a strawberry patch at him.

"Good lad." To young Ben, he added, "Now don't you go shooting me, will yer, son?"

The kid was concentrating on the scene below him and did not appear to hear. "Keep an eye on him, Fred, do me a favor. Where does that come out?"

"Somewhere in them ruins over there," a bobby offered.

"Right, I want someone to find out if there are any plans of the drainage system round here." The policeman hurried away in the direction of the road. "Fred? Get three lads round the other side," George continued. Several policemen stepped forward. "Take some of the Home Guard with you," George said to them. "And fetch some more netting from them allotments and block up the other end of that pipe. Lively now, lads, we ain't got all day."

"You're a bloody nut case!" Medford said.

"That's a ten-year-old kid down there, Fred. I don't want to kill it unless we have to." Medford gave George a questioning look, but held his tongue. Motioning to the assembled onlookers, George went on, "I'm not into public executions of children. That's what them Nazis do, isn't it?"

With evident disgust, Medford motioned to the netting George held in his hands. "You think that's gonna stop it?"

"You got any other bright ideas? Just make sure we got somewhere to put it after I get hold of it. I want a doctor and an ambulance standing by. It isn't going anywhere now."

Medford began snapping orders at assembled policemen who were trying unsuccessfully to keep back the crowd. Brusquely, George motioned to two constables and said, "You two. Round the other side. I'm gonna distract it, and when I do I want you to get them two out of it."

The coppers exchanged glances, clearly unhappy with their lot, then hurried to get into position.

George started the slow diagonal descent to the floor of the grassy crater, traversing the slope away from Nevil and the Gypsy, making sure the creature held him in its gaze. The whispered hush from so many assembled people was eerily unsettling.

As he descended to the floor of the crater, George could not rid himself of the images of the children in a hospital ward in Epping Forest; tried not to think about his own child's condition; tried to blot out everything but staying on his feet and keeping the creature's attention. He half slid to the bottom, his gaze firmly fixed on the creature. It was turning its head this way and that, not yet decided what to do.

George stood up, swaying from the effort, the netting a tangle in his hands. He watched two policemen slide down the opposite face toward Stimpson and the Gypsy and start to haul up the injured man, who cried out from pain. As they neared the top others pushed forward to help.

The creature sniffed the air and turned in Stimpson's direction. George shouted, but when the creature paid him no attention, remembered it was probably deaf. He moved nearer, shaking out the netting. The motion attracted the creature's attention and it turned toward George once again, quickly backing into the duct, growling louder, baring its teeth.

George glanced up at Medford and young Ben, shaking his head. If it retreated any farther they'd be able to trap it. As if sensing its fate, the creature shrieked, the echoes reverberating through the piping. Then it lunged.

□   □   □

The policemen had been distracted—and that was when Nevil seized his opportunity. He didn't know why he had to go into the crater, but that's where he headed, making for the injured Gypsy, believing somehow that he could get between the child and the injured man and prevent any more violence. After all, it had its quiet moments, Nevil could attest to that. *After it has eaten,* he reminded himself; but by then it was too late. He heard someone behind him shout, "Oi, you stay where you are," but he just ducked his head and pressed on.

Keeping an eye on the child, he began to talk soothingly, not so much for the benefit of the child, which he didn't think could understand him, so much as for his own well-being. The sound of his own voice at first quavered, but became calmer as his determination hardened to see this thing through. What he was doing felt right—it was what he was supposed to do. He'd spent too much of his life being afraid of his instincts. He helped the policeman hoist up the Gypsy, but stayed behind in the crater. They were too busy to notice until it was too late. Nevil watched Llewellyn shake out the netting and the child swing to face him once more, ignoring Nevil for the moment. Nevil stepped closer, the child turned back to him snarling, strands of hair writhing like snakes in the chill breeze, arthritic, clawlike hands with long twisted nails held out before it as it crouched and quickly shuffled back into the duct before cautiously emerging once more.

Nevil paused and watched the policeman step closer to the pipe, the netting hanging loosely in his hands. Realizing what the copper intended, Nevil stepped closer too, hoping he could help force the child back into the duct.

Perhaps they won't have to kill him, he thought. Perhaps all this had been leading Nevil to redemption after all—he'd been sent by the Mad Arab to save the child!

Sensing it was trapped, however, the child shrieked, then lunged for the policeman.

Nevil stood transfixed as he saw the copper smash to the ground with the child on top of him, both becoming entangled in the netting. It backed away to free itself when a shot rang out, its echo reverberating around the crater. The child screamed and twisted away, blood spouting from a wound in its thigh. It bent to lick itself when a second shot whined off a rock buried beneath the earth. The child hurriedly backed into the pipe on all fours, alternately howling and snarling. Nevil approached cautiously, then, as it lashed out at him, quickly stepped backward.

He saw Llewellyn lying where he had fallen, though with no immediate signs of injury. He dropped beside him, pulling away the tangle of netting. He was joined a moment later by Fred Medford.

Weakly, George said, "I told you that bugger couldn't hit the side of a barn, didn't I?"

"You all right?"

"Yeah. I think I busted my stitches though. Vera's gonna be right pissed off."

"You're lucky you'll be here to listen to her. And here you were, giving me an earful about Herbert Williams playing silly buggers. Who do you think he gets it from, you daft sod?"

George tried to sit up, but was forced back by Medford. George allowed his head to loll to one side, trying unsuccessfully to see the pipe opening. "Where is it?"

"He went into the pipe," Nevil said, "but he's hurt. Badly

I think, I'm not sure." He paused, then said, "I want to go in after him and bring him out—alive."

"Out of the question," Medford said. "You'll be lucky if I don't throw the book at you. I told you to stay put, didn't I?"

"I'm the only one who c-can," Nevil insisted. "You're all t-too big to fit in there." Turning to George, he said, "I found it once before, you see, only I didn't know what it was then. I carried it to a safe place. Don't you understand, somehow it let me help it. I want to try again. Do you really want to kill it?"

George glanced at Medford, then said, "No. I think he should try if he wants. I'm in no shape to go in there. You want to do it? Or one of your lads?"

Medford's steely silence was a clear enough rebuke. Grabbing hold of Medford's arm, George pulled himself to a sitting position. "Someone's gonna have to go in there."

Medford grunted, his surly attitude showing he was acting against his better judgment. He said to Nevil, "You got ten minutes, right? After that we'll pump some gas in there or something, do it that way."

Nevil stared at George, somewhat dazed at the turn of events. The enormity of what had just happened slowly dawned on him.

"Here," George said and handed Nevil one of the silver knives he still carried in his coat pocket. He and Nevil stared at each other for a moment, a communication— something—moving between them like a spark, gone almost the moment it was born. Yet its existence reverberated within Nevil. "Give him your flashlight," George said to Medford.

It wasn't until Nevil had ducked into the pipe and been swallowed by the darkness that he realized what he had sensed was respect—from that man of all people. Forgetting his fear for a moment, Nevil smiled.

□   □   □

Nevil played the flashlight beam around the coffin blackness that surrounded him; he was squatting like a Cossack dancer, one hand bracing himself against the slimy surface of the interior, his head barely clear of the roof, a rope tied around his waist and trailing behind him like an umbilical chord. As the beam swept the interior for a few meager feet before him, he saw that the earth jutted through huge gashes in the pipe's cast iron. A slimy rivulet trickled downhill toward the entrance, and the echoing of dripping and tiny splashes unnerved him. He blanked his thoughts as best he could, trying to follow a noise ahead that sounded like weeping and growling. The darkness was overpowering, especially knowing what his fate could be if the child attacked him now.

Nevil hefted the netting before him, knowing it would be unlikely to save him from danger, but with little else to protect himself. He forced himself to concentrate on the moment, the suffocating tomblike smell of damp and decay, the slick surfaces threatening to upset his precarious balance, the slosh of ankle-deep, stagnant water, stumbling several times on unseen piles of earth that had fallen on the floor of the pipe like miniature sandbanks. He peered once behind him, but the light of the entrance had disappeared. That meant he must have turned a corner somewhere, though he hadn't noticed. His isolation was complete now, the claustrophobic feeling bringing back vivid memories of that dark understairs closet, crouching, hungry, sniffling and exhausted from weeping, crying out to his mother that he would behave from now on, the sounds of what he thought were rodents scurrying by in the wainscot—in his imagination, rats the size of housecats had peered at him in a darkness as complete as this, a darkness they could see through and he could not, sizing him up as a meal—all melded together until he could recall neither time nor place, aware only of a dripping echo in a familiar, malevolent, suffocating limbo.

He paused to ease his aching thighs and the tightness of the rope around his waist, his umbilical to safety—or at least, to the fresh air and the waiting police—but forced himself to move on, knowing if he stopped for much longer he would not be able to continue. It seemed he had been inside the piping, heading toward the very bowels of the earth, for hours, though logically Nevil knew it could only be a few minutes. The fractured sounds ahead, like crystal chimes, were barely audible but frighteningly real, nevertheless.

The piping suddenly arrived at a T-junction, and Nevil realized the police might not have managed to block up all the exits as they had supposed, making his mission even more necessary. Things could not go on like this any longer—too many people were getting killed.

He ventured down one of the branches, but had to backtrack after a few moments when he came across a landfall blocking off the way ahead. Returning to the main branch of the pipe, he continued ahead, suddenly finding himself able to stand at a crouch, the sounds of the child now clearly audible just ahead of him. Had to be!

The piping had broken cleanly in half, and he clambered up a muddy slope to continue on. The remaining pipe angled downward, and Nevil had to brace himself against the slimy walls to stop from sliding into the black maw below him. He knew he was drawing closer because the stench became overwhelming and, gagging, Nevil covered his mouth and nose with a handkerchief, without much noticeable effect.

He emerged finally into a small natural cavern created by an upheaval of the broken piping, where he was able to continue standing at a crouch, catching his breath. The sounds of the child had become subdued, no doubt because it had heard Nevil approaching.

Nevil swung the flashlight around the miniature cave, maybe five feet at its highest, finally catching sight of the child curled in one corner, its eyes feral, its bearing clearly threatening danger if he came closer. Nevil paused, allowing his eyes to adjust further to the dim, almost phosphorescent light thrown by the flashlight which he placed on the floor.

The child kept leaning over itself, and only when Nevil cautiously took another step closer, noting that if it leapt for him now he would barely have a chance to defend himself, he saw it was licking at its thigh, an animal tending a wounded limb.

Nevil pulled out the silver knife, and began talking soothingly, forcing himself to remember that he had got close to the child once before without mishap, that finally he had a chance to do something important—he couldn't blow it!

The child looked up again and growled loudly, baring its teeth, pulling itself tighter into the wall. But the motion caused it to move its injured leg and it cried out from clearly excruciating pain.

Continuing to talk soothingly, more for his own comfort than anything else, not knowing what he was saying, not really caring, hoping that somehow his nonthreatening, counterfeit calm would somehow transmit itself to the child, Nevil took another step closer.

The child sniffed the air and made a strange whine, as though it might have recognized Nevil from before. Drawing encouragement that it might work out after all, Nevil gingerly held out his hand, as he would to a strange dog before petting it. Keeping his movements painfully slow, he examined the child visually. The blood that still oozed from the thigh was smeared on the child's face and body.

Carefully, so as not to alarm the child, Nevil turned away to mask what he was doing, using the knife to slice two-inch strips from the bottom of his overcoat and the inner lining, continuing to talk in a soothing tone, even when his face was turned away, realizing the sound of his own voice was as much for himself—so he would not scream with terror and run from the vision before him—as an attempt to reassure the child.

He moved closer still until only an arm's length separated them and crouched to the child's level in the hope of making himself less threatening in appearance. The child growled again, hissing, its knees pulled tight to its chest and a fresh stream of blood pouring from the bullet wound. "It's bleeding to death," Nevil thought.

Closing his eyes for a moment in what he was certain was a final prayer to his Maker, Nevil cautiously wadded one of the tweed strips and, taking a deep breath, moved alongside the boy. There was nowhere else for the child to retreat to, and although it made some clearly frightening and threatening sounds, it allowed Nevil to place the wadding on its thigh. Nevil felt the blood pumping from the wound onto his fingers. Keeping the wadding in place with one hand, he placed the knife beside him and used the strips of coat lining to wrap around the wound and the wadding. The child cried out and moved violently, slashing at Nevil with its long fingernails. He scurried backward, feeling the seeping of his own blood from deep gouges on his arm where the claws had raked him. The child stayed where it was, eyeing Nevil warily, then leaned over and licked its wound once more.

"Don't be afraid, there's nothing to be afraid of," Nevil continued to mutter, not certain any longer who he was addressing. He untied the rope around his waist and left it lying on the ground, then prepared more strips and tried once again. This time, perhaps because of the growing familiarity and Nevil's timid gentleness, he managed to put the new wadding in place and loosely wrap around it and the thigh a long strip of lining. The child was in obvious pain and continually growled in warning, but as if understanding Nevil's purpose, allowed him to wrap a second strip of lining, this one with its end split and knotted to allow it to be tied in place. All Nevil had to do now was finish the field dressing and somehow drape the rope around the child. Then, if all else failed, they would be able to pull it out relatively unharmed—or at least, still alive anyway.

His hands shaking almost uncontrollably, Nevil nevertheless managed to tie the first loop of a bow. "There you are," he whispered, "right as rain again." He pulled the ends together, and as the makeshift bandage tightened the boy screamed with agony, and with a snarl lashed out with a clawed hand, catching Nevil across the face.

He fell back in blinding pain with a scream of his own, feeling blood well up and stream across his face, suddenly blind in his left eye, then, before he could recover, felt the crashing weight of the child as it hurled itself on top of him. Nevil found himself on his back, the weight of the child crushing him in the confined space. He struggled to hold it off while the boy's jagged, misshapen teeth snapped inches from his face, its breath dragonlike.

If the cave had not been so cramped, Nevil might have managed to hurl off the child, his fear and panic having now taken complete control. One hand groped in the muddy earth, even as he struggled to rise. He slipped in the floor's ooze and with stark insight knew he was not going to make it out alive, even before the child's teeth fastened on his throat and, clamping shut began to rip. The Mad Arab's message was finally clear—that afternoon with Camilla Stepan, Nevil had been shown his own death.

In a primeval instinct for survival, Nevil tried to grab the boy's head, twist it, crush it, anything to stop what was happening. His groping free hand fastened instead on something hard and cold. The child snarled and continually twisted its head, finally tearing free, its mouth filled with flesh.

Nevil tried to speak, but all that emerged was a wet gasp. The child lunged once more, its eyes wide with savage victory, and, not even aware of what he was doing, Nevil jerked up his hand to keep it at bay.

There was a howl, and Nevil felt the silver knife judder in his hand as it sank into the boy's chest, its blade long enough that its point emerged through a shoulder.

Nevil heaved off the child's dead weight, and the boy lay fetally where he fell, still alive but unmoving, his breathing a lung-flooded gurgle. Nevil clapped a hand to his throat and felt the tide of blood pour from the gash in his neck; the boy had killed him. With his remaining strength Nevil crawled over to the child and lay beside him, ignoring the whimpering growls, cradling him, as much for his own comfort in the loneliness of imminent death as for the child's. With that final gesture, as he tried to summon up the forgiveness and compassion that had been denied him, Nevil felt his body start to chill, and his legs shudder of their own accord while his blood pooled beneath him, and he smiled as the world faded away; and for the first time he faced the darkness of that understairs closet unafraid.

FRIDAY

January 10, 1941

You can't erase the past, George thought. *You can only come to grips with it.* It was a perception that had plagued him for the last couple of days since his healing injuries had forced upon him a brooding, bedridden inactivity.

He found himself admitting, perhaps for the first time consciously, *that's* what he had been avoiding all these years. *We don't exist without history. It's what we are, even when we hate what we've become. If we're going to survive, all we can do is try to embrace the shadow within us and hope that's enough to save us from ourselves. Confront the monster, like we're now confronting Hitler. There are no other choices.*

The implications of the "London Werewolf," as the Stepan case had been nicknamed by the press, reached deep into George's psyche—deeper, indeed, than he had ever wanted or intended to plumb, plunging him into a bottomless well of ugly self-awareness. He had been forced to stare at himself, and he had flinched.

George peered out of the window of the Green Line bus as it rolled past bare fields, spiky clumps of denuded trees,

266

and a general landscape of barren, chilly despair while they drew ever closer to the Mary Kitteridge Home.

What Stimpson had done disturbed George profoundly. Being so wrong about him, both now and five years ago—after George had been so certain, so *sure*—had become a source of distress that had seized George by the throat, chopping away his own belief in himself as effectively as if he had lost all power of movement. If he could be so wrong about Stimpson, what other mistakes had he made—and would he make?

Such were George's churning thoughts as the bus neared the stop by the gates of the home. He was squeezed into a window seat, feeling the occasional brush of warm bodies with the woman sitting next to him. George tried to take his mind off his morbid thoughts by thinking about the date Vera Armstrong and he had tomorrow evening. But the thought became one more strand woven into a tapestry of despair. He had toyed with asking Vera to come with him on this trip, but it was one of those late-night ideas, dispelled in the cold morning light by the knowledge that his daughter was a responsibility he could not share, however close Vera and he grew to each other. He had lost his temper with Gwenyth, and Wendy had got in the way. He hadn't even known he'd hit her until it was too late. Never again, he swore . . .

George had spent the last two days recuperating in hospital, and even though they had let him go home yesterday lunchtime, his mood continued to be dour. Fred Medford put it down to stress, sparked off by the Stepan boy. George had asked Fred to make a point of seeing that both Stimpson and the child were buried with some dignity; it seemed a fitting if belated recognition of such troubled lives. It made sense to play up Stimpson's heroism and play down George's unfounded suspicions of him, if for no other reason than to prove the police once more infallible in their even-handed guardianship of the public and help boost the morale of the war effort, make some attempt to ease George's troubled conscience.

The war news was not good: Several battleships and several hundred sailors had been lost in naval clashes in the Mediterranean over the last couple of days. Control of the sea there was slipping away from the Allies. It was clear to George, and many others now, that far from being able to end this war quickly, as they had once hoped, it was time to settle in for the long haul—years perhaps, transforming the world in the process, brutalizing it, metamorphosing it in a cauldron of blood and fire.

What happens to one, happens to us all, George thought, reminded of fiery Sunday Chapel sermons that had made him cower in his mother's skirts as a child, never before believing the truth of it. He was undergoing a change that frightened him, for it meant admitting he was vulnerable, open to pain; exactly those raw sensitivities that had always been the bull's-eye his father unerringly struck when domineering his younger son, faulting him for being too much like his mother. It was why, George now saw, Vera had become important for him. He had shut himself off from so much within, using the shield of law enforcement, the way those scared of making fools of themselves dancing often become musicians, safe on the periphery, taking part only on their terms.

The London Werewolf case was neatly tied up for the politicians, the chief inspector content with the conclusion because Downing Street was, and with the threat gone, the only person who still seemed disturbed by what had happened was George. Who else had the time to think of such things but the recuperating wounded?

George's role in all this had more to do with himself, he

was beginning to see, than what he could objectively say was the truth. For Truth is shaped not by what happens, George thought, so much as by what we believe is happening. Our perceptions are blinded by our inadequacies . . .

He was still entangled in such ideas when he rang the bell to the home and was once again greeted by the blowsy teenager.

"Whatchuwant?"

George pushed past her into the entrance lobby before saying, "I'm here to visit my daughter. That a problem for you?"

She didn't reply, just jerked her head in the direction he was to follow and led the way along the squeaking echoes of the hallway's linoleum floors, pursued by harsh whispers and strident shrieks.

At the door to Wendy's room, George paused, dismissing the attendant with a frigid, though silent demand for privacy, which she obliged. He turned to stare at the figure hunched in the chair pulled up to the barred window. He knew he would never be able to breach the chasm that separated them, though like some Herculean labor he had to pursue it. He felt a sharp pain in his chest and choked for a moment, gasping for breath.

Gradually, the feeling eased.

Once recovered, he pulled up a chair beside Wendy and, taking up her cold hand, began the familiar routines of his visits.

"I was in a bit of an accident the other day," he said after a while. "Nothing to worry about, but it's made me think a lot." He turned from her a moment, muttering, "Not that I wanted to.

"I think I understand your mother a little better now. Whatever else happened, I got you out of it. That's something I treasure, even if it has to be like this. I've got

269

this lady friend now. She's nice. You'd like her. I'll bring her to see you one of these days. I'll come more often, too.

"I didn't . . .your being here like this, it should never have happened. It was my fault, not your mam's. Life with her was just so damn hard. I felt she deliberately crushed my dreams. The only power she had to be herself derived from her ability to thwart me. Confounding me somehow made her whole, in some strange, perverse way. I think it was when she realized that, that she decided to leave. It seemed the longer we went on, the more things soured between us. She started drinking, I started staying away from home, punishing her, I suppose, by making her look after you, avoiding that cloying, evil atmosphere day after day, night after night . . .

"Between the two of us you didn't stand a chance, did you?"

He paused, stroking the cold hand, peering up at the blank expression, seeing not emptiness but a chastisement that forced him to turn aside for a moment.

"You were such a *happy* child. I remember, I used to bounce you on my lap and you'd laugh and hiccup with glee, say 'more' all the time. I don't remember when it all changed. I just woke up one day and it had. Not around enough to try and find out, I suppose. Hiding. If I hadn't avoided dealing with your mother, if, if, if. Pointless though, isn't it? But I can't get it out of my head that it's all my fault.

"You see, my da' . . . that was the only way I knew how to be a father, a husband . . ." He choked, feeling the burning flush of tears well up in his eyes. He took a moment to sniff and blink them away. "He was a *hard* man. Had a hard life. But he'd take it out on us, see, my mam and me, and my brother; blamed us, and I hated him for it. The thought that you could hate me as much as I hated him . . .

"He's dying, see. My da'. And seeing you like this, wanting to heal this hole in me that hurts so much, it's made me realize some things. I was like him, I thought I was enough for you all. That I should have been enough. That I was the point of your lives whenever I deigned to be around.

"Perhaps, I don't know, maybe if I can try to set things right between us before it's too late, make the effort anyway, I keep thinking—can't get the thought out of my head these days—that maybe if I make the effort to reach him, you'll try to reach me. Stupid, I know.

"So anyway, I've decided. I'm going home for a few days, back to Wales. Try and make my peace with him. He'll probably spit in my eye on his deathbed. It would be like him. But it doesn't really matter, does it?"

He continued to talk, about Gwenyth and his da' mostly, his soft voice eventually becoming hoarse, his thoughts free-flowing until finally he expended himself and sat quietly, head bowed, her limp hand loosely between his sweating palms.

Eventually he rose, stiffening his shoulders and loudly blowing his nose. It was only when he leaned over her in a gesture of farewell, kissing her forehead and standing back for one last, painful look, that he noticed something different about her. He peered closer, and it was only then that he saw a teardrop slowly trailing along her nose. With one finger he reached forward and gently wiped it away. He licked the salt wetness of it, and the smell and taste of her emphasized the vast distance between them. He knelt down and embraced her, blanking his mind of all else save the comfort he drew, a wondrous hope welling within him, despite his cold understanding that what had just happened meant nothing.

He was still rocking her gently and crooning a song his mam had sung to him as a child when the attendant came to tell him visiting hours were over.

This time, however, she kept silent, and after standing indecisively for several moments left them alone, softly closing the door behind her to make certain they would not be disturbed.